I0673337

FERAL WOODS

M.C. ROTH

Feral Woods
ISBN # 978-1-80250-507-8
©Copyright M.C. Roth 2023
Cover Art by Kelly Martin ©Copyright January 2023
Interior text design by Claire Siemaszkiewicz
Pride Publishing

This is a work of fiction. All characters, places and events are from the author's imagination and should not be confused with fact. Any resemblance to persons, living or dead, events or places is purely coincidental.

All rights reserved. No part of this publication may be reproduced in any material form, whether by printing, photocopying, scanning or otherwise without the written permission of the publisher, Pride Publishing.

Applications should be addressed in the first instance, in writing, to Pride Publishing. Unauthorised or restricted acts in relation to this publication may result in civil proceedings and/or criminal prosecution.

The author and illustrator have asserted their respective rights under the Copyright Designs and Patents Acts 1988 (as amended) to be identified as the author of this book and illustrator of the artwork.

Published in 2023 by Pride Publishing, United Kingdom.

No part of this book may be reproduced, scanned, or distributed in any printed or electronic form without permission. Please do not participate in or encourage piracy of copyrighted materials in violation of the authors' rights. Purchase only authorised copies.

Pride Publishing is an imprint of Totally Entwined Group Limited.

If you purchased this book without a cover you should be aware that this book is stolen property. It was reported as "unsold and destroyed" to the publisher and neither the author nor the publisher has received any payment for this "stripped book".

Pride Publishing books by M.C. Roth

Single Books
The Drumbeat of His Heart
A Song for His Heart
Karma's Kiss
Greedy Boy
Feral Woods

It's a Kink Thing
Kinked Up
Unkinked
Kinks and Crosshairs
Dupli-Kinked
Getting Kinky

Collections
Secret Santa: Daddy's Secret

FERAL WOODS

Dedication

For Q

Chapter One

Cambry

Cambry grasped the curtain, pulling it away from the polished glass of his bedroom window. The fabric was soft and heavy in his hand — something from the latest designer his mother had fallen in love with. Instead of the previous indigo, it was now a deep blue that blended in with the softer tones of his room.

A fountain spurted beyond the window, its waters guarded by a black gate that matched the fence that surrounded the property. There were grass and trees, too, beyond those gates, not that he ever got the chance to enjoy them.

An alpha retreated along the concrete walkway, his back rippling under his thin T-shirt. Each movement was like a feral dance of instinct and desire. There was a streak of red across his shirt that hadn't been there when he'd arrived. The alpha had been big, strong, attractive and sweet — everything a proper mate should be.

But Cambry's plan had been disastrous, like a spectacular firework that had failed to launch and exploded in his face instead. The second the alpha had shown any intent that wasn't exactly platonic, Cambry's instinctive side had reared up and taken him out.

Sighing, Cambry let the curtain fall shut, the filtered light dimming to a sparse glow. Luckily, the alpha was only leaving with a scratch and a black eye instead of a broken arm like the last one — or the broken collar bone from the one before him. Maybe it was because Cambry had warned him?

Most alphas sneered at the warning — hence the broken arm and collar bone — but this one had seemed different.

"When you try to touch me, I'm going to react...badly." Cambry couldn't remember how many times he had said those same words. He guessed that the first few alphas had assumed that Cambry would react like any other omega was supposed to — with slick and a burst of pheromones.

They hadn't been expecting violence.

Walking to his dresser, Cambry pulled the top drawer wide, fumbling with a pair of boxers and tugging them up his thick legs. The fabric was smooth and silken and clutched his soft package like a fitted glove. They were worth spending his tiny allowance on, that was for sure. *Thank goodness for the little things in life.*

The little things being both his package and the expensive underwear.

His old friend Aubrie had asked him why he always splurged on the things if he had no one to show them off to. He had his own mirror, thank you very much, which added ten pounds, even on the best of days. But it was always honest about the boxers, which looked a hell of a lot better than they did on most omegas.

"Why don't you give up, Cambry? It kills me to see you like this. If an alpha hasn't induced a heat in you by now, it's not going to happen."

Aubrie had probably had the best intentions when she'd said that, but it had pierced Cambry's soul like a dull pencil crayon. Or maybe that was why Cambry's father had chosen her as his friend…to wear him down a bit more.

There was only so much loneliness he could take before he tried to be with someone again, hoping that everything would finally work the way it was supposed to. It wasn't the sex as much as it was everything else. He couldn't hug someone or even hold their hand without his feral side acting out.

His skin prickled as his door slid back, light footsteps moving across the floor behind him. And there was *that*.

"Your father is upset," said his mother, her meek voice slapping him harder than any blow. He couldn't look at her and see the same disappointment that was in his soul.

He could hear her shaking, her teeth chattering softly as she stayed as far away from him as she could. He was surprised that she had even managed to step into the same room as he was in.

"I tried, Mom," he said, pulling a second drawer wide and tugging a shirt over his frame. He had to get alpha sizes, seeing as nothing for omegas fit his frame. His father was upset about that, too.

The alpha sizes were shaped differently than he was, though — the shoulders a touch too wide and the waist not quite narrow enough. Nothing had fit him well since he'd hit puberty.

The steady thumps of his father's steps approached, and he hurriedly pulled a pair of jeans over his legs. They at least fit a bit better, his thighs stretching the fabric to its brink as it cupped his ass. The only place with too much room was the crotch, but he was almost glad that nothing ever touched him there.

He looked at the mirror above his dresser, scowling at his reflection. Fellow omegas were terrified of him, and alphas treated him like he was a strange cousin to the human race who needed to be broken or beaten until he fit into a different shape than what he had been born into.

He sniffed, slamming the drawer shut before his father could step into his room. There was no use crying, no matter how frustrated he was.

"We've tried it your way, Cambry. These alphas can't stand to get close to you, let alone allow you to bond with them," said his father as he hovered at the edge of the door frame. He was a few inches shy of Cambry's height and had lost his alpha muscling to his age long before Cambry had been born. Like most alphas, he never got too close to Cambry — just close enough to hurt with words.

Cambry wondered if he would ever forget his father's *way*. The restraints had dug into his wrists as a strange alpha had approached him from behind. Guided by an overdressed and undereducated doctor, Cambry's father had hoped to kick-start Cambry's omega nature with some good ole fashioned alpha cock. They hadn't counted on Cambry breaking his own arm as he shifted, turning on the alpha and ripping a chunk of flesh from his throat.

The alpha hadn't died — thank goodness — but they had never tried to restrain Cambry after that. And they had finally listened to him and had let him try on his own terms by picking up an alpha from a bar. It was about as romantic as a one-night stand could have been.

But it had resulted the same way — minus the shifting and massive blood loss, at least.

"It almost happened, Dad. I was so close," said Cambry, touching his belly. He'd been naked, which had been a first. And the alpha had managed to touch him once before Cambry's beast had risen to the surface and socked him in the face. Biting the alpha's gland to bond with them had been the last thing on his mind.

"Close isn't enough," said his father, the snarl in his voice enough to prickle the hair on the back of Cambry's neck. He'd never attacked a family member, but he had come close enough times that his father rarely approached him without backup. It was probably why his mother was strategically between them, shivering with her eyes downcast.

"Your heat could kill you. You're already so much older than you should be for your first one, and there's no way you can manage it alone," said his mother, the edge of a sob in her voice. Cambry turned, his heart falling as he watched the tears stream down his mother's face. She, at least, cared for him. His father was more interested in seeing him out of the door in a different alpha's house — with some financial benefits for himself, of course.

"I'd have to *have* a heat first." Cambry turned away as his father's dark eyes glared into him. Most omegas had their first heat when they were still in high school, the late bloomers sprouting by eighteen at the latest. Cambry had turned twenty-two three weeks before, and he still hadn't experienced a heat. He was hardly an omega at all by some standards.

But his mom was right. Those that had monthly heats had the mildest cycle, still able to continue their day-to-day lives with only a mild fever and a bit of slickness. Some of Cambry's classmates had been that way, and he'd scarcely been able to tell.

Those who had heats once a year had to isolate themselves for nearly a week, their scent and instincts so uncontrollable that they could kill any stranger who attempted to approach. They *needed* a mate to ease them through it, more with their presence than their knot, from what his mother had explained.

For Cambry not to have had a heat at his age meant that his first would reduce him to nothing more than a feral beast that would kill and fuck without conscious thought. The idea was terrifying, especially since he was already so close to feral that an alpha couldn't touch him.

"I've tolerated this abnormality of yours for long enough," said his father, his mother's spine stiffening.

"Dear, you promised," she said, her voice pleading.

"No, he'll be going to *them*, and that's final. That doctor wasn't worth his degree, but a colleague of mine gave me the name of a facility that he swears by. If one alpha can't handle him, then maybe two can snap him out of this phase." He tossed a business card into the room and it fluttered end over end before settling upside down on the floor. Turning, he stormed from the entry.

Cambry finally took a breath as his father disappeared, skirting by his mother to grab the business card. It was deep forest green with the name *Feral Woods* inscribed along the middle with deep gold lettering.

He flipped it over, his eyes going wide as he read the services listed on the card. "Instinctive therapy? What is that?" It sounded terrifying and alluring at the same time.

His instincts were everything that was wrong with him, though. As much as he wanted to listen to the little whispers in the back of his mind, he knew if he did, he would be alone for the rest of his life. *Therapy* brought to mind cages and bindings, the hair on his arms and chest thickening at the thought.

If it had been his father's idea, the latter was probably exactly what was involved. His colleagues weren't much better in Cambry's experience, either.

"I hear they are very good," she said softly, her voice trembling as she took a step back. His heart broke under the weight of her fear.

His parents were terrified of him. Maybe he should be locked in a cage for the rest of his days until they found someone who could make him submit. *Or two someones.* He quivered.

"When do I leave?" He took a shuddering breath as he looked around his room. What would he be allowed to bring? His collection of rocks from his younger years? *Probably not.* His romance novels? He should probably give them a proper burial before he left, because his father would burn them and disown him if he found them hidden under the floorboard.

Just another layer of his *abnormalities*. His father would have a heart attack if he ever read one of them or even caught sight of the cover. They were the only things that Cambry had ever intentionally rebelled with, and they could cost him everything.

"Your father pulled some strings." *Because of course he did.* She cleared her throat. "You're leaving in an hour."

So his father had *expected* his plan to fail.

"There are single omegas, Mom. Why can't he just let me be?" Cambry sighed, drawing a hand down his arm as his fur retreated, prickling as it pulled back under his skin. Others described shifting as painful, and even his mother could hardly bear to do it. But to him, it was a release he only ever found when he was in that form — wild and without the presumptions of a society that hated him.

"You know why," she said, not even looking at him. He hadn't noticed the exact moment that she had given up on him, but it had been a long time ago — perhaps when he had matured into an omega, only he hadn't stopped growing like he was supposed to or maybe when the first alpha had offered him a mating contract and Cambry had bitten clear through his hand.

"I'm sorry," he said. The reasons were too long for her to list, and he knew them almost by heart. "*Your father has so much pressure at work. People are wondering why you haven't mated yet. People will talk, son, and your reputation will be ruined. We can't let them know that you're...unnatural. Your heat will kill you, and if it doesn't, your father...*"

They did have a slight point. He had no desire to die, especially since he hadn't seen the world except for his tiny slice of neighborhood and the bit of lawn within the black gates. The unmated omegas he'd seen were considered strange anomalies in the circles his father traveled in and were best to be left alone and shunned.

As if they couldn't function without a knot to drool over.

Cambry rolled his eyes. The idea of a knot made him a bit nauseous. He had no desire to bend over and *take it* like he was supposed to. His feral side agreed with toothy gusto.

"You should pack. I'll give you space." She set a duffel bag on the floor before she swept from the room, the loss of her presence barely palpable in the quiet house.

She was his polar opposite. His beast refused to be compliant and meek, even when he tried so hard to overcome that part of himself. He didn't want to be his mother, who was a shadow of a human being ruled by society more than her education and emotions.

Sighing, he looked around the room before grabbing the bag. If he were lucky, he would have just enough room to pack his books under a thin layer of clothing. Then, at least, he could take everything that meant something to him.

He looked at the business card one last time. *Alpha and omega instinctive therapy sessions. Two hundred acres of supervised development.*

Well, on the bright side, he would probably get to see some hot alpha ass. A smile tugged at his lips. He could have a positive attitude. At least he was getting out of the house. And two hundred acres would give his beast a lot more places to run, even if he was *supervised.*

Checking to make sure the coast was clear, he lifted the floorboards just inside his closet. His collection of books that he'd spent years gathering barely fit in the space anymore. The pages were worn from being read so many times, the front covers smudged from his fingers. The covers gave away everything that his father didn't need to know. Two men, bigger than even himself and twined in a primal embrace, painted a steamy picture that made his mouth water. *Forbidden Alphas.*

Heat flushed his cheeks as he packed them out of sight, zipping the bag shut with a hard pull. He balled up a pair of socks and underwear, jamming them into the side pouch to disguise the corners the books had created.

There. All packed. I hope I never come back.

Chapter Two

Bryce

Bryce tossed the plunger over his shoulder, growling as the toilet continued to overflow. Luckily, it was only water seeping into his sneakers and socks, but it was still making a heck of a mess on a floor that wasn't waterproof in the least. He would have to truck the dehumidifier and fan out of storage to try to save it from mold and mildew. And his shoes would have to go into the trash.

"Jake!" he shouted as the toilet glugged and stalled, the waterfall pausing for the moment before it started all over again, sloshing onto the ground and seeping into every wooden crack.

"Here."

Bryce started, whirling at Jake's voice as it came from right behind him. Jake was glowering down from his two-inch height advantage, a few drops of water dripping from his forehead and the orange plunger gripped in his white-knuckled fist.

"Umm." Bryce looked from the plunger to Jake's soaked forehead. "Did I hit you in the head with the plunger?"

Jake grunted, tossing the plunger toward the corner of the room.

"I'm surprised it didn't stick." Bryce snickered as Jake growled. He was a good shot, but maybe not when he wasn't looking.

The toilet gurgled, and Bryce took a step back, his feet sloshing in the growing puddle. "Ah, just stop, you stupid thing. No one has pooped here in months, so why are you even plugged?" Bryce dove for the plunger again, depressing it a few times in the bowl and taking another shower in freezing toilet water.

"Why don't you turn the water off?" asked Jake, his arms crossed as he leaned against the threshold. His dark eyes glimmered beneath his grumpy veneer, his lips almost hidden by his beard.

"Because..." Bryce dropped the plunger, reaching behind the toilet and turning the water off. The flow ceased immediately, the automatic fan clicking on overhead as it sensed the growing humidity. It wouldn't have been so bad if the water wasn't so cold, his toes aching like he'd dipped them in the freezer.

"Because I didn't think of that." Bryce bit his lip, scratching the back of his head as he turned to Jake. "I just don't understand how it could be plugged." The cabin had sat vacant for months because they only ever used it for when Bryce managed to overbook them. It was deeper in the woods—deeper than most of the couples wanted to be when there were rattlesnakes about.

Jake strode past him, taking up all the extra space in the bathroom with his presence. Luckily, Bryce was used to it. His own feral side had no qualms with stepping to the side and letting Jake emasculate him by taking a look.

Jake lifted the back of the toilet, setting the porcelain top in the bathtub before splashing his way back to look at the complicated inner workings. Dual flushes were absolute genius until Bryce had to fix one.

Bryce crossed his arms, leaning back against the wall as he prepared to gloat. That had been the first thing he had checked, as well as the third when the plunger hadn't worked.

"Did you check the exterior vent?" asked Jake as he placed the lid back onto its spot. "If the air has nowhere to go in this type of system, the whole thing will back up."

Bryce slumped his shoulders, refusing to look up at Jake. "I don't know what that is. Like a chimney pipe or something?"

The first hint of a smile appeared on Jake's lips.

"Or something. Give me three minutes." He turned from the room, his rubber boots squelching with each step. At least he had come prepared, and his socks were probably ridiculously dry unlike Bryce's, which were now sodden past his ankles. Cotton was just like a wick, apparently.

Chuckling, Bryce grabbed the plunger, giving it a few cursory swishes around the bowl. Sure, he orchestrated the retreat and planned every square inch of the property, but Jake was the real mastermind behind the operation. Without Jake, Bryce would have lost everything during the first spring thaw.

With a glug and a strange plunking noise, the water started to drain, the level in the bowl dropping until it was right around normal. Bryce let out a happy squeal, clapping his hands once.

"You got it!" he shouted over his shoulder before turning the water back on and flushing a few more times, just to be sure. Thank goodness he had checked. He didn't want to imagine how one of the couples would have reacted to the same scenario.

"Yeah, I got it," said Jake as he stepped back into the bathroom, his boots sloshing through the water. He dangled something in front of Bryce's face — something furry that smelled like a bloated carcass.

"Oh no, it's Frank," said Bryce, taking a step back. The soaked and furry body twirled as it hung from Jake's fingertips. "I was wondering why he hadn't come for treats lately. Poor little guy."

Frank was one of the first chipmunks that Bryce had taught to take treats from his hand. Usually, he warned any visitors about feeding the wildlife, but come on... Chipmunks were the cutest rodent out there.

"Yeah, he had about fifty peanuts stuffed into the pipe, too," said Jake before he marched back outside, setting the deceased chipmunk on the porch and shouting over his shoulder. "You should stop feeding them or it will happen again."

So *maybe* Bryce had more than a dozen chipmunks that visited, each one with a name and its own special treats that he set aside for them. Thank goodness Jake didn't know about the fawn he'd been petting in the woods.

"Do you have time to talk about something?" asked Bryce, stepping through the pool of water and heading for the mop that hopefully had less mouse damage than the tea towel had. He hated setting out traps for the little guys, but sometimes he didn't have a choice.

"I already know you overbooked us again," said Jake, rubbing the back of his hand across his forehead as he let out a deep sigh. "As long as you think you can handle them, then I've got no problem with it."

"Yeah, about that." *How do I say this?* "I took on another project after the last cabin was booked." Bryce cringed, readying himself for Jake's glare that was already headed his way.

They'd been through the same kind of conversation more times than he could count. He just wanted to help people. So when somebody called him up and the retreat was fully booked, he always tried to make room for them.

"You going to put them both out in a tent somewhere?" asked Jake, wiping his hand on his pants before crossing his arms.

"Uh, no. It's only one person actually," said Bryce, wincing as Jake's glower deepened. *No turning back now.* "And I'm going to put them up in the second bedroom at our place."

Jake flexed his jaw, twitching his hands before curling them into fists.

"You know the Parsons? It's their son." Bryce gripped the mop handle, ready to use it as a shield if necessary. The Parsons were real dicks, in his humble opinion, but he wouldn't turn away anyone in need.

"No." Jake's voice was strained between his clenched teeth.

"You can't just say no, Jake. I already told Mr. Parsons yes." *Completely true.* "And he could probably bankrupt us if I refused." *Not going to worry about that.* He clutched the mop tighter, the rough wood nearly splintering in his hands. "It sounds like his son really needs our help. He's already hurt a few people."

Mr. Parsons had been awful sketchy on the details, but it had sounded like he was certain that his son was some kind of deranged beast.

"This is a couple's resort, Bryce—for couple's therapy. You can't just take on every little project because of someone's sob story." Jake's scowl deepened, his expression darkening. "I can't have another alpha in our home."

Bryce took a deep breath, squinting and offering his most apologetic look. Between him and the mop, one of them was about to get mauled. "It's an omega." *Oh God, he's going to kill me.* "And I said that you could be their temporary alpha for the therapy program."

Jake's mouth flopped open before a look of utter rage crossed his face. He flushed red before he turned on his heel and stormed from the cabin, slamming the door shut with a crack that startled a few nearby blue jays.

Bryce winced. He should have waited until after Jake had helped him clean up before he dropped that bit of news. He hadn't been able to keep it from him for another moment, though. Secrets were never meant to be kept by him for longer than three minutes—even less if it was from Jake.

Mr. Parson had sounded enraged when he had called Bryce a few weeks earlier, declaring that his omega son would be put through their program, no matter what the cost. He actually sounded pretty close to begin a dick, and Bryce had been about to tell him to piss off, but then he had thought about the poor omega. If the guy spoke to a stranger about his son like that, then how did he treat his actual son?

If there was one thing that Bryce could never condone it was abuse, no matter what form. A little rough play was fine…but never abuse.

Jake would just have to forgive him. Maybe he would after hearing how much Bryce had charged Mr. Parsons for his son's treatment.

He had been a dick, after all.

Whoever the omega was, he was probably desperate, lonely and close enough to the edge that he could already feel the wind on his face. Bryce had heard it before, and he'd promised himself never to turn anyone away who needed help.

It would be good for Jake to get borrowed for a bit and attend the sessions himself, too. It had been a long time since he'd joined, and maybe it would pull him out of his permanent grump.

Bryce huffed as he finally got the water off the floor, then dragging the fan and the dehumidifier out of storage before setting them to maximum. With that done, he went around and did his other checks of the building. Starting up the fridge and the water heater went off without a hitch, and the rest of the towels were still intact.

The others would be here before he knew it, then Jake would see. Bryce wasn't the only one with the bleeding heart.

Chapter Three

Cambry

Cambry took a deep breath as he stepped out of the taxi, his lungs filling with the scents of earth, pine and something wild that called to the deeper part of himself. Rubbing at his sternum, he pulled his bag over his shoulder. Three seconds in and it already felt like he was about to get in touch with his feral side.

There was no fence or gate like he'd expected, but a simple dirt road that disappeared into a thick canopy of trees. The mailbox at the end of the lane was battered, as if it had gone head-to-head with a few snowplows.

What will they do when I lose control? Not if…when.

He looked back at the cab, the driver already paid and just waiting for his signal to leave. His father had been too busy to see him off, and his mother hadn't appeared when he'd dragged his bag downstairs. She probably hadn't wanted to be caught in a cab with him when they'd be close enough in the back seat to touch.

"Hello there."

Cambry turned to the sound, his heart pounding as he sized up the alpha headed his way — and he definitely was an alpha. Cambry didn't exactly fit societal norms, but there was no way a man that large could be anything but a testosterone-fueled alpha in his prime.

Most of their house staff were omegas, and his father wasn't exactly in his prime anymore. The few alphas that he'd tried to date had nothing on the man before him.

Cambry took a step back, clutching his bag as the corner dug into his thigh. His mouth was dry as he tried to swallow, his heart pounding and his beast shifting in his chest. *Holy crap.*

He had a few inches on Cambry and probably close to fifty pounds of muscle, with dark hair and eyes that were crinkled at the corners from his friendly smile. Smiles could be deceiving, though. Cambry's father had a smile like the devil — pure and genuine until it came time for payment.

"Hey, none of that," he said as Cambry took another step back, the cab halting him in his tracks as he pressed against the door. "I know I'm a big guy, but don't worry. I'm slower than I look." He gave Cambry a wink as he walked up to the driver, mumbling a few words before sending him off.

"I'm Bryce," he said, holding out his hand as the cab started to pull away. "And you must be Cambry. Your father told me all about you."

I doubt that — especially if Bryce was offering his hand. Unless he was one of those overconfident a-holes who thought six inches was nine. Just because Cambry hadn't had sex didn't mean he hadn't seen a few dicks up close. They just never got close *enough* for it to count.

Cambry looked down at the proffered hand, his skin prickling at the thought of touching the alpha. His chest clenched, his breaths coming faster as he clung to the strap of his bag, holding on for dear life. Dropping his gaze, he looked to Bryce's feet and the thick leather sandals. They fit right in among the greenery that surrounded the property like a life force.

"We'll get there," said Bryce, lowering his hand. "Most of the couples are already here. I'll show you to your room so you can get settled. Orientation is in an hour, so you'll have time then to meet everybody. I'll see if I can round up Jake so you can meet him before that." Bryce chewed on his lip before he turned away. He looked back when Cambry didn't follow after a few steps.

Who is Jake? Maybe he was supposed to know and his father had simply forgotten to tell him. Maybe he'd been matched and mated already, and the therapy was simply another name for making sure he went through the whole process until he was broken enough that he was as meek as his mother.

With the cab gone, silence had descended, the constant city traffic replaced by a few early cicadas. His choice of jeans and a T-shirt may have been a bit overzealous. He was already starting to sweat, the mugginess of the forest sinking in.

The two hundred acres that had been on the business card were closing in around him fast. He hadn't even known that trees could get that tall. And Bryce was heading straight into the forest as if the darkness between the trees wasn't the most terrifying thing that Cambry had ever seen.

His beast liked the idea, though, begging him to step into the shadows and shift. *Mind your manners.* Hopefully, it listened.

"You coming?" Bryce called over his shoulder as he paused at the tree line.

Cambry looked down at his clenched hands, stretching them out as they began to ache. He was scarier than anything in the forest—except perhaps the strange alpha—but that was what terrified him the most.

In the city it was easier to keep control. His feral side wanted nothing to do with his computer or books. It found his life even more mind-numbing than he did. Out in the wild, there was nothing to hold him back. They would never see him coming.

But he didn't want to hurt anyone else. There were only so many strikes he could have before the courts got involved and his father couldn't smooth it over. After that…who knew?

"It's okay, kid," said Bryce, slowly moving back toward Cambry. "Nothing here is going to hurt you. Well, except maybe rattlesnakes, but they hardly ever come up to the main house. You're here for a reason, right?"

Cambry swallowed, glancing up at Bryce's soft eyes before darting his gaze back to the ground. "I don't want to hurt anyone else."

Cambry wasn't sure what his father had said about him. It would have been easy enough to live a secluded life and not attempt to mate anyone—but not if his last name was Parsons. And not if his first heat would kill him if he didn't have a partner.

"I won't let that happen. We've had hundreds of people come through here and no one has ever gone home in a body bag. Sure, there have been scratches and the like, but that's all part of the fun."

Fun? His life was so far from fun that Cambry couldn't even comprehend the word. His stomach shifted as his feral side perked up, taking the reins and forcing him toward the canopy. Bryce gave him a quick smile, turning and stomping his way along the dirt path.

Glancing into the trees, he tried to find signs of fences and cameras. The fences should have been easy to spot, but he couldn't make anything out. There had to have been cameras *somewhere*. The card had said two hundred *supervised* acres.

"I'll give you the first tip for free," said Bryce, shooting a smile over his shoulder. "Wherever you go, make as much noise as possible." He stomped his feet extra hard as if to prove a point, a branch cracking under his sandal. "Snakes will sense the vibrations and take off if you step hard enough, and the noise should keep any of the real bears at bay."

"Real bears?" asked Cambry softly, peering to the side as they passed a cabin. It was small, with probably enough space for a bedroom and a bathroom but not much else. The exterior was made of crisp logs that looked freshly cleaned and stained. A spider-free electric light dangled from the peak of the roof, casting some much-needed light in the permanent semi-darkness.

It was nicer than he had expected. Then again, he'd expected a jail cell, so anything other than that was a step up.

"Yeah, there are a few bear shifters about," said Bryce with a wink, "but the real bears can be a bit grumpier than them, and they are harder to keep out of the trash. Don't leave any food out and travel with your partner—and you should be just fine."

Partner. The back of Cambry's neck prickled. *Not mate.* That was a good sign. Maybe his father was a touch nicer than Cambry had given him credit for.

"I've never— I mean, I don't have a partner…not a real one. I need to be able to get my feral side under control so I have a chance with someone without trying to rip their throat out." Cambry flushed, dropping his gaze when Bryce shot him a strange look.

"Don't worry, kid. Jake will help you out with the couple's exercises. You'll be in the main cabin with us if you need anything else. I would have offered up my own alpha services, but I can't teach and be paired up at the same time."

Cambry swallowed as they passed a few more cabins, each one looking a little darker than the last. The lights made up for it, but they only did so much to take away the ominous glow.

Alpha services. So that's what they were calling it these days. When Cambry had been in school, sex had had so many different names that it had made his brain ache. Some days, it had been all that any of his classmates could talk about. He hadn't understood it until he'd found that first novel and had delved deep into his forbidden desires.

"This is the hall where we'll have our meals and some of our scheduled activities," said Bryce as they passed a larger cabin that looked to be about four times the size of all the other cabins he had seen so far. The front door was open wide, the sound of music filtering out. Cambry let out a sigh of relief. The music was almost comforting.

"And this is home," said Bryce, as he turned off the path and headed for a building that looked more like an actual house than any of the others. It was in the middle of a slight clearing and had two floors peaked with a blue metal roof and a brick chimney along the side. The entire exterior was brick except for the porch, which was cut from the same logs as the cabins. The forest parted around it, leaving a small space for a firepit beyond the porch.

"Jake and I will be shacking up in the same room, so you can have the second bedroom. They are connected by the only bathroom, so we will have to share. I hope that's okay. It's not the usual set-up I like to keep for our guests, but we were already overbooked when I got the call from your father." Bryce scratched the back of his scalp as he stepped on the porch, holding the front door wide for Cambry.

"I'm sorry," Cambry whispered, eyeing a spider that scurried along the porch. His father had obviously thrown his weight around to get him into the place. It was a surprise that Bryce was being so welcoming.

"I hope our scents aren't too much for you. I opened up the windows before you came."

Cambry stepped through the door, taking a deep lungful of air as he took his first look around. A pile of two different-sized shoes were off to his left, along with more jackets than seemed reasonable. Beyond the front hall, he caught sight of the edge of the kitchen and what looked to be a stainless-steel stove. Stairs jutted off to his right, the dark-stained wood leading to the second floor.

"I've never had a problem with alpha scents," said Cambry, easing his bag off his shoulder before setting it down beside him. "Just everything else." *Like touch, taste and the mere idea of a knot.* His skin prickled, his beast growling just underneath his skin. He ran a hand down his arm, brushing the goosebumps away.

"Good," said Bryce. "I had a hard time at first with Jake because he can fill up a room, if you know what I mean. I'm sure you'll acclimatize in a day or so."

Cambry slid his running shoes off, setting them on the corner of the mat so he wouldn't leave too much dirt behind. His socks looked like they were already picking up some filth from the floor, but it wasn't surprising, given the state of his shoes after the short walk through the bush. Burrs and dirt clung to the laces, the soles more stained than they had been, which was saying something.

"I'll show you your bedroom." Bryce gripped the banister, taking the first step before he paused. "You are under no pressure to stay here. If it doesn't work out, I'll figure something out with one of the other couples in the cabins."

Pausing, Cambry glanced to Bryce. *Are you serious?* Did Bryce think that he had a choice? He shook his head. It didn't matter. His next stop was prison or a sanitorium if he put up any fuss.

The stairs creaked under their combined weight, the carpeting along the middle worn and stretched. There wasn't much to the upper floor except a hall and a few doors, one of which Bryce held open.

Cambry glanced around his new bedroom, clutching his bag close just in case Bryce decided to inspect it. There were a few pictures on the walls along with a single bed squashed into the corner with blankets that were neatly made. The air was stale and cool, despite the heat.

Setting the bag on his bed, he slowly explored, trying not to wince as Bryce's stare pressed on him. The alpha seemed nice—one of the nicer ones he had met, but he was still an alpha, which meant he had to be on guard.

"Since the bathroom is shared, just make sure to lock both doors when you are in there—and unlock them when you're done." Bryce hovered in the doorway, his bulk filling most of the frame. "I'll go track down Jake so you two can get acquainted." He scratched the back of his head before he turned away.

Cambry looked up from the bed. "Bryce, wait." Bryce paused, shifting as he chewed his lip. "Thank you." Something bloomed in Cambry's chest as Bryce smiled, the crinkles at the corners of his eyes furrowing.

"No problem, kid. I look forward to getting to know you better."

Even if he wasn't telling the full truth, Cambry struggled not to believe him. Glancing around, he tried to find a spot for his bag that was out of sight. It was doubtful that Bryce would be as kind if he stumbled upon Cambry's books.

He'd just finished tucking them under his bed when a knock at the door startled him upright. The door squealed as it swung wide, and Cambry's breath caught in his throat.

The alpha—it had to be Jake—was somehow even larger than Bryce, his massive figure filling the doorway and beyond. He scowled, his dark eyes going even darker as his nostrils flared and he took a deep breath. A growl rumbled from his throat, the sound making every hair on Cambry's body stand on end.

It was the reaction he had been expecting from Bryce when he'd first seen him. A powerful alpha usually reacted badly to someone like him, especially when he looked them in the eye.

Dropping his gaze, he stared at the floor, clenching his hands with the effort of keeping his beast back. His teeth suddenly felt too large, his mouth watering as the growl came again. If the alpha touched him, he wouldn't be able to stop his shift, no matter how hard he tried.

"Omega?" Jake asked, his voice low and thick.

"Alpha?" Cambry trembled as the word appeared on his lips. He'd never called anyone alpha before, not even his father. He curled in on himself, trying to appear smaller as the alpha's presence threatened to become overwhelming. He longed to bite something, his jaw aching with the need. Energy raced along his limbs and his hands twitched.

Jake cleared his throat, surprisingly giving ground as he backed out into the hall. "We're introduced, then. I'll see you for orientation."

The door slammed shut and Cambry dropped to his knees, fur bursting along his limbs as his beast struggled to surface. Biting his lip, he pushed it back, tears springing to his eyes as the shift went from pleasant to painful in a heartbeat.

He was used to fighting his beast, but it wasn't used to losing. *I can't give in.* Fear trickled down his spine.

If he shifted, Jake would probably come back and tear him apart before he had his way, mounting and fucking into Cambry's hole like an animal bent on claiming.

He rocked back, wrapping his arms around himself as tears spilled onto his cheeks. The fur receded, his nails going dull.

"I want to go home," he whispered into the room. No one answered. There was no one to save him now.

Chapter Four

Bryce

Bryce winced as a door slammed shut upstairs and Jake stormed down the stairs and past him, pushing his way out of the house. Hopefully, he was headed to the hall for a quick snack and wasn't disappearing into the forest. Or maybe he was off to give Frank a proper burial, the poor thing.

Which reminded him...

Strolling over to the fridge, he added peanuts to their grocery list. When they only went into town every other week to get supplies, he had to keep track of what he needed or he'd be out of luck.

He glanced at the clock, peering outside to the little area around the firepit. He always did orientation outside, not only because of the fresh air and sunshine but because sometimes things got a bit...hectic. The first session was always the hardest.

He wandered out, briefly looking around for Jake and coming up empty. Slapping his hands together, he tossed a few logs into the firepit, crumpling some paper before striking a match. As it caught, he piled on some smaller dry timber, building the flames around the larger logs.

Most Boy Scouts would probably slap him for his terrible fire-building technique, and Jake always stared at him pointedly as he went through three newspapers' worth of paper to get one started. Personally, he liked the little bit of extra smoke that clung to his hair and clothes. It always made him feel more authentic.

That, and the smoky fire helped alphas and omegas who were sensitive to smell. He had dried herbs to the side for the extra punch that would hopefully squash the rest. He wasn't worried about most of the couples, but Cambry had seemed legitimately terrified that he was going to hurt someone.

Cambry was big, sure, but he certainly didn't look the part of the feral omega that Wilfred Parsons had warned him of.

Bryce had heard of feral omegas, of course, and he'd taken an entire semester's worth of courses on them during his counseling education, even though they were incredibly rare. It was that one-in-a-million shot that nobody understood.

Most of the families put them in facilities meant more for criminals than people with a mental illness. Usually, their stays were short-lived, some lasting only months before they passed away from either injury to themselves or a situation where they had to be put down.

Bryce remembered touring one such facility, the state of the people inside bringing tears to his eyes. When his teacher had noticed his sympathy, he'd pulled Bryce aside as the tour ended. Mr. Duncan had always been a little *out there* and had taken Bryce under his wing after that moment, teaching him a different side to things that wasn't exactly 'curriculum approved'.

"People have two layers, kid," Mr. Duncan had said, casting a sad look back to the facility. *"The first layer is what we used to be – our instinct and our will to live. The second layer is what society has created to break us."*

Zack hadn't understood it then, but the more he worked with people, especially couples, the more he realized what Mr. Duncan had meant. People came to him with an expectation of how things *should* have been, without understanding that things were exactly the way they were supposed to be.

Tossing on a few more logs, he waved as the first couple approached. It was a rare pairing of two omegas, something that wasn't exactly smiled upon in society but was just as natural as an alpha and an omega, as far as he was concerned.

"Hello there!" Bryce called out as they approached, motioning them over to the fire. They were both small, even for omegas, and almost demure. People had probably come down on them hard in the past, but he hoped he could help them cope with that.

"Welcome, gentlemen. You're welcome to have a seat on the grass while we wait for the others to arrive." The dark-haired omega glanced at the grass, his nose wrinkling, even as the blond dropped to the ground, patting the spot beside him with a shy smile. Grumbling, the brunet sat stiffly, folding his hands in his lap.

Bryce chuckled to himself, grabbing a stick and poking at the embers that had started to form. *This is going to be fun.* It was always the grumpy ones who ended up being a hoot.

The other couples arrived shortly after, all alpha-omega pairs who gave the omega pair a second glance before seating themselves around the fire. They were quiet, looking around at the surrounding forest with a touch of trepidation.

Well, all except one alpha, who puffed out his chest like a little dodo bird who was unaware that he was about to go extinct.

Bryce held his breath as Jake emerged from the forest all at once, his shadow concealed in the trees until the last moment. He didn't look quite as angry, but he still glowered at Bryce as he emerged, glancing around to the other couples. His nostrils flared once before he looked to the house.

Cambry was on the porch, clutching a supporting log like it was the only thing keeping him standing. He really was the most unique person Bryce had ever seen. His scent indicated that he was an omega, the sweetness like a fresh peach clinging to his skin. But there was something else beneath it that was molten and dangerous. It made Bryce's skin prickle every time he caught it.

In appearance, Cambry was more like an alpha — taller than any of the other alphas present besides Jake and himself. He was thick, too, with muscling that put most gym-goers to shame.

He could see the moment that Cambry's scent reached the others at the fire, a ripple going through the couples like a wave. The omegas looked worried, and the alphas looked like they were ready to fight. Even Jake looked like he was barely holding on to his control, his nails cutting into his palms as he stared at the fire.

Cambry's dark hair fluttered in the breeze as he lowered his head, his blue eyes that were so pale they almost glowed, disappearing as he closed them.

"There you are, Cambry," said Bryce, his voice easy and smooth even if his beast was rumbling beneath his skin. "You are welcome to join us at the fire. Jake saved a spot for you." Bryce motioned to the space that Jake had left when he had given the other couples a wide berth.

Cambry slowly shuffled over to Jake, his gaze never lifting from the lawn. Jake visibly stiffened further with each step the omega took, his nostrils flaring and his eyes flashing.

Bryce tossed a handful of dried herbs on the fire, the powerful perfume soaking the vicinity in moments. It was a nice trick to have when it looked like people were going to start killing each other. It eased the tension like a rippling swell.

"Thank you, everyone, for coming — and welcome to Feral Woods," said Bryce, smiling at each person in turn. The blond omega looked a touch woozy as he inhaled the perfumed smoke that wafted his way.

"So, I'll tell you a bit about myself, then we will go around and introduce ourselves before we start our first session." He gave another soft smile, watching the alpha out of the corner of his eye, who seemed to be puffing his chest out even farther. His omega rolled his eyes and Bryce barely contained his laughter.

"My name is Bryce. I'm an alpha, and I've been running these therapy sessions for ten years now. My hope here is to help every one of you with your goals, and teach you how to listen to your instincts instead of denying them." He motioned to the omega pair, the blond perking up.

"Hi, I'm Jeremiah, and this is my husband, Brandon. We've been mated for just under a year," said the blond, a shy smile on his lips. He was even cuter when he blushed. A warmth settled in Bryce's chest.

"And why are you here?" asked Bryce.

Jeremiah hesitated, looking to his husband, then the other couples around the fire.

Bryce cleared his throat. "I can tell you one thing for certain. If you aren't honest with us, then you have no accountability to be honest with yourself. This week will be about being truthful to you and your inner beast."

Flushing, Jeremiah looked away, fiddling with his hands in his lap. "We've been having trouble — uh — in the bedroom. I can't…perform, I guess you could say? I want to, but every time we try, I just…" He trailed off, moisture gathering on his eyelashes as he slumped. Brandon reached for him, placing a hand on his shoulder.

"Thank you, Jeremiah. You were very brave to tell us." Bryce turned to the alpha with the puffed-out chest and his snickering omega.

"I'm Braxton," said the alpha, his voice deep and his neck bulging as he pushed his voice lower than it was naturally meant to be. "I mated my omega three years ago. He doesn't get slick for me."

There's always one in every group. Bryce struggled not to face-palm. "And what are you hoping to accomplish this week?" *Here it comes.*

Braxton looked at him like he was an idiot. "He's my omega. He should get slick and ready for me whenever I want to take him."

What is this? The eighteen-hundreds? "And what's your name?" asked Bryce as he turned to the omega in

39

question, plowing on as if the alpha's statement hadn't been one of the most offensive he'd heard in the last month. He'd heard worse, and he'd taken down bigger alphas.

"Does it matter?" Braxton growled. "He's my omega and that's all you need to know. Now fix him." He crossed his arms, his biceps bulging as he flexed.

An awkward silence settled in the clearing, the only sound the snapping of the fire. *Okay. That's enough.*

"Do you know how omega slick is produced, Braxton?" asked Bryce, digging his claws into the grass to keep calm. His beast was ready for a fight, but he was hoping to avoid that.

"Of course I do."

Bryce waited a few moments, huffing when Braxton didn't continue. "Then, by all means, explain it to us." He struggled to keep his sarcasm under control. Sometimes wondered who the fuck was teaching people these days. The internet couldn't be responsible for every mess.

"Omegas get slick when they are exposed to an alpha. Everyone knows that," said Braxton, his chest puffing out a tad more as he turned to the other couples around the fire.

"I see," said Bryce, tugging a dandelion free and blowing the seeds toward the fire. He turned to the omega pair with a smile that was probably a bit diminished. "Brandon, do you get slick for your husband?"

Brandon's head shot up, his brow furrowing. "Yes."

"Interesting," said Bryce, tapping his chin. He turned to Jeremiah next. "Was your mother an alpha?" He'd gotten that vibe from the man. If he was right, both of Jeremiah's parents were alphas.

"Uh, yeah. How did you know?" Jeremiah's gaze cut to the side.

"Did you ever get slick for your mother?" asked Bryce, keeping a straight face, even as the others shifted uncomfortably. Therapy wasn't about being comfortable. It was about changing the views you had about yourself.

"Ew, no, of course not." Jeremiah screwed his face up, giving Bryce a little glare.

"Even more interesting," said Bryce, looking back to Braxton, who had gone red in the face, the veins on his neck standing out. "That's because slick has very little to do with pheromones, and everything to do with sexual arousal. If your partner isn't slick and there is no medical cause, then it's probably because you don't know the meaning of foreplay."

Bryce waited for one beat, his beast prepared to intervene if things got out of hand, which they usually did at this point. He didn't exactly enjoy humiliating people, unless they deserved it. And hell, if anyone deserved it, it was Braxton. His omega snickered, not even trying to hide his laughter.

He glanced at Jake, who had a hint of a smile on his lips, his broad shoulders more at ease with the herbs cutting down on Cambry's scent.

"Moving on. What's your name?" he asked Braxton's mate.

"Edward," he said, another snicker sneaking out. "I've been mated to Braxton since our parents arranged it, and my goal here is to help my alpha figure out that I'm his husband and *not* his call-boy." He shot a look at Braxton, who wilted immediately, his red face going nearly purple.

If only every omega in the same situation could be so strong and endearing. Bryce grinned. His job had just gotten a whole lot easier.

The third couple introduced themselves with zero fanfare, before Bryce turned to Cambry, who was holding himself stiff on the grass, his arms wrapped around his legs as he leaned as far away from Jake as possible without falling over. Jake looked to be in a similar state of duress as the wind direction changed, every line in his body taut and ready.

"I'm Cambry," he said softly as Bryce looked at him. His unique eyes shot around to each of the couples as he spoke, never staying on anyone long. "I'm unmated, but I have a temporary partner while I'm here." He looked to Jake, wincing under his gaze. "And I hope that I can touch someone without hurting them."

Oh dear. Bryce let out a breath, trying to ground himself. Wilfred Parsons had obviously left a few things out. "Have you ever been with anyone, either alpha or omega?"

"No." Cambry fiddled with the edge of his shirt. "No one can get close enough to touch me, and if they try...my beast doesn't like it." He pulled his arms tighter across his legs. His scent thickened, even through the herbs, and Jake's eyes glowed.

"Thank you for your honesty, Cambry." Bryce pinched the base of his nose, hoping the smoke would shift Jake's way again soon. Cambry's scent made his own docile beast grumble, so Jake's more aggressive one had to be ready to tear free.

"Okay, everyone. The first session is always the hardest, so some of us might feel a bit low after today. But don't worry, it's all better after that. Just remember that what happens here, doesn't leave the property.

You've all signed non-disclosure agreements, and believe me, I do have a lawyer. There's no reason to be embarrassed about anything that happens here. We are all trying to get in touch with our beast so we can pave the way for a better life for ourselves."

He clapped his hands, startling Edward, who seemed to have started to drift. Bryce used to drone on for half an hour until he'd realized that even adult attention spans were only about three minutes. "Without further ado, I need everyone to get undressed and shift."

Silence followed his statement, and a few uneasy glances were exchanged. No matter what group he was dealing with, they always had the same reaction. "Come on, guys. Omegas first. Let's see some awesome beast forms."

Some people considered their forms to be deeply private and expressions of themselves that no public eye should ever see. But Bryce was going to do his best to change that.

Jeremiah let out a small laugh before he tugged his clothes from his body, his cheeks flushed red and he averted his eyes. He was thin, but not overly so for an omega, and his slim hips and small cock fit perfectly for his gender. Bryce's beast ignored the display.

Aw, a bunny. Bryce grinned as Jeremiah shifted before him, his human form bleeding away to a small fluffy bunny with long flopping ears and brown patches against his white fur.

His clinical training kicked in as he looked for any problem signs. There was more than one reason that he asked couples to shift during their first session. While a person could hide something, their beast-form couldn't. Substance abuse would show up as bedraggled fur and physical or mental abuse would be glaringly obvious.

Brandon went next, a small hedgehog appearing a moment later. Braxton was a golden retriever, which was slightly hilarious.

Omegas were *always* prey animals and alphas predators, but a golden retriever was smack dab in the middle. It was no wonder he tried to put on a brave front when he was just a slobbery puppy.

Some groups claimed that omegas were prey because they were supposed to be hunted and claimed, but Bryce and his teacher had had a different opinion. Prey animals survived because they were faster, smarter and better evolved. The predators had to earn their way to the top and failed more times than not. Only a smart fox managed to catch a bunny.

But dogs were in between — not really predators or prey, and more of a friendly and slightly stupid neighborhood goof. Bryce nodded his approval. Their relationship could be worth saving after all.

Edward went next, revealing a chipmunk that made Bryce's heart pang with loss. He did look a lot like Frank, and Bryce wasn't made of stone. The chipmunk darted up the dog's leg as soon as he shifted, settling on Braxton's fluffy head. Perhaps there was some love there after all.

The next alpha was a fisher, which was a touch surprising because he had appeared to be the calmest of the alphas, and fishers were notoriously vicious. His omega was a deer, though, so more than able to stomp him if need be. The deer took a longing look at the forest that made Bryce grin.

"Soon."

"Okay, Cambry, you're next." Bryce's beast perked up, just as curious as Bryce was.

"I'm not safe," said Cambry, his trembling obvious even from across the fire.

Aw, honey, don't be scared. Bryce wanted to run a hand through Cambry's hair and pull him in for a much-needed hug. The poor kid had been through way too much if he was this afraid. Wilfred Parsons was definitely on the naughty list.

"Jake and I won't let anything happen to anybody, okay? I can ask Jake to shift first if that will make you more comfortable." Bryce gave Jake a quick look that spoke volumes. Moments later, a grizzly bear appeared.

Damn, he looked fantastic. Even pissed off, Jake always managed to dazzle him. His coat was thick, and Bryce knew it was coarse except for around his ears, which were baby-soft. His dark eyes glowed nearly gold, his lips hiding his impressive teeth.

He was one of the most intimidating forms that an alpha could have, which was probably why the bunny looked ready to take off and the hedgehog had curled into a tight ball of spines. Even the golden retriever had tucked his tail.

Luckily, Jake had better control over his beast than most. Even if Bryce had pulled him out of the garbage once or twice, he'd never been intimidated by him. His own beast-form probably helped with that, though.

"See? You won't be able to hurt anyone," said Bryce as Cambry's eyes went wide and he shifted away from the bear.

Cambry looked down at himself, touching his shirt before closing his eyes and letting out a shudder. He bit his lip as he started to tug at his clothing.

Bryce had the strangest urge to look away as the first bit of skin was revealed. Frowning, he looked at the fire. He'd seen hundreds of naked people and had always managed to look at them with a clinical detachment, but something seemed different about Cambry. Bryce's beast grumbled, drawing his gaze back.

Oh. He was thick, broad and hard — everything that an alpha typically was. His thighs were thicker than Bryce's and his ass — *oh God*, his ass. Saliva flooded Bryce's mouth and he had to shake the feeling off. He caught Jake's look that mirrored his own, swallowing thickly.

When Cambry started to shift, it didn't happen like any of the others. There was no hesitance once he was naked and kneeling — and no apparent pain. He let out a soft sigh instead, his breath so close to the edge of ecstasy that Bryce had to bite his lip to stave off his body's reactions.

He swallowed as a wolf stared back at him where Cambry had been moments before. At the shoulder, the wolf was more than half the size of Jake's bear, with a steady gaze that would put any alpha predator to shame.

A predator omega was completely unheard of. Bryce couldn't even recall anything like it from school, and they had gone through hundreds of cases of unique shifter types.

It made sense — the strangeness of Cambry's scent and the violence that Cambry was terrified of. Omegas weren't *supposed* to be wired to fight, but Cambry was, down to the very feral being of his soul.

Bryce blinked, pushing back his surprise as he struggled for words. His run-on speeches failed him, every encouraging word drying up. *Now, what am I supposed to do?*

Everything happened so quickly that Bryce barely had time to comprehend it, let alone react.

Cambry turned to the largest alpha in the clearing, drawing his lips over white teeth that looked sharp enough to kill. The fur on his hackles rose until he looked nearly as big as Jake, and he curled his tail over his back aggressively.

Jake lumbered forward, grunting like a pig before he bellowed once, his breath bursting out as he flattened his ears back on his head. Cambry followed suit, snapping his jaws as he wagged his tail slowly, and licking his lips as drool started to form.

Before Bryce could blink, Cambry had lunged for Jake's neck, his teeth sinking in with a roar from Jake that sent a bolt of ice straight to his heart.

Cambry couldn't hold on for long. Jake swiped at the wolf with one great paw, knocking him to the side with a startling yelp. Cambry snarled as he hit the ground, writhing as he tried to get to his feet.

Jake was on him before he could stand, pinning him with one foot and snapping his jaws close to Cambry's ear. It should have made any alpha submit, let alone an omega, but the wolf wriggled until it freed itself, launching itself onto Jake's back and grabbing his scruff in his teeth.

The scene was as startling as it was eye-opening. Jake was close with his beast, enough that his animal instincts were almost stronger than his human ones, but Bryce had never met someone who was as melded with their beast as Cambry was.

Just because a person could shift didn't mean they had the same instincts as their feral side. In fact, some could hardly coordinate their paws, let alone fight.

Bryce tore his shirt off, shifting and ruining his favorite pair of sandals as his limbs grew rapidly. He didn't have time to mourn them as Cambry managed to grab Jake's ear in his jaws, tearing a strip from it with a burst of blood that had Jake bucking and clawing.

A shiver burst over Bryce's skin as he lunged at the pair. While he wasn't nearly as impressive as Jake, he was still a brown bear and had the same claws and teeth that could kill in the right circumstances.

Rearing on his hind legs, he grabbed Cambry by the scruff, sinking his teeth in until he could taste blood. Cambry yelped, clawing and snarling as Bryce tossed him off Jake. Darting after him, he restrained Cambry before he could recover, his teeth piercing new holes into Cambry's flesh.

For all of Bryce's efforts, he still wasn't fast enough. His body lagged for a single moment, giving Cambry the reprieve to roll to his feet and aim his jaws at Bryce's face. Bryce flinched, Cambry's teeth skirting off his muzzle just as Jake managed to lumber over, grabbing Cambry from behind and holding him to the ground one final time.

Blood poured from Jake's ear onto the prone wolf, soaking into his fur as Jake forced the wolf belly-up with his teeth around Cambry's throat. Jake bit down until Cambry gurgled and turned his head to the side.

Gasping, Bryce shifted, his heart pounding and his skin covered with sweat as his fur receded and he stood as a man. Marks from his claws were wedged into the earth, mixing with the blood strewn on the grass.

Cambry was still snarling, not ready to give up, even though he was overpowered. It was the closest Bryce had ever come to disaster.

"Like I said," said Bryce breathlessly as he pushed himself to his feet. The other pairs had scattered during the fight, moving to the far edge of the clearing with the bunny and fisher at the head. He turned to them, his chest heaving as he rubbed his hands together. "The first session is always the hardest. It's all up from here."

Jake grumbled in agreement, and Cambry let out one last whimper before he went limp. Cambry's tongue lolled out of his mouth as he panted, his eyes half-closed and almost peaceful. A touch of bright pink on his abdomen had Bryce looking away.

Shaking his head, Bryce scolded himself. He had seen it all—literally. He had helped couples that had wanted to, well…couple…in their beast-form, and he'd seen all forms of feral arousal. A little wolf dick was nothing new.

With a shake of his head, Jake licked the blood from Cambry's fur with long drags of his tongue.

Heat pooled in Bryce's groin at the sight, and he cleared his throat before reaching for his partially-shredded pants. The waistband was mostly intact, but the seams had burst from the knees down where they'd been caught inside-out.

Maybe I should have charged Mr. Parsons more.

"Thank you everyone for coming today. If you have any questions, you are welcome to stay behind. We will be focusing on individual sessions tomorrow, and you all have your schedules. Feel free to come up to the house anytime if you need something, but I do ask that you knock. Jake can get a bit…territorial." He glanced to the grizzly, who had moved onto Cambry's chest. The wolf was arching into each lick, his eyes closed.

"Have a good night!" Bryce waved them off before turning to Jake and threading his hands through the thick fur of his scruff. Jake grumbled, nosing Bryce's leg before returning to his grooming.

"Thanks, buddy." Bryce leaned on the grizzly for support as his knees wobbled. Fur brushed against his naked ankle that was way too soft to be Jake's. *Cambry.* His unreal eyes were staring right at Bryce.

Chapter Five

Cambry

It was the first taste of freedom that Cambry had ever had, and it had been while two bears mauled him. Perhaps *mauled* was a bit of a strong word. He wasn't missing any limbs or half an ear like Jake was. *Will Jake ever forgive me?* His gentle licks felt a lot like forgiveness.

His beast had never been at peace before. It had always been fight or flight — usually, fight — when there was another person nearby. The second Cambry had shifted, he'd felt the rage coming on, the presence of so many alphas like fire on a stripped nerve. His beast hadn't taken no for an answer when it had demanded that they take out the largest alpha first.

Jake was massive and covered in dark golden fur that gleamed in the sunlight. And he'd fought like a demon, snarling and slapping Cambry aside with massive paws that Cambry would be feeling for days.

And just when Cambry thought he'd finally gotten the upper hand, Bryce had shifted.

Cambry sighed, and his fur melted away, drawing under his skin as his limbs changed and his paws flowed into hands. His skin was molten under Jake's tongue as he cleaned the blood, more dripping from his torn ear with every movement. Cambry's belly-flopped with each touch, his groin pulling tight.

Glancing down at his naked form, he balked, closing his eyes and thudding his head back onto the ground. He threaded his fingers through Jake's scruff, desperately trying to tug him away. His limbs were weak, his beast fighting him to submit like never before.

But he was...*hard*. He flushed, mortification flooding every part of him. Of course, the first time he responded positively to an alpha was with a *borrowed* alpha, in front of a crowd of misfits like no other, with another alpha looking on as he waved the crowd away. At least he wasn't slick.

Cambry rolled, trying to curl into himself as he peered up to Bryce. Jake grumbled, his teeth grazing over Cambry's side with a burst of heat that had his cock throbbing.

"I-I'm sorry," said Cambry, shuddering and trying to convince his weak limbs to respond. He shouldn't have been in such a prone position. He shouldn't have been hard with an alpha in his beast-form, either. It was wrong on so many levels, even as his wolf purred in contentment.

Bryce lowered himself to a crouch, bracing himself against Jake. "Why are you sorry, Cambry?" he asked softly, his gaze uncannily steady. He was nearly naked, too, with his pants shredded to bits.

Cambry gasped, his entire body flushing as Jake leaned away and started to shift. Jake furrowed his forehead, obviously feeling more discomfort than Cambry ever had when he shifted. Fur receded under his tanned skin, his body shrinking, but not nearly as much as Cambry's had. Even in his human form, Jake was still huge and thick, the hair on his chest curly and dark.

"I'm sorry," said Cambry again, closing his eyes and tilting his head to the side. The posture was completely foreign to him. Tears gathered in his eyes as his cock throbbed to the beat of his pounding heart, pre-cum oozing past the slit as Jake loomed over him. Jake was beautiful in his beast-form, but his human form was like no other. Cambry couldn't look.

With a grunt, Jake withdrew. Cambry cracked his eyes open, his heart falling as he saw Jake stand and turn away from him. His wolf whimpered at the blatant rejection, the grief striking Cambry deep until the heat in his groin felt like every kind of wrong.

"Don't apologize," said Bryce, glancing over his shoulder at Jake's retreating back before he looked to Cambry. "Everything that just happened was completely natural and exactly how it was supposed to be."

Cambry swallowed. Bryce had to be full of shit. The only time violence had anything to do with mating was when two alphas were vying for the same omega. Polite society insisted that the omega make the choice, but on the uncivilized side of the world, where people didn't give a shit about right and wrong, it didn't matter.

Cambry had managed to sneak out of his home to attend a cage match once before, and it had shown him exactly that. He'd spent the day reading one of his novels, and his blood had been thrumming for some alpha on alpha action. It was too bad that he didn't have a credit card of his own to peruse the internet, and his browser history was tracked by his parents, who were *concerned for his wellbeing.*

But his friend Aubrie had told him about cage fights before and their testosterone-filled brutality. When Cambry had heard whispers of one from the house staff, he had been determined to get there.

He'd caught the tail-end of the fight when he'd made it to the abandoned warehouse, the smell of blood and pheromones enough to drive his beast wild. Both alphas had been bleeding with matching bruises along their cheekbones, although one looked a touch worse off.

He'd watched as the stronger alpha had pinned his opponent to the floor, snarling as his teeth elongated in an illegal threat. The alpha beneath him had tapped out, and the omega prize had rushed into the ring to be claimed.

Cambry hadn't stayed to watch the victory round, despite the cheers of the crowd. He couldn't fathom volunteering as a prize, giving himself over to a beastly alpha as others looked on. His cock had been hard when he'd fled back to the house, though, easily concealed under his clothes.

The cage fight could have been called natural. Alphas fighting for an omega had been the underlying theme through most historical conquests.

But there wasn't one legend or recollection out there that had an alpha fighting an omega. The concept was completely ludicrous. Bryce had to be out of his mind.

"Don't try to make me feel better when I already know I'm a freak," said Cambry quietly, curling in on himself as his hardness finally started to fade. He took a breath of grass and earth spiked with trees, the smells calming his whimpering beast.

Bryce sucked in a breath before letting it out slowly. *Does he see my tears?* Most people left the moment they caught the first hint of a breakdown.

"Don't use that word," said Bryce. "People used to use it all the time behind my back, and I know how much it hurts when you start to believe it's true."

Cambry blinked, slowly turning to Bryce. He hadn't expected the look of grief on the alpha's face. He couldn't believe it, either. "You're everything that an alpha is supposed to be. How would you know what it feels like?"

Bryce chuckled, running a hand through his dark hair before rubbing his chest. The sweat that was beaded on the hair, soaked into his skin as he scrubbed, refusing to dry in the heavy air. He pushed himself to his feet.

"People ask a lot of you, and if you give in, even a little bit, they'll never let you back down again. You can refuse to let them change you, or you can try to be like them. I had a hard time, kid, but I promised myself a long time ago that I would never pretend to be something I'm not." Bryce shook his head, his jaw flexing as he clenched his teeth. "I'm going to check on Jake before he breaks something. You're welcome to get dressed and explore, eat or rest a bit if you like. We'll talk again tomorrow during our one-on-one."

Cambry swallowed at the obvious dismissal that had him even more off balance than his shift. Waiting until Bryce had followed Jake into the bush, he pulled his clothes over his damp limbs, shuddering even with the warm summer air.

Heading to the house, he darted up to his room, diving straight into the bed. He bounced once on the dusty sheet, the tiny particles shimmering around him as they floated in the air. He closed his eyes, hoping that when he woke, it would all be a dream.

Chapter Six

Bryce

"How did you feel about our exercise yesterday?" asked Bryce as he watched the two omegas for any sort of reaction. Brandon turned his head to the side, raising his chin just a touch while Jeremiah flushed and squirmed.

The air of the hall was much cooler than outside, the crispness hardly ever receding. It was one of his favorite buildings, styled exactly like the cabins only larger, with an office to one side for private meetings.

He'd kept everything minimalistic, with an armchair for himself and a couch a short way away. The two throw pillows that he'd meant as decoration, often ended up in the arms of someone during a session. Jeremiah reached for one as he watched, pulling it into his lap before hugging it tight.

"It was kind of weird," said Jeremiah, sending a brief look to his husband. "I think we've only shifted once in front of each other. I almost forgot what it felt like to hop like that. And my skin always feels so weird when I'm in that form, like it's not even connected to my body."

Bryce held back a grin. How did bunnies always manage to be his cutest clients? "When you were like that, could you smell Brandon more clearly? Could you feel his presence close by when there was danger?"

Jeremiah nodded, his eyes going wide. "I hid under his belly when Cambry shifted. I was so terrified. And Brandon just held me tight, curling into a ball with me inside so his quills protected both of us."

Brandon huffed, the corners of his lips twitching. "I got you, baby."

Awwww. Bryce loved omega couples. They always seemed almost overbearingly loving, even if they had some mechanical issues sometimes. A child raised by them rarely had any mental or social concerns either, which made his job that much easier.

"So, you expressed some concerns about mounting your husband and erectile dysfunction, is that right?" asked Bryce, his heart melting further as Jeremiah went bright red. "What about non-penetrative sex?"

Bryce frowned, turning to the door as a knock sounded. Whoever it was, it had better be important. Therapy sessions were something that weren't to be interrupted unless it was an emergency.

"Sorry." Standing from the couch, he opened the door, sliding out and closing it behind him. He eyed up Jake, a frown on his lips as he took in every taut inch. He'd never managed to catch up with Jake after he'd taken off into the woods, and he hadn't come back to the house the night before. Bryce had hoped that he'd gone to sleep it off in a cave somewhere.

"We have a problem," said Jake, keeping his voice low. He furrowed his forehead, drawing his dark brows together as he grumbled in his throat.

"Did another toilet plug?" asked Bryce, scratching the back of his head. "I swear I didn't give Petunia those almonds after what happened in the last cabin." *Complete lies.* Bryce had given her at least a dozen almonds that morning, but he had chopped them in half so they were less likely to jam up another pipe.

Jake gave him a long look, his frown morphing into a glower. *Oops.*

"I can't go into the house," said Jake, crossing his arms and taking a step back. He looked to the side, a bead of sweat dribbling down the side of his face. He was in the same clothes that he'd worn yesterday, which Bryce had folded and left on the front porch for him when he hadn't returned. His ear was crusted and black with dried blood, a streak of it down the side of his neck.

The scent. Cambry's scent had changed overnight, from something enthralling to something treacherous. Bryce had burned a few vanilla candles the night before, burying his head in his pillow that smelled of Jake. He should have realized that it would affect Jake even more.

"Does your beast want to claim him?" asked Bryce, trying to keep his voice steady. He'd never seen Jake so out of control before—not since they'd first met in a war of teeth and claws.

"It wants to kill him," said Jake, a growl in his voice. "Yesterday was different—when he submitted—but now?" He shook his head, clenching his jaw. His claws, which hadn't fully retracted, bit into his skin as he flexed his fingers. His eyes still had a touch of yellow in them as well, which was a sign that he was close to losing control.

"What do you need?" asked Bryce, holding the doorknob behind his back just in case the omegas thought to follow him.

Jake looked away, moving from foot to foot. He mumbled something under his breath that Bryce couldn't hear. But he didn't *need* to hear the words. He'd known Jake long enough to understand most things about him — more than Jake probably understood about himself.

"Let me wrap my session up, and I'll meet you on the front porch." Reaching for Jake's hand, he squeezed it, wincing at the sharpness of his claws. Jake nodded once, the tension in his shoulders easing just a tad before he turned and shuffled away.

Taking a deep breath, Bryce let himself back into the room. Brandon gave him a bored look, chomping on a piece of gum that he'd gotten from who knows where, while Jeremiah flushed and dropped his gaze.

"So, where were we? Oh yeah, who wants to try a mounting exercise?" Bryce grinned as Jeremiah flushed even brighter.

He tried to keep his attention on the couple as he went through the motions of the exercise, showing the couple different methods of mating that didn't have to lead to penetration. They kept their clothes on after he decided that Jeremiah would probably burst into flames if he turned any redder. Even Brandon had a hint of a blush when he settled on top of his husband between his legs. Their groins lined up, his feigned boredom dropping away to arousal.

Some days, Bryce wished he could eliminate every sex-related standard in society — like the one that declared that you had to have penetrative sex with your mate because that was how it was done. That *wasn't* how it was done...or how it had to be.

He took his job as a sex therapist seriously, and he had yet to meet someone who hadn't realized that they didn't have to follow a set of rules and recommendations to be with the one they loved. Whatever happened to doing what felt right and natural?

Easing out of the room after sending them a quick farewell, he couldn't help but feel a tad triumphant. If only every couple was so easy to treat and work with. If only every person was brave enough to go against what society expected of them.

Unfortunately, Bryce could picture the trials they had ahead of them.

"Two omegas? How unnatural and deviant! Who's the alpha in the bedroom, huh? You need an alpha to show you how it's done."

Bryce shook his head. There were reasons he lived in a two-hundred-acre forest. The first reason was that he had loved *Winnie the Pooh* as a child and had always vowed that he would live in a hundred-acre-wood one day. The second was the man who was waiting for him on the front porch.

Jake's temporary ease had obviously disappeared as Bryce had finished up his session. He was pacing the porch of their home, his arms looking a tad bigger and hairier than usual and his shoulders nearly touching his ears. He growled as Bryce approached, whipping his head around to glare with yellow eyes.

"Hey, buddy," said Bryce, holding up his hands in mock surrender. "You want to go for a run with me first or are you ready to go inside?"

"I want a fucking shower," snarled Jake, scratching at the side of his neck where there were still remnants of dried blood.

Oh, grouchy, grouchy.

"Okay. We can make that happen." Bryce threw all caution to the wind, like he usually did with Jake, strolling past him and throwing the front door open. Slapping his hand to his face, he covered his nose and mouth as Cambry's scent assaulted him. If anything, it was worse than it had been the night before.

He would never be able to have a garage sale again. No one who had any sense of self-preservation would ever want a couch that smelled the way Cambry did at that moment.

It was still a touch sweet, but the sweetness of caramel that was seconds from burning, the sugar bubbling and turning dark, even as he frantically turned off the stove. There was the spice of rage that had been there the night before, but now there was meek sorrow that was so strong that his breath caught in his throat.

No wonder Jake hadn't been able to step inside. Bryce could barely get his feet to move, but he kicked his sandals off all the same.

Forcing a smile on his face, he turned to Jake. "All clear, bud. No omegas in sight." He closed the distance between them, wrapping his arms around Jake and pulling him down so his face was nestled in Bryce's neck where his scent was second strongest. The strongest spot was off-limits because he didn't think Jake would be happy with a face full of dick in the front hall.

"I don't want to hurt him," Jake mumbled into his neck. He smelled of the forest, sweat and fear, the dried blood leaving a film over Bryce's tongue. A shower was definitely the best idea.

"I won't let you hurt him," said Bryce, taking a step into the house and dragging Jake with him, his face still firmly against Bryce's collar. "I mean, have you seen my beast? He has a few pounds on you, and honestly, you wouldn't stand a chance."

Jake chuckled—a puff of air over Bryce's skin. His skin peaked from the contact, heat moving over his flesh in a wave that sank straight into his gut. Perhaps Jake wasn't the only one influenced by Cambry's presence.

"I could chew you up and spit you out for breakfast," said Jake, gripping the banister as they reached the stairs.

He had a point. Jake's grizzly wasn't quite as heavy as Bryce's brown bear, but he had muscles that were built for brawling, where Bryce's beast was always more interested in chomping on flowers and sleeping in the sun.

"You shouldn't play with your food," said Bryce, slipping past Cambry's closed door and into their bedroom. He nearly shouted with joy when he saw the bathroom door open, even if it was open on Cambry's side too. The room beyond was dark, the air thick and still. Cambry's scent coated everything, but there was a chance that he wasn't even in the house.

"In you go, bud," said Bryce, helping Jake step over the lip of the tub before he started the water and let it run through the lower tap as it started to warm. Bryce glanced over his shoulder as he assisted Jake with his clothes. The door was too far out of reach, and he didn't want to leave Jake alone for a moment.

He pulled the plug on the tap, forcing the water up into the showerhead as soon as it had warmed to the perfect temperature. Jake hissed as the first hint of cold touched his skin, dropping into a rumble as steam started to rise.

Bryce's cock shifted and he swallowed, shaking his head. With the sight of naked and wet skin, especially on a man as beautifully rugged as Jake, it was a natural response. Unfortunately, it was the worst timing possible with Jake barely hanging on.

"Tell me what you need, buddy." Bryce took in a deep breath, the oppressive scents lost in the steam.

"Get your ass in the shower. I want you clean," said Jake as he ducked his head under the water, tilting to the side to rinse his ear. He winced as the water touched it, the dark blood finally washing free.

Bryce glanced once at the open door to Cambry's room. *Fuck it.* It was his house after all, and Cambry was a guest. If he didn't like it, he would just have to close the door himself.

"I'm coming, buddy," said Bryce. His cock flexed as he undid his pants. He should have known better than to fight against his nature in the first place. His beast may have been lazy, but he made up for every moment of sleep with excessive horniness.

Chapter Seven

Cambry

Cambry burst from his dream with a wail. He fisted the sheets, drawing them tight and pressing the fabric to his cheeks to soak up his tears. The air was so thick that he could scarcely breathe, the talons of his nightmare still holding him close.

The dream was the same one he always had when life seemed its lowest. It wasn't even a dream as much as a memory, the fear just as real as it had been years before.

He could remember the moon and crisp air on the day his parents had checked him into a facility for *troubled* omegas. It was a place where omegas went in as shy little rogues and came out dead inside. The walls had closed around him as they'd stepped inside, the door locking shut and cutting off his escape.

His father was rich and had a reputation to uphold, so they had gone under cover of darkness and non-disclosure agreements. Cambry hadn't been there to stay—not that time—just to learn. It only took him a few moments to see his future laid out before him.

He'd watched an omega in the throes of heat, strapped down so he wouldn't be able to resist the alpha behind him or tempt the alpha to mate with him. The omega hadn't even done anything wrong in Cambry's book, unless loving another human being was wrong.

The human being just happened to be the wrong *kind*.

They had strapped Cambry to the table, too, just to show him how it would feel. The quiet helplessness that they had told him was supposed to be comforting was anything but. When the alpha doctor had approached him, with the honest intent of releasing him, Cambry had broken his own arm before shifting. The rest was a blur of heat and blood.

His father had covered up the incident with money, and Cambry hadn't seen the outside world since except for his few trips to the bar in search of a mate.

It was the helplessness that haunted his dreams. The sheets wrapped around him and pinned him to the bed like a memory of the restraints. Sometimes, he couldn't move for fear someone was watching.

Tossing the blankets back, he let out a shuddering breath as the cool air soaked into his sweat-slicked skin.

It took him a few moments to realize that it was no longer dark in his bedroom. The blinds were still shut tight, but light filtered in from the bathroom, steam pouring into his room along with the sound of running water. He hadn't tried the shower earlier because he'd been too nervous that one of the alphas would be able to get inside, even with both doors locked.

Tugging on his single pair of jeans, he crept toward the light, his breath catching when he heard a voice. It was hard to tell over the sound of water, but it sounded like Jake.

A shudder ran through his body as he thought of Jake—Jake, who had pinned and groomed him like some sort of actual animal, before turning away as soon as he'd shifted. The memory left a lump of searing heat in his belly, curbing any appetite he may have had.

The first time he'd been beneath someone—really beneath them—and they didn't even want him.

He paused as a moan cut through the sound of running water, heat spreading across his skin at the cry. He tried to scent the air, but his sense of smell had always been crap, and paired with steamy body wash, he couldn't pick anyone out.

Had Jake brought one of the omegas back to the cabin? Maybe he was giving the golden retriever alpha some pointers? Cambry bit his lip at the surge of jealousy that he definitely shouldn't have had.

He looked back to the bed and the novel that was still sitting on his pillow. He'd buried himself in the pages, reading by lamplight until his eyelids had drooped low and his vision had blurred with the need to sleep. His book thudding against his forehead had been the final straw before he'd set it down and pulled the sheets up to his shoulders. The drawing of the two alphas on the cover never failed to get him hard.

A second softer moan didn't help the situation either. He palmed his cock, adjusting it in his pants until it pointed up to his belly. The sound of water cut out, leaving only panting and quiet moans behind.

He curled his fingers into the door frame, his sharper-than-they-should-have-been nails cutting into the wood with ease. Paint peeled from the frame, sliding beneath his nailbeds until his fingertips ached.

He could smell them as soon as he pressed his cheek against the wall. The arousal would be hard to miss, even if his nose wasn't a dud. It was thick, his mouth watering at the heady scent that he'd only caught a few times in his life.

He smothered a gasp as he finally managed the courage to peer around the corner and into the bathroom. Naked and slick skin was partially concealed by steam, so it took a moment before he realized what he was seeing.

Bryce and Jake were in the shower, the curtain pulled wide and the floor tiles soaked and probably slippery as all hell. They didn't seem to mind the mess, but that was probably because they were engrossed with each other. And by engrossed, he meant... something else entirely.

Cambry blinked, still unable to catch up. Bryce strained his thick thighs, flexing his ass as he pushed Jake against the wall, their lips sealed as they moaned into each other's mouths. Their hands were roaming, mapping out thick muscle and skin that looked so warm that *they* were the source of the steam and not the shower.

The kiss was like nothing Cambry had ever imagined two alphas could have. In his mind and in his stories, it was always brutal with a hint of barely suppressed rage as the alphas clawed and bit each other, drawing blood in their heated passion.

But Bryce looked so gentle as he sucked on Jake's tongue, then nibbled on his lower lip until Jake gasped and tilted his head back. When Bryce dropped his mouth to Jake's neck, he kissed and sucked, drawing patterns with his tongue and not his teeth. He didn't try to bite, in fact, there was no violence in anything he did. Even his hands looked gentle as he moved them down Jake's waist, cupping his ass and urging him closer so their groins touched.

Cambry's breath left him in a whoosh as Bryce moved lower, sucking Jake's nipples into his mouth one at a time while he curled his fingers in the chest hair between Jake's pecs. Cambry's mouth watered and his hand twitched. He longed to feel that hair for himself to find out how soft it was.

Even Jake's belly was worshiped by Bryce as he crouched and swirled his tongue in it. Jake let out a groaning laugh, flexing his abs as he moved his hands down the damp shower wall. Water dripped from his hair, blazing a path along his rigid body where it was caught by his chest hair or lapped up by Bryce below.

"Here's my favorite guy," said Bryce as he went to his knees and wrapped his hand around Jake's cock. It was the first good look that Cambry had managed to get of Jake's cock, and his mouth went dry at the sight.

He knew that alphas were bigger, and he'd seen it in the few flashes of flesh he'd had in horrible places, but there was something about seeing one that he actually *wanted* that made all the difference.

Cambry's might as well have been a finger compared to Jake's cock that was flushed, thick and dripping in Bryce's grip. Even Bryce seemed impressed as he licked at the head, gathering a few drops of pre-cum with his tongue before he stood and brought their lips together again.

Cambry imagined the taste they shared, probably so much stronger than his own. He'd tried it once, just to see what all the buzz about blow jobs was about. He had gagged and spit his cum into the bathroom sink before he'd brushed his teeth twice. The flavor had still clung to his tongue.

"Tell me what you need," said Bryce, drawing his hand down Jake's side, and dipping into every little crease with his fingers. "Can I take you to bed?"

Jake nodded, his eyes still partially closed as he stared at Bryce.

Bryce threaded their fingers together before tugging Jake into their bedroom where they disappeared from view. The light flicked on a moment later, and Cambry caught the sound of something shifting in the room.

"What are you doing?" asked Jake, his deep voice thrumming against the walls.

"You'll see."

Relief and disappointment had never been so close together. Cambry longed to see more — see everything — but he was resolutely terrified of what would happen if he did. He'd never known two alphas to be together, except for in his books.

He braced his hand on the counter, his feet getting soaked instantly as he stepped through a puddle. He grabbed a towel, dropping it to the ground to soak up the mess before he took another step. He couldn't *not* look. He had no choice, even though his wolf was strangely silent about the ordeal. Perhaps it was as shocked as he was.

When he peeked through the bedroom door, he slapped his palm over his mouth to keep from moaning out loud. Bryce was laid out on the bed beneath Jake, his head tipped back and ecstasy written across his features. Jake hovered over him on his hands and knees, tracing Bryce's ear with his lips.

Jake's cock throbbed visibly between his parted legs, swaying slightly as he shifted over his lover. The sight was more mesmerizing than a metronome. It looked so heavy and hard. *How is it not uncomfortable for him?* It looked hot, too, and so red that it was nearly purple.

"You can take a seat if you're comfortable," said Bryce, looking toward the bathroom door.

Jake froze, turning his wide-eyed gaze on Cambry. It took him a full three seconds before Cambry realized that Bryce was speaking to him.

Growling, Jake perched over Bryce protectively before covering his body with his own. Cambry's heart pounded, more from the sight than from the growl that his beast ignored like a harmless fly.

"How long have you been watching?" asked Jake, his anger thick and palpable in the warm room. Cambry shuddered. How was he supposed to answer without enraging Jake further? His leg collided with a chair as he stepped back. It hadn't been there when he'd scoped out the room earlier.

"Almost since the beginning," said Bryce, cupping Jake's cheek and pulling him into a brief kiss. "Take a seat, Cambry, or leave and close the door."

Heat broke out along Cambry's skin. Bryce was inviting him to what? Watch? His curiosity was nearly as strong as his nervousness, but it was his aching groin that won out.

He took two steps to the bathroom, flicking the light off before he very deliberately walked to the chair and sat down. The cushion creaked under his weight, the frame groaning as he leaned back to try to give his erection a tad of extra room to be comfortable. With what little he had upfront, he couldn't imagine how uncomfortable it would be for an alpha to be trapped within their pants.

Bryce had looked a touch panicked when Cambry had first stepped toward the bathroom, but a slow smile spread across his face as Cambry sat. Jake seemed to somehow relax, too, but maybe it was because of the line of pre-cum leaking from his cock and dragging over Bryce's skin.

"Can you smell him?" asked Bryce, looking to Jake before leaning up to nibble on his uninjured ear.

Jake grumbled a reply, and Cambry flushed as he realized they were talking about *him*. Sniffing his pits self-consciously, he only detected a touch of sweat and maybe a hint of body odor. He hadn't exactly had time to bathe since he'd woken from his nightmare.

"I'm sorry," Cambry said softly, sinking into the chair before bringing his knees to his chest. The chair groaned at the added weight, the antique wood creaking.

"You smell delicious," said Bryce with a smirk. "The best you've been since you got here. Your arousal is sweet with a touch of citrus. It's the opposite of your fear."

Cambry swallowed as his eyes burned. In all his life, no one had ever told him he smelled good. He'd been told he was overpowering, which was why the doctors figured he had such a poor sense of smell. Even *they* had been hard-pressed to get close to him with the way he *reeked*. His father had gone as far to describe him as 'week-old garbage'.

A moan pulled him from his thoughts. Bryce had flipped Jake onto his back, pinning his arms above his head as his chest heaved. Jake's legs were spread wide, giving Cambry the perfect view of his cock as well as the barest hint of his furled hole. It twitched when Bryce said something into Jake's ear.

Cambry half-expected Bryce to guide his cock into Jake at that moment. His nails bit into the arms of the chair as he waited for the impending fight — or at least a rushed fuck like he'd read about so many times before. Perhaps he was reading the wrong books, because Bryce didn't seem to be in any sort of rush.

"Have you ever watched two alphas together?" asked Bryce without turning to look at him. He lowered his lips to Jake's neck, sucking a sloppy line of kisses along the reddened column.

Cambry flushed as he glanced back at his bedroom to where the book was still on his pillow. *Did Bryce know?* He hadn't exactly hidden it well. "I've read about it. It didn't seem like this."

Jake whimpered under Bryce's obviously skilled mouth, arching his back as Bryce skimmed his thumbs over his nipples. Cambry throbbed, his throat on fire as he struggled to hold back his own sounds. Maybe this was exactly how it was supposed to be.

"No matter what gender or secondary gender your partner is, it's always about trust," said Bryce as he paused his kisses. "I have to trust that Jake will tell me what he needs, and Jake has to trust me that I will do my best to give it to him. Right now, he needs to be cherished, and that's exactly what I'm going to do." He moved to Jake's hip, sucking the skin into his mouth. He nibbled until Jake's cock flexed, fluid oozing from his cock and pooling on his belly. It wasn't there long before Bryce licked it up, scraping with his teeth and tongue.

Cambry moved his own hand on himself along the same path as Bryce's tongue. He could almost imagine that it was another's touch and not his own. His nerves prickled, his balls going heavy as his cock throbbed.

He'd never considered touching himself like that, other than to bathe. Sex was about mounting, fucking and making babies. It wasn't about exploration or being cherished, right?

But Jake looked so peaceful, even as he writhed, his cock bigger and harder than Cambry had ever imagined. He didn't long for that cock inside him, but he wanted to touch it, taste it and feel every inch of Jake's skin.

"What does it feel like?" Cambry asked softly as he leaned forward in his seat. Bryce didn't respond, nipping at Jake's groin only a few inches away from his cock.

"Good," said Jake, his voice barely more than a growl.

Cambry shook his head, unable to look away. "I mean for Bryce. What does it feel like?"

Bryce paused, furrowing his forehead for a moment before something seemed to dawn on him. "If you were one of us right now, Cambry, who would you be?"

Cambry edged closer to the brink of his seat. His imagination was working overdrive to try to satisfy his curiosity in both instances, but a part of him didn't want to be prone on the bed. He would rather be the one over Jake, touching every part of him and *tasting*. A shudder ran up his spine.

"Bryce. I would want to be touching and..." He trailed off, unable to finish. Jake let out a long groan at his words, bucking his hips until Bryce was nearly thrown off.

"Would you like that, Jake?" asked Bryce, pinning Jake's hips with his hands. "Would you like Cambry on top of you? Inside you?" He dropped his hand lower, pressing between Jake's cheeks to his hole that had disappeared out of sight.

Growling, Cambry clutched at the arms of the chair, his claws digging deep into the antique furniture. He'd felt himself inside once, cringing at the pressure that his thick fingers caused, but he still remembered the heat and the longing to push deeper, despite the twinge.

Bryce chuckled, spreading Jake's legs wider before moving them so Cambry had the perfect view of everything he longed to see. Reaching for the drawer, Bryce grabbed a clear bottle, popping it open and spreading some of it over his fingers.

"Like some omegas, alphas don't produce their own slick, so you have to use the artificial stuff. Some are flavored like an omega in heat, but we prefer the unscented. I never want to be removed from the fact that I'm fucking another alpha." Bryce grinned, spreading the slick over Jake's tiny hole.

There was no way he would fit. Even his fingers looked like it would be a tight squeeze. Alphas just weren't meant to be fucked like that.

"Are you going to treat this entire thing like a fucking documentary?" grumbled Jake, hissing as Bryce slicked his swollen sac.

"I owe you two a session today, so yes." Bryce dipped his finger inside, disappearing through the tiny ring until he reached the first knuckle. Jake let out a breath, clenching his abs tight as his cock twitched.

"He looks tight," said Cambry, unable to stop himself. He left the chair, kneeling at the foot of the bed. The air was thick with arousal and the smell of sweat that was beading along their skin. The sheets were rumpled and already damp beneath them.

"He *is* tight," said Bryce, sinking farther until his finger was all the way inside. "You have to prepare an alpha the same way you would prepare a virgin omega. You need to take your time. If you rush, you'll tear something, especially if you knot them."

"Ah, fuck." Jake tossed his head back. "Right there."

Bryce chuckled again, crooking a free finger to summon Cambry closer. Cambry inched forward on his knees, the flooring scuffing to the point of pain.

Up close, he could see the glisten of lube against Jake's rim, the artificial smell of it drawing him in. The heat of Bryce's body blazed right next to him, soaking any remaining cold from him.

"Every man had something called a prostate, and it's a lot like a G-spot on a woman. If I press here" — he flexed his finger and Jake let out another groan — "it stimulates Jake's prostate and makes him leak."

There was a growing pool of pre-cum on his belly, and as Bryce moved his finger again, more fluid joined it. At least his novels had *that* part right. Cambry nodded to show his understanding, licking his lips as he inhaled.

"Come on, Bryce. I'm dying up here," said Jake, the sound of tearing sheets spiking his continued moans.

"Do you like it?" asked Cambry, pushing the heel of his hand into his cock as it surged. It was almost surreal to have an erection with an audience. He had to keep checking to make sure he wasn't dreaming.

Bryce shrugged. "Sometimes. I really get off on making love to Jake. Mounting him is the biggest high in the world." He snuck a second finger inside, spreading them wide before he added a third. "My favorite thing is tasting his skin and licking the sweat from him as I get him hard, knowing that I'm the one who did that. I like taking care of him and showing him that he has more control than he thinks."

"Well, I'm about to lose it up here if you don't fuck me in the next twenty seconds. Then Cambry will really get to see two bears going at it." Jake grabbed the pillow from behind his head, lobbing it at Bryce and smacking him across the face.

"Just for that," said Bryce, curling his lips back before running teeth along the underside of Jake's cock.

Jake hissed and tried to pull away, but Bryce stopped him by clamping down on his hips. Lube shone on Jake's skin from the fingers that had been inside him moments before.

Cambry cringed in sympathy. His cock was sensitive, and the idea of teeth touching him there was electrifying.

Bryce slowly made his way up Jake's body, pausing at every contour to suck and nip until Jake looked like he was barely hanging on. Their bellies were slick with pre-cum, their skin sliding smoothly together as they humped and ground.

At last, when Cambry had decided that it would never end, Bryce finally parted Jake's thighs, slipping his cock between Jake's cheeks. Bryce flexed, his ass going taut, and Jake suddenly cried out, their bodies moving closer until they touched as intimately as possible.

Cambry let out a gasp as he realized that Bryce was inside Jake, buried to the hilt with his massive alpha cock. Slipping his hand into his pants, Cambry wrapped his fingers around himself.

"Does it hurt?" asked Cambry, one elbow on the comforter as he stroked himself.

Bryce shook his head, gasping and closing his eyes. "He's so tight and hot around me. If we wouldn't have used lube, it would hurt us both. Jake's being stretched wide...wider than his body knows he can take. It never remembers how good I split him, and how I can make him burn for it."

Oh. Oh. Camby stilled his hand, his groin throbbing with the need for release. He didn't want to let go and risk missing anything that was happening before him.

"Fuck! Knot me." Jake dug his nails into Bryce's back, bloodied lines appearing on his skin. He bucked, driving Bryce deeper inside.

"I didn't get you ready for my knots, buddy. You'll have to be happy with just my cock today." He turned to look at Cambry, his face flushed and his mouth open in a pant. "My knots are almost as big as my fist, so I have to do a lot of extra prep if Jake is going to be able to take them."

Jake snarled, bucking and twisting until he managed to grab Bryce and throw him down on the bed with a thud. Bryce grimaced as his cock withdrew violently, the throbbing flesh pink, slick and shiny. Jake settled on top of him a moment later, almost dwarfing him with his bulk.

Grabbing Bryce by the cock, Jake lowered himself all the way to the base, flexing as he took every inch. "I said knot me, *bitch*."

The word seemed to do something to Bryce, who snarled and lunged before sinking his teeth into Jake's throat. Cambry's heart stuttered as Bryce wrestled Jake off him before rolling him face-first into the mattress. With a slap of wet skin, he grabbed Jake by the hips, pulled him to his knees and sank all the way inside in one long thrust.

Jake cried out, his face contorting as he turned to look at Cambry. There were so many emotions that Cambry could hardly decipher them, but one reigned over the rest. There was pure satisfaction with every grunt as Bryce slapped his groin to Jake's ass. And Jake wailed in what sounded like delight when Bryce grabbed him by the neck, pushing him into the bed.

So maybe the novels had been right on par.

"Don't call me that," said Bryce. His words were peaked with anger for the first time.

"It's what you are," said Jake, gasping as Bryce landed a slap on his ass. "You're my *bitch,* and you'll knot me like you're told. I can take it, but can you give it?" A grin touched Jake's lips as Bryce pounded faster, seemingly losing himself.

Cambry swallowed. What the hell was he even seeing? Jake *wanted* Bryce to go harder and faster?

"Doesn't it hurt?" he asked softly, not sure if Jake would even hear him. Jake blinked lazily, his grin nearly infectious.

"I love it when he loses it."

Bryce suddenly slowed, and Jake furrowed his forehead before he shut his eyes tight. Cambry moved along the bed to where the couple were connected.

Jake was stretched so wide, his rim pale and thin as Bryce fucked into him. But Bryce's cock had changed, with two small bulges forming along it as he slowed his thrusts. He paused for a moment, pulling all the way out before he plunged back inside, forcing Jake even wider. His hips stilled as he bottomed out, grinding as Jake started to whimper in earnest.

"You'll take it," said Bryce, biting Jake's shoulder as he heaved in a breath. Loosening his teeth, he turned to Cambry, his pupils blown wide. "Did you see them?"

Cambry nodded, his entire body throbbing as Jake's cries got louder. He scrambled over the bed to see Jake's face, which had flushed red, his brows together in concentration.

"Some alphas have one knot, but others have more than one," said Bryce, reaching around Jake's hip to stroke his still-hard cock. He jerked rapidly a few times before stilling at the base and clenching it tight. Jake went wild beneath him, the base of his cock swelling in Bryce's palm as cum oozed from the slit.

"Jake has one knot at the base." He squeezed it as he pulled Jake upright, giving Cambry a better look. It grew rapidly, until it barely fit into Bryce's hand. It was dark red with veins lining the surface when it finally stopped expanding. Bryce held it tight as Jake pulsed, his sac clenching with each shot.

"Jake's is big enough that I really can't take it unless he fists me first," said Bryce, nearly breathless. "Mine are a touch smaller, but I have two — one at the base and one closer to the tip. Alphas can't come unless our knots are stimulated. I could pound into Jake for days, but he would stay right at the edge until I wrapped my hand around him. It's worse for him right now, because my second knot sits right over his prostate."

Jake cried out as Bryce ground his hips, cum spurting from his cock in a torrent. Cambry stared, completely mesmerized as the sheets went from stained to ruined in the span of heartbeats, and still, it kept flowing.

"He comes a bit more than I do, but not by much — probably because he only has one knot. Alphas with multiple knots tend to come less." Bryce's voice had gotten a touch steadier and he lowered his forehead to Jake's sweaty back. "You okay, bud?"

Jake grumbled softly, arching his back as he sank his face into the rumpled blanket. "Hurts."

"Uh-huh." Bryce leaned back to rub along Jake's lower spine, presumably trying to ease the tension. "Will you let me prep you properly next time?" He shut his eyes for a moment, and Cambry caught the flex of his ass along with the twitch of his balls.

He's still coming? Cambry peered under Jake's belly where most of his cum had soaked into the sheets. His cock was still dribbling from the tip in a steady stream. Bryce eased his grip, and the stream stopped abruptly.

"Any questions?" asked Bryce, scratching the back of his head before he patted Jake once on the ass.

"Yeah. You fucking done yet? I'm getting too full," Jake grumbled, crawling forward until they both hissed and Bryce pulled him back.

"Don't be like that," said Bryce, smoothing over Jake's belly as he stilled. Cambry nearly balked as he noticed that he could barely see the definition of Jake's abs anymore. He was completely filled with Bryce, enough that his belly swelled.

"If I try to pull out too early, it could hurt us both. Twice as bad, actually, because I have two knots. These babies won't go down for a while yet, so Jake will just have to be patient." Bryce patted Jake's other ass cheek, grinning as his lover groused.

"Can you not talk about me like I'm not here? It makes me feel like a science experiment," said Jake, grumbling again as Bryce laughed.

"You know I love you, sweetheart."

Oh God. Everything was wrong. Cambry's heart pounded as his palms went slick, his stomach turning over as he struggled to swallow.

Cambry moved from the bed, slowly standing and heading for the bathroom. He managed to hold back his tears until he closed the bathroom door behind him, the sound of Bryce's concerned voice cutting straight through him.

Jumping into bed, he buried himself beneath his blankets, digging his claws into the sheets so he wouldn't touch himself. He waited until his heart slowed before he finally let the sobs out.

Chapter Eight

Bryce

"Okay, everyone," said Bryce, slapping his hands together sharply before looking to the gathered group. His omega pair looked a touch tired, so hopefully they'd been having some marital success after his one-on-one session, but they didn't seem nearly as exhausted as Cambry. Bryce didn't doubt that Cambry hadn't slept at all.

Bryce had miscalculated, and not just a bit. He'd smashed the brand-new suspension bridge that he'd erected between Cambry and Jake.

His knot had taken forever to go down, and when he'd made it to Cambry's room, Cambry hadn't responded to him. He'd fallen asleep to the gentle sound of Cambry's distant sobbing.

"So, if you liked our first exercise, you'll love this one." Bryce forced a grin on his face, even if it was the last thing he wanted to do. He couldn't give up. Cambry wasn't the only one who needed him, even if he'd already managed to carve a spot for himself in Bryce's chest. His heart twinged as he looked at Cambry, who was staring resolutely at the grass with his knees drawn up.

He was still in the same clothes as the day before, and the day before that—and it didn't look like he'd showered either. His pale eyes looked even stranger with the dark circles under them. His scent was muted as well and barely discernible against the fresh trees.

Jake shifted uncomfortably and Bryce grinned. He loved it hard or soft with Jake, but what really got him going was a good wrestling match where he ended up knot-deep with Jake aching around him.

"Everyone gets to keep their clothes on today if they want to, but they are completely optional. There is one rule, though. No boner shaming. If I see one snicker or hear a single comment, you're not going to like what happens."

Bryce pulled his hoodie off as the sun peeked through the clouds, pulling his hat down to cover his eyes. As much as he loved the outdoors, he hated the in-between days when it was too cool for a T-shirt but too hot for a jacket, and the sky couldn't make up its mind which shade it wanted to be.

"Questions first. Who here has been mounted by an alpha?" He watched as every omega raised their hand except for Cambry. "Come on, alphas. Don't be shy. I'm not talking penetration here, just the mounting part. I don't think I've ever met an alpha who hasn't been mounted in a play-fight."

Jake begrudgingly raised his hand, letting out a sigh as he shifted on the grass. The fisher alpha raised his hand next, but the retriever kept his hands locked together in his lap, despite his mate's eye roll.

"Just put your hand up." His mate elbowed his side, despite his alpha's glare. "What about that fight in the alley last year? I saw the whole thing." The alpha didn't move.

"Oookay, thank you to our honest people who don't think a bit of mounting is emasculating. It's not, by the way. It's too fun for that." Bryce grinned as a few omegas snickered. "Now, who has ever been mounted by an omega?"

His omega pair raised their hands, to no surprise, but every other hand stayed down. Braxton let out a snort.

"You can't be serious," said Braxton, rolling his eyes and managing to look much less attractive than he had with the puffed-out chest. "Omegas aren't built for mounting. They couldn't do it if they tried."

"Says the one sitting beside an omega pair," said Bryce, throwing his hand out as Braxton turned a sneer at Jeremiah and Brandon. "I won't tolerate any disrespect or shaming here. This is a safe place for every individual, which is the only reason I haven't ripped you a new one." Braxton turned his glare on Bryce, and Bryce let out a laugh. "You really think you could take me, puppy?"

Okay, so maybe Cambry is still affecting me. Jake was smiling, though, which made his unprofessionalism just a tad better in his mind. He would do literally anything to make Jake smile.

"I'm actually glad you brought that up, Braxton, because today is your lucky day. Today will be the day that your omega mounts you for the first time."

If Braxton turned any brighter, he might spontaneously combust.

Bryce moved over to his omega pair, kneeling before them. "If you want, you can practice with each other and just take turns, or I can have Braxton volunteer for you. Totally your choice."

Jeremiah reached for his husband's hand before pulling it to his chest. "Just us, please."

"Remember that this isn't about comfort zones. It's about trying new things and breaking down barriers." He moved away, leaving it for them to decide. In all honesty, he loved mounting Jake, but there was no way he wanted to be on top or underneath Braxton.

He moved to Cambry next, kneeling before the omega. Cambry didn't look up, his gaze entwined with the grass as if he didn't realize Bryce was there. Bryce rubbed his own legs, smoothing the goosebumps that had risen at Cambry's presence. His beast shifted, more bothered than Bryce would ever let on.

"This is something that needs to be taken slowly, so I understand if you want to sit this one out. Jake is almost a stranger to you, but I also think this might be good for you. It may not show you how everything feels, but it might give you answers to things you have questions about." Bryce looked to Jake, holding his gaze long enough that Jake nodded and waved him away.

"Thank you for volunteering, Braxton. Edward, let's give it a go. Put your mate on his hands and knees and hop up." Bryce moved to the fire, tossing on a handful of herbs. Things were bound to get heated, and the herbs would take the edge off.

Braxton crossed his arms over his chest, his facing turning nearly plum as he let out a pathetic growl. Bryce's beast growled in return, already on edge from missing out on his regular amount of sleep.

"Ah, I see. You mean, you don't just get yourself ready whenever your mate wants you?" asked Bryce, keeping his voice even as Braxton's eyes went wide. It was the exact reason that he always did the exercise. There was always the same revelation for alphas, like a pheromone-filled veil was lifted from their eyes.

Braxton looked to Edward, who was gazing down at the grass, a frown tugging at his lips and his eyes glassy with unshed tears. It was the first time he had looked truly serious.

"Is that...really what it's like?" asked Braxton before he reached for his mate and pulled him close. "I thought that was the way it's supposed to be."

"You don't put someone on their knees and complain when they aren't receptive every time," said Bryce, addressing every person in the crowd. "Your partner always has the right to say no. Are you saying no, Braxton? Are you denying your mate the same thing he's given you over and over again when you didn't even ask if it's okay?"

"He doesn't hurt me," Edward cut in, a single tear spilling over as Braxton hugged him tighter.

"I know you're here because your relationship is worth saving. You're good people—even you, Braxton," said Bryce, stepping back to give the couple space. "Any other volunteers while we give these two a few moments?"

The fisher alpha dropped to his hands and knees, his omega giggling as he jumped on top from behind. The alpha smiled, turning his head to kiss his mate, before leaning back and scooping him into his arms.

Cambry still hadn't moved, his gaze on the grass as Jake went to his knees and looked over his shoulder expectantly. A blip of panic coursed through Bryce's veins. He'd already managed to fuck up with Cambry once, and he had no desire to do it again so soon. He caught Jake's gaze, giving a shrug.

Maybe Cambry was as doomed as he believed he was.

Chapter Nine

Cambry

How many shades of green was the grass? More than he'd originally thought. Cambry had figured maybe a dozen or so, but he'd been looking for so long that it seemed more like thousands. Every blade was a slightly different color, the tip just a tad lighter than the breadth.

He grasped one in his fingers, ripping it in two. The tear bled darker, oozing the scent of freshness that made his eyes sting.

"Cambry?"

He heard Bryce's voice for about the dozenth time, but he hadn't exactly been keeping track. He'd been doing everything possible to avoid him, as well as Jake, even as his beast tried to pull him toward them. He wouldn't go. *I won't.*

They were everything he could never have. He'd been living in a fantasy world for far too long, and it was time to face reality.

"You can play with us."

A soft voice had him looking up, blinking as blond hair filled his gaze instead of the steady stream of green. It was the bunny omega. He couldn't remember his name. Either way, it didn't matter.

Shaking his head, he looked back to the grass, trying to find the blade he had split open between his fingers. "I don't want to hurt you. You saw me yesterday."

"Yeah," said the bunny as he moved closer. "That was actually the coolest thing I've ever seen." He let out a soft chuckle, and Cambry couldn't help but look to see the blush across his delicate face. He was cute in a soft and innocent kind of way.

"I'm Cambry." The words left him without his permission, and the bunny gave him a soft smile.

"I'm Jeremiah. My husband is Brandon. Would you like to come sit with us?"

Cambry looked across the fire to where Brandon was glaring back with about ten percent of the enthusiasm of his husband. His dark brows were furrowed, his delicate features about as fierce as they could probably get.

"Oh, don't mind him. He likes to put up a brave front, but he's just a pussy cat. I mean, he can't even watch horror movies without me and his stuffie." Jeremiah laughed, and it was such a soft, sweet sound that it settled something deep within Cambry. Brandon scowled, obviously able to hear every word.

"I guess, but I don't know what I can do." Cambry looked to Jeremiah's extended hand, slowly placing his palm there. He dwarfed the other omega.

"I really just want to sit next to the guy who was able to take on two huge alphas and win." Jeremiah tugged him until he stood, leading him around the fire to his husband.

"I didn't win," said Cambry, shaking his head. On his back, hard and wanting, was not a win.

"Oh, you totally did," said Jeremiah, pulling Cambry down before sitting crossed-legged next to him. Brandon grimaced before rubbing at the bottom of his nose. "I mean, taking on two alphas, then disappearing into the house with them later on? Win, win, win. It was a victory for us, too, because that was the hottest show we've ever seen."

Cambry flushed, peeking at Brandon, who had also turned a touch pink. He glanced at his hand where Jeremiah was still holding him tight. The last omega he had touched was his mother and that had been years before. Maybe he'd been expecting more, but there was…nothing.

It wasn't the fluid heat of Jake's tongue or the jagged slice of nerves when their bare skin had touched briefly. It just…was. There was no heat, no cold and his beast still slumbered.

"You, okay?" asked Jeremiah, touching Cambry's chin with his other hand and tilting his head up.

"I've never touched another omega who wasn't family before." Cambry clung tighter to the hand in his grip, dreading the moment when Jeremiah would pull away. "It's not like I imagined." He looked to Brandon, who was staring at him with wide eyes.

"What do you mean you haven't touched an omega? We're fifty-one percent of the population. Were you surrounded by alphas all your life?" Brandon deadpanned, his eyes narrowing.

Cambry shook his head. "They are usually afraid of me. My smell is really strong. And as for the alphas, only a few got close enough to touch me...and not for long. My beast doesn't like to be touched. Jake was the first who managed to pin me, and he wouldn't have been able to do that without Bryce."

"Oh, you poor dear." Jeremiah brought Cambry's hand to his lips, kissing the back of his knuckles. The spot tingled, the touch of moisture tickling his nerves. "Let us introduce you to an omega snuggle-pile. Usually we'd be naked, but let's try with clothes first."

Throwing his arms around Cambry's neck, Jeremiah pulled himself close and perched in Cambry's lap. "Lie back."

Cambry shuddered as Jeremiah's breath tickled his ear. Everything in his mind was telling him to shift and flee, but his beast only grumbled slightly before turning its attentions elsewhere. Lowering himself to the ground, he let out a breath as he settled against the grass with Jeremiah's weight on top of him.

"Come here, sweetness," said Jeremiah, waving Brandon over as Cambry's heart pounded. His eyelids were heavy, sleep calling to him as he slowly relaxed in Jeremiah's arms. Brandon snuggled up to his side, throwing an arm and leg over both of them. His warmth soaked in immediately, leaving only the coolness of the grass beneath them.

"I'm getting naked," said Jeremiah, his breath huffing over Cambry's neck. He squirmed and kicked, almost nailing Cambry twice with his knee before he managed to peel his clothes off. Brandon followed suit, his naked skin like a winter jacket on a cold day. Cambry trembled beneath them, his eyes burning as a calm like no other soothed his soul.

He didn't fight the hands that pulled his shirt over his head, or the ones that went for his pants. He could hardly swallow through the purr that made its way up his throat. Jeremiah responded with his own softer sound, Brandon chiming in with a slightly deeper one.

Cambry fluttered his eyes open as he sensed another presence moving close. Edward had left his alpha's side. He stripped the clothes from his body before sliding between Jeremiah and Brandon. Cambry opened his arms wider to welcome the new weight, tears flowing freely down his cheeks. When the last omega in the group wiggled his way into the pile, his beast let out a purr that could probably be heard for a mile.

He'd never purred before. Even when his mother had held him as a child, he'd never had the involuntary sound creep up his throat. He couldn't have stopped it, not that he wanted to try.

If my father could see me now. His father had always looked down on omegas in general, so Cambry could imagine his reaction to a snuggle-pile. Maybe he would describe it as beastly and unrefined, but maybe that was exactly what Cambry was.

What he couldn't figure out was when the other shoe was going to drop. His father had picked out his therapy. There was no way he would have approved paying for something like *this*. It just didn't make any sense.

Edward snuggled closer, snuffling against Cambry's ear before letting out a contented hum. Cambry clutched him tighter and slid their legs together. Edward was soft against him, just like the rest of the omegas. The contentment was so complete that it was nearly boring.

Something shifted as an alpha approached. Cambry forced his eyes open, letting out a low growl as Bryce came into view. Bryce held up his hands in surrender, taking a small step back, even as Cambry's beast calmed at the familiar presence.

It was strange. Bryce was still unfamiliar, but his beast seemed to prefer him over his own father.

"I'm not here to stop anything, but may we join you?"

Cambry flushed under Bryce's stare, looking over his shoulder at the alphas who had started to close in. Jake was there, his dark gaze steady as he licked his lips. The strain of his pants was more than obvious. *They're aroused? Why?*

His mouth went dry as Jeremiah grumbled before turning to his husband and locking their lips together. Brandon thrust against Cambry's hip in response, going from soft to hard in record time.

It was like a chain reaction of touches and groans, omegas writhing against him and near him as the snuggle filled with pure intent. His own cock hardened, his vision narrowing to Bryce and Jake. Without realizing it, he nodded.

Pulling Edward harder to his chest, he let out a sigh of relief when Braxton didn't try to take him away and instead settled his knees on the grass, licking a strip up Edward's spine. Edward gasped against Cambry's chest.

The thick smell of his slick filled the air, and he wasn't the only one. There were so many scents, sounds and touches that Cambry could hardly keep track. He closed his eyes, holding as much skin close to him as he possibly could. If they left him, he was sure to float away.

A touch of a warm hand landed on Cambry's hip and he let out a gasp as his cock throbbed. The touch felt like Jake—hot and powerful but yielding at the same time. He opened his legs wide, not sure who had settled between them. Edward gasped in his ear, the sound so filled with pleasure that Cambry had to look.

Braxton was behind his mate, pushing Edward's cheeks wide as he licked his exposed hole and drank his slick. His eyes were blown wide and nearly black as he bobbed his head over and over.

Jeremiah was on Cambry's opposite shoulder, Brandon now on top of him and grinding their groins together with gasp-filled moans. The other omega lay across Cambry's belly, his alpha nuzzling his neck.

Then there was Jake, his dark eyes narrowed as he touched every available part of Cambry. Cambry tried to find Bryce in the pile of limbs and longing, finally spotting him off to the side. Maybe he was observing, with his lip caught between his teeth and his cock poking his pants with an obscene bulge. He was the only thing that was missing.

"Bryce," Cambry called out, hoping that he could break the last of the alpha's restraints. Suddenly, Bryce was there, pressed against Jake intimately and slowly easing his clothes from his body. Leaning in, Bryce bit down on an exposed part of Cambry's leg, his nerves surging to life at the flash of pain.

He'd never been so hard in his life, not even when he'd watched Bryce and Jake together on their bed. But he'd never been so stimulated with every inch of skin belonging to someone else. He closed his eyes, letting his head fall back into the grass.

Someone licked his inner thigh, the sensation bringing a laugh to his lips. He squirmed, his thigh sliding along a rigid hardness that wept against him.

Edward gasped in his ear, crying out at whatever his mate was doing.

More. More. More.

Finally, there was a hand on his cock, stroking from tip to base with the perfect amount of pressure. It was slick, and it took him a few moments to realize how much pre-cum he was actually leaking. Slick splashed onto his hip, the taint of arousal like cotton candy on his tongue.

Someone crept between his thighs, stroking between his cheeks with blunt fingers. There, at least, he was dry. It was probably the only spot on him that wasn't soaked in some sort of fluid.

A flash of terror pushed through his mind as they probed deeper, touching his entrance with steady pressure until he was sure his body would give way. Whimpering, he tried to close his thighs, clenching his cheeks so his hole would lock up tight. His heart beat wildly as he wondered if they would push inside anyway.

They retreated, sliding over his sac and teasing his balls one by one instead. Sighing with full-bodied relief, he bucked as something warm, which had to have been a mouth, descended over his cock, sucking him all the way to the base with the most powerful suction he could have imagined.

Crying out, he threaded a hand through someone's hair, tugging once before searching for something else. He shuddered when he found it—the long, hard shaft that was almost too thick for his hand. He moved his other hand along the sea of bodies, searching until he found the matching cock that somehow felt even bigger.

They leaked into his palms as he squeezed them tight before moving up and down the shafts one at a time. He moved slowly, mapping out every vein, even as their owners bucked. He moved faster, doing his best to remember what he liked.

"Squeeze the knots for us, baby." It was Bryce's voice in his ear, urging him to move his hands down to where cock met groin. He squeezed harder than he would ever dare to on himself, gasping as the hot flesh started to swell. He almost let go out of pure shock, until he felt Bryce's hand over his, gripping his second knot that was farther up his shaft.

Look, dammit! He pried his eyes open, immediately finding Jake, who was bent at the waist and snarling as he licked someone's pre-cum from Cambry's chest. His knot was swelling impossibly in Cambry's hand as he started to shoot, cum pouring down Cambry's arm until it dripped from his elbow.

Bryce had bitten Jake's shoulder, his teeth sinking deep a few times and leaving rosy circles all over the muscle. A few were there from the night before, bruised and dark like a bullseye.

The mouth on Cambry's cock swallowed and he looked down frantically. He had expected Jake or Bryce to be the ones on him, but blond hair greeted him as he looked down. Jeremiah's eyes were half-closed as he sank down on Cambry over and over, his purr vibrating along his shaft better than any toy. Brandon was behind him, pumping his hips as he presumably fucked into his husband. Jeremiah's cock was already covered in cum and starting to soften.

It was too much. As Jeremiah took one last suck, Cambry shattered, his grip going hard on the two alpha's cocks in his grasp and his balls drawing up as he poured into Jeremiah's mouth.

A universal groan seemed to go up in the group, and Braxton snarled, sinking his teeth into Edward's neck as Edward emptied himself on Cambry's skin. Somehow, some made it into Cambry's mouth, coating his tongue with ecstasy and sex as his orgasm peaked.

There was a moment where he thought he might shift, his wolf howling so close to his skin that his teeth ached. Then it was gone, receding as fast as his orgasm and leaving him so utterly sated that he never wanted to move again.

The tied alphas hovered over their mates as they snuggled close to the mutual slick and body heat. Brandon pulled out and squirmed his way to the center of the pile on Cambry's belly. Jake leaned down, licking the slick and cum from Cambry's skin and getting every speck that he could reach as Bryce ran his hand through Cambry's hair.

He let his eyes fall shut again and took his first real breath in his life. Sleep called to him, easing the coolness of the grass as someone big, that had to have been Jake, pried him high enough to slip underneath. Bryce never left him, even as he finally let himself slip away.

Chapter Ten

Bryce

He'd been on edge for the last twenty-four hours. He'd skipped his one-on-one sessions with each couple to let them recover after the epic mating pile that Jeremiah had so wonderfully started. He had always hoped to experience one in his lifetime, but it had never come forth in any of his therapy sessions.

They just weren't accepted anymore except on the fringes of society. People were born and raised to believe that monogamy was the only way and that pack life was a thing for the Neanderthals of the past. Even though the benefits, both mental and sexual, were numerous, they were still frowned upon.

Maybe it was something that he could make mandatory for every one of his week-long therapy sessions?

He glanced at Jake as he stared off into the woods, his jaw set and his mind probably wandering to the same place his own was. *Cambry.*

The pile had lasted for hours, omegas and alphas seeking their pleasure until there were so many fluids that they all had to go have showers. Cambry had been in the middle of the pile, the true center who every person had navigated to, including Jake and himself.

When he'd set Jake up with Cambry, he had hoped to get the bear out of his comfort zone just long enough that Jake could see how far he'd come. Sometimes, Bryce was certain that Jake still thought of himself as the feral alpha he had been when they had found each other, ready to rip limb from loin.

He hadn't expected himself to get involved with a client. Cambry was his charge, but he was also his patient, and no matter what kind of silly ideas Mr. Parsons had about Feral Woods, Bryce was going to treat Cambry until he felt like more than just the shoe that everyone trod on.

Glancing back to the house, he let out a deep sigh, hanging another scent trap before he nodded at Jake to move on. They were setting up for the final couples therapy challenge, one that he treated more like a game than anything else. There would be one more one-on-one session after that, then the groups would move back to their daily lives — all except Cambry.

"You keep him until you fix him." Bryce had barely kept his few choice words to himself when Mr. Parsons had said that to him. Bryce was fine with any client staying as long as they needed, but with Cambry, it was different.

He'd never met someone so damaged, and it didn't seem like Cambry had even had a choice about coming to Feral Woods. He wasn't dangerous. Okay, maybe he was a *bit* dangerous. Feral Woods was the best place for him, and he couldn't imagine Cambry just leaving.

He just hadn't figured out if that was because he didn't *want* Cambry to go, or if his professional opinion was that it wasn't safe for Cambry to go. He had Jake as his mate and life partner — something many in society wouldn't understand or accept. He'd never gotten off with a client in his life, and it was fucking up his point of view.

If it got out that he was mated to an alpha, he wasn't sure if his practice would be ruined by bigoted assholes or if more hesitant couples would seek him out for advice and counseling.

"He was wearing the same clothes again today," said Jake, startling Bryce from his thoughts. Jake rubbed his back against a nearby tree, spreading a fresh scent to further confuse the alphas in the final couples' session.

Five days and Cambry had donned the same shirt and jeans each morning. Even in the afternoon when the temperature climbed and everyone had donned shorts, Cambry still shuffled into the hall for dinner in the same clothes, sweat clinging to him.

"He's showered, though," said Bryce, scratching the back of his head. "Do you think it's a phobia thing? There have been a lot of other things that have come up that I wasn't expecting."

Jake gave him a sharp look. Maybe he was thinking the same thing. Bryce hadn't expected to blow his knot and watch Jake lick his cum from an omega's skin. He hadn't expected to be with another man, period. Jake was perfect for him and exactly enough.

"Does he *have* other clothes?" Jake asked.

"He brought a duffel bag, and his dad's loaded. It's not like he can't afford clothes." Bryce shrugged, pulling a sprig of lavender from his pack. He struggled not to sneeze as the oils soaked into his skin, slipping straight up his nose.

"Just because your parents have money doesn't mean they take care of you the way they should." Jake turned away, his words ringing in Bryce's ears. *Darn.* He should never have said something so callous.

Jake's history was almost as bleak as Cambry's, only Jake had started cage fighting so he could support himself when he'd struck out on his own. There was no government funding for schooling when a parent pulled in six figures, whether or not they believed in using their money for education.

When Bryce had found him, Jake had owned two shirts and as many pants, with zero boxers to his name. The ragged pair of socks that he'd worn had disintegrated shortly after they'd met.

Hanging the rest of his scent traps as quickly as he could, Bryce rushed back to the house, taking the stairs three at a time before heading into his and Jake's shared room. The bathroom door was open on both sides and Cambry's light was on.

He chewed his lip as he slowly approached, listening carefully so he didn't interrupt whatever Cambry was doing. One thing he was going to have to do was convince Cambry to spend more time outside. It wasn't healthy to lounge indoors while you tried to get in touch with your beast. It just led to confusion and pent-up emotions.

He rounded the corner slowly, blinking when he found Cambry reading on his bed. He'd spotted the book out of the corner of his eye before, but he'd never actually noticed Cambry reading.

He was lounging against the headboard with every pillow jammed under his back so he was propped upright. The book looked tiny in his large hands, but he held it gently, carefully turning the page. He furrowed his forehead in concentration, his cheeks dusted with a faint flush. The scent of arousal reached Bryce a moment before he noticed Cambry's hard cock peeking through his open zipper.

He *was* wearing the same clothes. It really was a shame, because Bryce had seen him naked and it had been a treat. Part of him wished that Cambry were lounging on the bed completely naked—a *big* part of him.

Bryce took another step, the cover of the book finally readable in the dim indoor light. *Forbidden Alphas?* Licking his lips, he cleared his throat.

Cambry shot upright, throwing his book to the bed and covering his groin at the same time. His eyes were wide and terrified, his scent thickening and turning with his fear. Bryce sniffed, rubbing the bottom of his nose uncomfortably as he took a step back.

"Hey," said Bryce. *Eloquent, as always.* "Just wanted to check on you. I didn't see you at breakfast." He sat on the corner of the bed, reaching for the pillow that had fallen to cover the book. Cambry squeaked and threw himself off the bed, darting to the door at a flat run.

Bryce blinked as Cambry disappeared from view, racing down the stairs in a whirl of thumps and bangs. The slap of the front door reached him a moment later. *Should I follow?* Cambry's run hadn't looked like an invitation.

He reached for the book instead, turning the cover right side up as he brought it before him. *Oh.* His mouth dropped open as he stared at two men, who were obviously alphas, naked and writhing so only their cocks were hidden.

He turned the book over, sliding his fingers along the dulled cover that was marked with thousands of overlapping fingerprints. The pages were frayed and yellow, the scent of omega arousal clinging to them.

"Families at war and two alphas bound by more than just a hatred that is generations old."

Bryce blinked, flipping open to a random page where the corner was creased as if it had been folded over more than once.

"Diego growled, pushing X into the bed as he sank his teeth into the back of his neck, slamming his knot to the hilt inside the other alpha with one brutal thrust."

Okay, so that explained a few things. He turned the book over again, tracing the cover. He hadn't realized that there were books like it out there. Every time he went to the bookstore for a good read, he found the shelves flooded with male-female alpha-omega romances. There was only so much he could take before he turned into a sap. If he searched long enough, he sometimes found a male-male pairing, but they were always alpha and omega as well.

Looking down at the open duffel bag beside the bed, he let out a laugh as he spotted the shadowed edge of a pile of books. He tugged on the strap, the thirty pounds of literature inside resisting him. It was no wonder the kid didn't have any clothes.

Bryce thumbed through them, his groin tingling uncomfortably when he saw that they were all the same theme. A few of the covers even looked like Jake and himself if he squinted.

He leaned back against Cambry's headboard, taking the same pose the omega had before inhaling the lingering sweetness. Flipping the book open to the first page, he started to read. It had been too long since he'd read a good book anyway, and maybe it would have some pointers for him and Jake—not that he was complaining.

It wasn't long before he had to pop the button on his pants, freeing his cock with the tug of his zipper.

Chapter Eleven

Cambry

He shifted into a wolf as he pushed through the front door, ripping his shirt to pieces as his body grew. Luckily, he managed to free himself from his jeans before his legs started to thicken. He didn't appreciate the sturdiness of denim against his groin during a shift, especially if the seams didn't burst right away.

He turned toward the forest, ready to dart within, before his wolf paused. Tilting his ears toward the sound of laughter, he inhaled, closing his eyes to give his dull nose a touch more power.

Cinnamon and honey. The laughter belonged to the sweetest man he'd ever met. A man who had taught him that nudity wasn't shameful and that it was okay to follow his instincts.

He let out a warning bark before he barreled toward the sound, yelping as Jeremiah came into view. Brandon's eyes went wide as he caught sight of

Cambry, taking a step back and looking about a second away from spurting quills.

"Hi, Cambry!" Jeremiah held his arms wide as if he weren't a bunny about to be snatched in the jaws of a wolf. "I was just wondering where you were. I didn't see you at breakfast."

Cambry slowed to a trot, bumping his head against Jeremiah's chest when he got close enough. Jeremiah brought a hand down on his head before threading through the scruff just behind his ears.

"Oooh, you're soft. Brandon, touch him."

If Cambry could have flushed, he would have. Instead, he lowered his head, letting out a humiliated whine as Brandon awkwardly patted him. His wolf grumbled with a touch of indignation, lifting his lip in a silent snarl.

"I get it," said Jeremiah, never pausing his hands. "You're the big bad wolf. Well, guess what, Mr. Wolfie, even you need a hug at least once per day. I need three, and Brandon has only given me two so far today. Can I give you a hug?"

Cambry huffed, turning away and wishing he could smile. There was something about Jeremiah that just calmed his beast. Maybe it was his innocence or the fact that Jeremiah would never pose any threat.

If you could see me now, Dad. The only ones allowed to visit Camby had been a long line of alphas and his one appointed friend. Omegas were never permitted in the same room with him alone, and even if they would have been, he doubted that they would have had the same bravery as Jeremiah.

"Brandon and I were going to check out the pond. We brought our swim trunks when we read about it in the reviews. I already asked Bryce, and he said we were fine to use it if we wanted to."

That sounded so much better than getting caught red-handed and red-cocked with a taboo book on his hands. His father would have sent him straight to a facility, but Bryce? Maybe the alpha would understand. It just wasn't something that Cambry had any desire to talk about.

He nodded once, padding along behind Jeremiah and Brandon as they strolled down an overgrown path. A few jays called in the trees, fluttering their wings every time they got close. The air was thick and close, but the trees kept the worst of the summer sun at bay, which was great when he was wearing the equivalent of three winter coats.

The trees parted along a rock ledge, revealing a small lake that looked like it had been put there completely by accident. A sturdy beaver dam held the water on one side with only a tiny wisp escaping at the base. A few skeletal trees drooped along the water's edges, like giant pieces of twisted driftwood. Tracks of every kind were stamped in the shallow reeds.

Cambry bent to sniff one, the scent and taste of a real bear rolling over his tongue. His wolf wagged his tail, keeping an eye on his companions as they stepped to the rock and looked out over the water. Jeremiah clasped their hands together, leaning his head down on his husband's shoulder.

"It's beautiful."

The loon on the water gave a whooping alarm as Cambry perked up, holding his tail erect as he spied the bird.

With a burst of water, it flapped its wings, calling to every instinct in Cambry's body to chase and run. He let out a bark, leaping into the water and splashing through the shallows. It beat its wings frantically, its red eyes locked on him as he surged toward it, his wolf taking over every part of his mind.

He snapped his teeth over its tail, and it called once more before it finally seemed to catch the air on its wings, tugging free as it powered ahead and lifted off the surface. Cambry growled, a single feather caught between his teeth as his only prize. He dipped in the water as he lost focus for a moment before his wolf took over, paddling in the way only a dog could.

Holding his head above the water, he turned back to shore, kicking his powerful legs and going fast enough to create his own little ripples. A few reeds tickled his paws as he went by, the cool water keeping the worst of the sun at bay.

Shaking at the shore, he strolled to Jeremiah, who was laughing again, the sound echoing across the clearing. He dropped the feather at his feet, nudging Brandon, who looked like he was about to set up an animal rights group.

"Oh, look, it's beautiful." Jeremiah lifted the damp feather into the sun, the white dots against black somehow so much more attractive than a crow. "Can you catch fish, too?"

Brandon elbowed his mate, snickering as Cambry nodded with enthusiasm. Cambry bolted back toward the lake, leaping off the rock and splashing into the reeds. His fur weighed him down in the dark water that was stained with iron.

A silver flash caught his eye and he splashed toward it, snapping his jaws and spluttering on a wet mouthful of mud. Prancing a few steps, he darted to the side as a leech undulated his way.

If there was anything in the world that he was afraid of, other than losing his freedom, it was leeches. They were like giant mosquitos, only they had no qualms about slipping under your clothes — and swatting them did absolutely nothing.

A weed tangled around his foot as he tried to escape, sending him face-first into the water. Cambry snorted, pulling himself upright before trotting back to shore. His tongue lolled out of his mouth as he panted, a laugh caught in his throat that his wolf would never be able to produce. Jeremiah was laughing for him, and even Brandon had a smile on his lips.

Sidling up beside them, Cambry let out a great shake, splattering them with raindrops and bits of muck.

"Ah, it's freezing!" Jeremiah shrieked, darting toward the rocky shoreline and running into the water. He paused when he got up to his knees, letting out a full-body shudder.

"So cold." He looked down at his toes as Cambry let out a bark before plowing back into the water and running after the freezing bunny. With a laugh and a yell, Jeremiah broke into a run, his strides so much shorter than Cambry's.

Checking Jeremiah's hip, Cambry tripped him into the water with a torrent of waves, spinning around to head back to Brandon. Brandon dipped one toe into the pond, shaking his head once before he muttered a low 'nope'. Cambry still got him with the second batch of fur-water, though. The hedgehog yelped, retreating to the large rock.

When he finally tired of chasing water bugs and tadpoles, Cambry trudged to the rock, his legs numb and exhausted. His heart was light, though, and he couldn't keep the wolfy-grin off his face.

"I never thought this week would be so healing," said Jeremiah as he pulled himself out of the water and followed Cambry up to the rock, lowering himself next to him before entwining his hands in Cambry's fur. "I was hoping Bryce could help us out with our sex life, but I feel like we've learned so much more. I never thought I would shift when I was an adult, unless it was an emergency situation. I never dreamed I would even want to."

He chuckled as Brandon joined them from where he had kept a vigil far away from the splashing, sinking down on the rock and stretching out with a groan. Jeremiah looked over Cambry's shoulders to his husband. "What do you think, dear? Better than you hoped?"

Brandon nodded, pressing his lips together as he looked over the water. He looked more relaxed than Cambry had ever seen him.

"I thought we were just kidding ourselves," said Brandon, his voice low for his slim build. "I mean, how long could we last, right? Everyone we've ever met has told us that we aren't meant to be together, no matter how much I love you. But maybe..."

He trailed off and Jeremiah let out a small sniff, closing his hands in Cambry's fur until it tugged uncomfortably. Cambry turned his head, dropping it into Jeremiah's lap in what he hoped was a comforting gesture.

"Fuck them, though," said Brandon, a hint of a smile on his lips. "I love who I love, and that's never going to change, no matter who has a problem with it. We're both consenting adults, and what we do with our lives is our business."

Jeremiah threw his arms around Brandon's shoulders, pulling him close until they were leaning over Cambry's back. Cambry let out an *oomph* at the sudden weight, even though he welcomed it.

His wolf receded so suddenly that it left him reeling, his fur slipping under his skin as his limbs went from canine to human in a heartbeat. He let out a low moan as his nerves thrummed beneath his skin, already confused with the building scent of happy omega so close.

"Did you guys want me to give you some space?" Cambry asked softly. He didn't want to go back to the house yet, but he wasn't sure if he was ready for another cuddle orgy so soon.

"Nah," said Jeremiah, lying out on the rock and throwing his leg over Cambry. Brandon sidled up behind his husband, hooking an arm over his waist before closing his eyes.

"Can I ask how you guys met?" He tried not to gaze at them longingly, but it was a test of futility. They were so in love that it was like looking at Jake and Bryce all over again, his chest pulling tight when he realized that feeling would probably never happen to him.

Jeremiah snorted, the corner of his lips curving up. "Of course. We've actually known each other since we were kids, but we didn't get *together* until we were teenagers. Our parents found out and married us both off to alphas." He turned his head, kissing Brandon's nose as he frowned.

"Once we were legal adults, we found each other again, got our divorces and got hitched in the Netherlands where our marriage was legal. It's not against the law here *now*, but this was almost fifteen years ago. Things have changed a lot since then."

"Oh." Cambry looked over to Brandon, who had reached for Jeremiah's hand and was holding it tight. The simple gold band on his ring finger shone in the sun, almost as if it were brand new. *Are Bryce and Jake married?* He hadn't noticed a ring, but he'd also done his best to avoid them.

"How old were you when you married the alphas?"

Brandon turned away, facing the sun as Jeremiah squeezed his hand and pulled him close.

"I'm sorry," said Cambry, dropping his gaze. "I shouldn't have asked. It's obviously not a fond memory."

"It wasn't as bad as you're thinking," said Jeremiah. "My first husband never forced himself on me, and he knew there was no love between us. He was a kind man, despite his reputation, and he didn't deserve to be stuck with me. I had just turned sixteen and my heart was broken because I'd lost my best friend in the world. Brandon was fifteen at the time, but his parents pushed the wedding off until his sixteenth birthday. His first husband, Sylvester, was an older gentleman who was looking more for a househusband than a lover. Their marriage was never consummated. Still, it's hard enough that our choice was taken away. That's why we started the shelter for omega runaways and those fleeing abuse."

He blinked, letting the silence stretch. For some reason, Cambry had never imagined Jeremiah and Brandon outside of Feral Woods. He hadn't realized that they would have lives and jobs to return to when he had nothing at all to go back to.

He'd heard of similar shelters before when he'd managed to catch snippets of the news. There were a few public and privately funded omega shelters, and there were even alpha shelters. He'd been so confused about the alpha shelters until he'd realized that just because someone had a certain secondary gender didn't mean they'd never experienced abuse.

"Thank you," said Cambry. "There was a time I thought I would end up in one of those places until I realized that my father would just track me down and drag me home." He let out a depreciating laugh. "Funny how he can't stand me but he still wants me under his control."

Jeremiah frowned, propping himself up. "Is your father the one who sent you here?"

"Yeah," said Cambry, blinking against the brightness of the sun. His skin was still tacky from the pond and sticky mud clung to his hands and feet. "He got sick of my abnormalities. I'm pretty sure both my parents are terrified of me, but at the same time, they don't want me to ruin their reputations. If Feral Woods doesn't work out..."

He trailed off, looking out onto the water. The surface was still except for the tiny ripples from the water bugs that had escaped him.

"He'll send you to a facility?" asked Jeremiah, letting out a shudder as Cambry nodded. "Those places should be outlawed. The only reason they aren't is because they are privately funded. You can always come to the shelter instead. You could be my little cousin with a new name and everything."

Cambry chuckled, trying to picture what freedom would actually feel like. Maybe it would just be like the pond and the two-hundred acres of forest. Or maybe it was just an illusion—a short trip before everything went south.

Chapter Twelve

Bryce

Bryce cursed as his phone hummed against his thigh, pulling him from the book. He blinked at the light streaming through the open window that was at a very different angle than the last time he'd looked. Glancing down at the book, he thumbed through the pages he'd already read, settling on the spot he'd left off before grabbing a tissue from the side table and using it to mark the page.

He was almost halfway done and had passed the spot he had skimmed earlier. He'd nearly had to pause earlier for a jerk-off session, but he'd plowed on through three cliffhangers instead.

He gingerly set the book beside him, taking the utmost care as he reached for his phone. Cambry had obviously read the book many times, and although it looked like he had no problem dog-earing the pages, Bryce couldn't stand the thought of doing any harm to it.

"Hello?" He brought the phone to his ear, wincing at the amount of static. He was a bit surprised that the call had even come through. Most times they had zero service at the house, despite the signal booster that Jake had installed for him. It was the same reason he gave two alternate numbers on his card and advertisements. The second went through a landline that was on low volume in the kitchen and primarily set up for voicemails.

He didn't exactly work in an emergency type of business. And if there was someone in desperate need, the authorities would probably help better than him.

"It's Wilfred Parsons calling to inquire on the progress with Cambry Parsons."

Bryce pulled the phone away from his ear, blinking at it in confusion. Would it have been so bad for the man to just say he was calling to see how his son was doing? Five seconds into the phone call and he was already grinding his teeth.

"It's only been a few days," said Bryce, trying and failing to keep his sarcasm at bay. "I'm a therapist, not a miracle worker."

Wilfred stayed silent for two long beats before he let out an angry huff, his breath splashing against Bryce's ear in a burst of noise.

"I was told by a trusted colleague that you were the best and that you were *discreet*. So, is he ready to be mated? Or do we have to string this along for a few more weeks before I send him to a facility? Frankly, my patience has worn thin, and I'm considering having him transferred there now to save time. Cambry's chances of a successful pairing drop drastically the older he gets."

Bryce took the phone away from his ear as Wilfred continued, setting it down on the bed so he didn't accidentally break it in his fists as his claws emerged unbidden. His mouth was suddenly too small for his teeth, the copper taste of blood on his tongue.

No one was touching Cambry—not his father or some two-bit doctor in one of those places where euthanasia was a blessing.

But the fact was, Bryce didn't have any power. He was nothing more than a therapist to Cambry, and that would be taken away the moment Wilfred changed his mind. Cambry had rights as an adult, but he had nowhere to go and no money if his father cut him off.

Taking a deep breath, he moved the phone back to his ear, letting out a loud cough to hopefully stall Wilfred's unceasing rant about how useless and hopeless his beautiful and kind son was.

"We are making progress," said Bryce, forcing his mouth closed before he started to swear.

"Has he been mated by an alpha?"

What? Am I running a brothel? He thought back to the snuggle-pile that had quickly turned into an orgy, swallowing his ironic laugh.

"Not exactly." Cambry had flinched away as soon as Jake had started to explore his entrance. Bryce had watched every moment, his own body burning with desire. *I'm a good therapist. I was paying attention.*

"Well, that's exactly what needs to happen. Do I make myself clear? You have one more week to see that he has been properly mated, and knotted, or you can drop him off at the facility yourself."

"I can't force him," said Bryce through gritted teeth. *Is this guy for real?* There had been a lot of progress in the last hundred years, but the last time Bryce had checked, rape was still rape.

"Your practice is called *Feral* Woods. I don't care if it's with a man or beast, but do your job." The line clicked and went dead, and Bryce couldn't hold back any longer. He threw the phone against the door with all his strength, denting the wood and shattering the device into a dozen pieces.

He couldn't—no—*wouldn't* let anything happen to Cambry, even if it meant losing his license or taking Wilfred to court. Cambry needed love and acceptance, not brutalization and terror-inducing threats. It was no wonder that he was so broken and submissive, and why his beast was so protective of him.

He needed to figure out a way...*now*.

Chapter Thirteen

Cambry

"Okay, folks, welcome to our final couples exercise," said Bryce, smiling as he looked around to each of the couples, settling last on Cambry and Jake.

Cambry tilted his head, furrowing his forehead as he looked at Bryce. He looked tense, with his shoulders taut and the veins on his neck standing out. Even his face was flushed and his scent, which Cambry could just barely detect, was off.

Dropping his gaze to the ground, Cambry couldn't hold back his soft whine. He had crept into the house a few hours after he'd left and Bryce hadn't been in his room, but his sheets had been rumpled and smelled of him. His book had been lying face down with a tissue marking it down the middle, his bag pulled open and his other books revealed. A change of clothes that were a size too big had been waiting at the foot of his bed.

He had hoped that Bryce wasn't angry. He hadn't seemed angry when Cambry had run, but maybe he hadn't gotten a good look at the book right away. But he'd obviously read it and now he was pissed, his eyes narrowed and his teeth looking a touch too big for his mouth.

Cambry jumped as a large hand came down on his shoulder. He whirled on Jake, a snarl in his throat before his beast calmed at the familiar sight of him. Cambry never thought he would have been able to say it, but since Jake had bested him, his beast had been almost *calm*. Maybe it was because it was the first time he'd lost a fight, or maybe it was because he hadn't been hurt. His few puncture wounds had healed up fine, with nothing more than flaking scabs remaining. Jake was worse off with his split ear that was still reddened and on the mend.

"You ready?" asked Jake, his hand still on Cambry's shoulder.

Cambry nodded. He hadn't heard everything that Bryce had said, but he'd caught something about scents and finding your partner in the woods. He knew there was no chance that he would ever be able to find Jake, but he didn't think he would be the one searching in the exercise.

"Good. I'll give you a ten-minute head start and a warning," said Jake, leaning in closer until Cambry could almost feel the grumbling in his chest as he spoke. "Bears have the best sense of smell on the planet, save for one animal, and you have the strongest scent of any omega I've ever met—in a good way." Jake added the last bit hurriedly, his cheeks tinting. "You're going to have to be fast *and* smart if you want to make this fun."

Nodding, Cambry turned to Bryce, dropping his gaze as Bryce's burned into him. Maybe he hadn't told

Jake what he'd found, or maybe Bryce was the only one who had a problem with it. *I mean, he fucks alphas, so why should he have a problem with it?*

"Okay, partners! The ones doing the chasing can stay put and the ones getting chased can go in three…two…one…*go!*"

Cambry darted for the trees, slipping into the shadows before any of the other omegas had even moved. He balked as he noticed Braxton enter a few steps behind him, Edward waiting in the clearing as Bryce continued to speak.

"We're rethinking things," said Braxton at Cambry's inquiring gaze. Cambry nodded once before he pulled his shirt from his body, tossing it up into the branches of a nearby tree. Hopefully, it would slow Jake down a bit.

The sound of crickets and cicadas closed around him, his breath close as the clearing fell away. A few branches snapped as Jeremiah and the deer omega sped by him, their footsteps like mini-earthquakes underfoot.

Jake wanted a challenge. Cambry smiled to himself as he peeled his borrowed pants and underwear from his frame, discarding his shoes in a nearby alcove before backtracking on the path he'd just taken. His wolf surged with joy beneath his skin as he bit down on his clothing and shifted, fur rippling over him like a tide.

His wolf was so much easier than his human form. It always managed to find joy in the little things, and it recovered easily from a rebuff, ready to entice the only alphas who had ever overpowered him. It also didn't care about Bryce's *mood.*

Cambry darted to the side, taking a path that ran parallel to the clearing, and only far enough away that it would shelter his movements. He doubled back a few times, heading out in a new direction until he had a dozen possible paths behind him that led to nowhere.

Even if he had no idea what he was doing, his wolf did. He had accepted the challenge even before Cambry had even realized what Jake was telling him.

Before it had been outlawed, alphas used to hunt for their omegas, claiming any prize they managed to catch. In ancient times, it had become entertainment at the omega's expense, pitting alphas against each other in brutal fights as the omega struggled to flee.

Cambry could imagine their terror and helplessness as their captors breathed down their necks, claiming them if they were ready or not.

But he didn't think that was what Bryce had intended. Every session before had drudged up unexpected results, changing the couples before Cambry's eyes in unexpected ways. He'd never expected Braxton to give in to his submissive side, hooting and hollering at a distance as he ran from his mate. He'd never expected to be able to touch anyone without reacting badly, omegas and alphas included.

He would never admit it to anyone, but running through the bush and fleeing a predator that he knew and trusted, was *fun*. He could only imagine what it would have felt like if there was a real bond between them.

He sneezed as he passed something hung from a branch that reeked of lavender. Every other smell was blown away beneath the overpowering oil, even the faint trace of Jake that his wolf had been subconsciously fleeing. Turning away from the herb, he looked toward a more familiar place. The pond called to him, its copper waters promising to soak the sweat from his thick fur.

Dropping the last of his clothes to the ground, he turned on his paws, darting to the abundant scent of water. Sweat seeped under his fur, so much hotter than it had been in the clearing. Running in the middle of summer while wearing a thick winter coat was like hot yoga—but not the fun kind.

He gulped in a few swallows of water as he reached the pond, curling his lips at the strong taste. His wolf didn't care that the water hadn't come from a tap. It was a beast of instinct, and it would fulfill itself with the nearest water source if it was thirsty. It was cooler than he remembered against his tongue as he lapped at the surface, settling like a stone as it flowed to his belly.

The sun beat down on him from above, the loon-less pond calling to him with hopes of cooling off. With a groan, he shifted, willing his fur back as heat thickened against his skin. Grabbing handfuls of water, he tossed it against himself, gasping at the sheer coolness of it.

It didn't seem to work. The sun cut into him until his head was floating, his vision blinking as magma surged through his veins. His mouth was so dry, even though he had just drunk his fill, and when he looked down at his hands, they were paler than the curled pages of his books.

"What?" He shuddered as a sudden wind picked up, every human hair standing on end as it stripped the sweat from his body, only to be replaced a moment later by fresh saltiness. His heart pounded and he shook his head with denial as a different kind of dampness made itself known.

He snuck a hand between his legs, touching the tip of his finger to his hole. He could feel slick oozing out of him, along with an ache in his belly that he hadn't noticed before. It was stranger than looking at a jar of pickles and feeling his mouth flood with saliva until he was nearly drooling, and he had the same amount of control over it.

Oh no. Swallowing, he eased into the pond, shivering as the chill sank into every part of him. He knew what was happening, even if he hoped it never would.

Maybe it was because his beast had found a viable mate in either Jake or Bryce, or maybe it was because he'd only ever been in the company of his family for extended periods of time, but it *was* happening. *My first heat.*

He had no desire to be the mindless breeding machine that the media portrayed, begging for a knot, even as his hole gushed with cum. He didn't want to take so much that his belly was round with it, his body cramping as it made space for an alpha's seed. He couldn't bring a child into a world where his father was in control of every moment of his life.

Ducking under the water, he blew the breath from his lungs, hovering beneath the surface until he could wait no longer. Breaking the surface and taking a deep breath, he pushed away from the squishy bottom that was still in reach, paddling out farther until only an occasional weed tangled with his toes.

His legs and arms burned with the effort of keeping afloat, but he couldn't return to shore—not with Jake looking for him in an artificial chase that was meant to bring couples together. What if he lost control? What if Cambry did, and his beast tried to bait him instead of fighting him?

"When I asked for a challenge, this wasn't what I meant."

Cambry turned toward the voice, his heart thudding as Jake stood on the shore, still dressed and without a hair out of place. He was scenting the air, his head tilted back as he drew in a deep breath. Hopefully, Cambry had gotten into the water before his smell had seeped into the rocks.

"I'll give you a gold star for trying, though. The scent traps would have worked if you hadn't made it so obvious. All I had to do was walk the path with the least number of prints and it led me straight to you."

Cambry swallowed, accidentally taking in a mouthful of bitter water. Coughing, he shook his head, even as his nose dipped beneath the surface. He kicked his numb legs to force his body upward, taking a deep breath as his lungs burned. Jake furrowed his forehead as he pulled his shoes off, dipping his toes into the water.

"You okay?" Jake asked. Cambry struggled to nod, getting a nose full of water for his efforts. It burned as it passed down his nostrils, every inch flaring as it sank into his lungs. Something pressed against his legs that didn't feel like a weed. More likely it was a horde of leeches in search of a fresh blood source. "Come back to shore," said Jake, pulling what looked like a phone from his pocket before setting it on a nearby rock.

Cambry shook his head. He wasn't even sure if he would make it to shore. His wolf was a good swimmer and hadn't had any trouble when he'd chased the loon, but apparently, *he* was the opposite.

"Now, Cambry." Jake dropped his voice into a growl, the grumble reverberating through the water. Cambry's belly ached momentarily, and he realized that more slick was seeping from him.

Hopefully, the leeches wouldn't be attracted to it. Something was already clinging to his toe and who knew how many of the little demons were in the water.

"The chase is over. It's time to go back. The other couples are already waiting for us." Jake's voice was softer this time. "I have the second-best smell of any animal, remember?" He tapped his nose. "I can smell an omega's slick from two miles away, and trust me, they are all slick right now."

Cambry kicked out, pushing farther away from shore. If Jake couldn't smell him yet, he would soon. He'd heard about alphas going into rut at the scent of an omega in heat. He hoped it was bullshit, but he didn't know what to believe anymore.

"Fine," Jake huffed, taking a step back before bursting into a run and leaping off the rock, splashing into the shallow water with enough power that every fish probably flinched. He grunted as he landed, letting out a soft shout as he stood, the water just below his waist. Wincing, he took a step deeper, water dripping from his clothes. "Water level is down this year. I haven't been out here yet this summer," said Jake as he stalked closer, his pace getting faster with each step until he was at chest level. He pushed off into the water, gliding toward Cambry with powerful strokes. "I don't care if you're naked. Don't drown over modesty." He spoke between strokes, each one bringing Cambry closer to his doom.

Cambry tried to struggle backward, but his adrenaline had officially worn out. It didn't help that his beast was fighting him with everything it had, trying to convince him to roll over and present his ass — as if it were even possible in the water. The frustration surged under his skin, growing thicker as Jake approached.

"Take my hand," said Jake as he paused to hover about a meter away, his shoulders bobbing up and down with each kick. "Come on. I won't touch you without your consent, but you're making it pretty tricky here. I won't just tread here and watch you drown because you're too stubborn to admit defeat."

So that's what Jake thinks this is? Cambry wasn't exactly stubborn in a traditional sense—he just listened to his beast more than most. But he couldn't listen when his life was at stake—he couldn't let himself or Jake be sucked into something against their will.

If Jake caught him, then he would be under Wilfred's foot, manipulated into some kind of shotgun mating that had no place in the modern world. Cambry couldn't let himself take Jake away from Bryce, just like Jeremiah had been taken from his husband.

The last of his energy sputtered out like an old-fashioned oil lamp in a mine. One moment, he was kicking, and the next, his limbs were frozen and he was sinking. He didn't make it past his nose before Jake wrapped his arms around him, pulling him back against his chest and the soaked fabric of his T-shirt.

Jake's breath was hot in his ear, puffing and blowing with every exhale. His chest was hard, each pec a rise of firm flesh against him. He wanted to struggle and push away, but he craned his neck to the side instead, setting his lips inches away from Jake's neck before letting out a low whimper. Jake grumbled in response, hugging Cambry tighter.

When the water was chest-deep, Jake slipped a hand behind Cambry's knees, lifting him bridal-style as he stepped toward the rocky edge. Maybe it was accidental, but he brushed against Cambry's ass before sliding along his back to support him.

Cambry whimpered again, his groin throbbing as slick leaked from him.

How could omegas stand it? It was disgusting, and it wouldn't stop, no matter how hard he clenched his cheeks together. His cock was one thing that he could explain away—the adrenaline rush from earlier was obviously still affecting some parts of him. But slick? There was only one reason for that.

Jake lifted him above the waterline with a grunt, not struggling much, even though Cambry was only a few inches shorter than him and not much lighter. His beast preened at the show of strength, a fresh flow of sickly sweetness dribbling from him as his body flushed with renewed fire.

Jake stuttered to a stop when he was ankle-deep, his lips forming into a surprised 'O'. He dropped his gaze to Cambry, his eyes going wide as he sucked a deep breath through his nose.

"Okay then," said Jake, his arms going taut as he closed the remaining distance to the shore. "Tell me what you need and it's yours."

A slopping, sloshing noise drew Cambry's gaze to Jake's feet as he stepped onto the rock. He was still wearing his boots, the tanned surfaces stained dark and water glugging over the rims with each step. More dripped down Jake's legs, adding to the mess at his feet. Some of that water was probably from Cambry, tainted with a sweetness that was coating Jake in a film.

What do I need? Probably what everyone in his life had always told him. He needed an alpha to knot and breed him through his heat or else he would lose his mind. The best would be if he mated an alpha, because that would halt his heat in its tracks before it had the chance to kill him.

His first heat had probably been brewing for years, waiting for a receptive alpha before it sank its ferocious claws into him. His wolf grumbled at the idea, clawing as it tried to escape.

"Don't take me back," said Cambry, thrusting his face into Jake's neck and hiding along his scent gland. It was heady under his tongue and thick with the smell of the forest. He hadn't even realized that he was tasting Jake until he licked the salt from his lips.

"We have to go back," said Jake softly, pausing for a moment to heft Cambry up when he started to slip. Cambry wrapped his arms around Jake's neck, doing everything he could to get closer. His teeth ached from the urge to bite, slick leaking from his hole and down his thigh with each breath of Jake's earthy scent. He'd never smelled anything so clearly before.

"I can't." He could barely think about dealing with one alpha, let alone the others. How many would he drive into a frenzy and turn against their mates? He clenched his hole at the thought. How many could he fight off before he had no choice but to submit?

"Let me take you to bed," said Jake. "Your bed." He added at Cambry's whine. "I won't take advantage of you like this, Cambry. I don't know what you've been told about me, but I'm not like that. I would never take you against your will...and neither would Bryce. As for the other alphas, they only have eyes for their mates."

Can he read my mind? Or am I thinking out loud? Jake chuckled under him. So maybe it was the latter. The trees around him were a haze, the only clear thing the breath of Jake into his lungs.

The alpha growled as slick dripped down Cambry's thighs to where they were touching, and Jake jerked away suddenly, dropping Cambry to his feet in a move so sudden that the earth threatened to tilt.

"Can you walk?"

Cambry nodded, his flesh on fire as Jake pulled away from him, the inferno creeping over him ten times worse than it had been before. His beast growled at the rejection, the sound slipping through his lips as he turned a glare on Jake.

Jake was still soaked to the bone, his T-shirt stretched tight across his chest and showing off two peaked nipples that were like islands in the ocean. Cambry couldn't look away, his fingers twitching with the need to touch and squeeze. He didn't know where the thoughts were coming from, but they were there, consuming every part of his being and pushing his hesitance to the side.

Maybe he had read one too many books because he could imagine more than a dozen positions in which Jake could take him, every one ending with his knot locked inside.

Taking a step back, Jake put another pace between them, the inches like a yawning maw ready to swallow Cambry whole. His beast snapped behind his chest, his nails lengthening into claws as Jake's eyes went wide and he moved farther away.

He could see it — the tent in Jake's soaked trousers. He could picture every inch with vivid detail as it oozed and twitched before squirting an alarming amount of seed. But Jake moved back again, his body taut and his chest heaving.

Cambry snarled, dropping to his knees as his beast took over his mottled mind, his dirtied limbs giving way to fur and paws. Snapping his jaws before they were fully formed, he lunged for Jake's leg, coming within inches of tearing flesh from bone. He wouldn't hurt him — not really, but Jake probably didn't know that.

Instead of backing away or turning to run, Jake shifted, his grizzly tearing his clothing apart until seams burst and his shoes ripped with utter finality. Pulling his lips back over his teeth, Jake growled low in his throat, the sound plunging the buzzing forest into utter silence.

Cambry knew he should have backed down — the grizzly alpha had already won the fight and had the right to claim him in his feral mind, but his wolf had taken enough rejection for one day. He could only be cast aside so many times before he responded with the fierceness of a mother protecting its young.

Footsteps thudded toward them through the still forest, a blue jay sending out a staggered alarm before it took to the sky. Cambry turned to the sound, his hackles raised and drool dripping from his teeth as he snarled, every hair on end as his wolf poofed up to twice its size.

Jeremiah slid to a halt between the trees, his chest heaving and his eyes wide as he looked at Cambry. He was naked, with slick on his own thighs, and a cock that was loose and flaccid. The sight enraged Cambry like he could have never imagined. The bunny was a friend, but he was too close, his scent too thick with Cambry's nerves already well past the edge of his tolerance.

Cambry took a step, then another, slipping across the ground until his jaws were poised over Jeremiah's thin throat. He could feel the pulse of Jeremiah's heart beneath his teeth and taste his sweaty arousal against his tongue.

"It's okay, Wolfie," said Jeremiah, his voice soft and sweet just like Cambry remembered. He didn't sound afraid, even as he trembled. "Jake here is going to take care of you, sweetie. Is this your first heat? The first one is always the hardest. There are so many thoughts and feelings rushing through your head, and none of them feel right."

Sinking his hands into Cambry's scruff, Jeremiah let out a soft hum, swallowing against Cambry's teeth. "I remember my first one as if it were yesterday. Brandon had just been taken from me and my new husband was sleeping in the bed beside me. I thought I was dying when the fever hit, and I almost drowned in the shower when I tried to cool down. It was so scary. Then the slick started, and I thought I would die of embarrassment, too." He let out a soft laugh, digging his fingers in until Cambry wanted to purr. "My husband took my hand and sat me down on the edge of the bed. He offered himself as relief, and every part of me wanted it but one. I was in love with Brandon, and I wanted so badly to spend it with him." The salt of tears struck the air.

Jake hadn't moved, his body frozen and maybe dreading that a single movement would set Cambry off.

"So you know what he did?" asked Jeremiah. "He went to my sock drawer where I had hidden a picture of Brandon. I didn't think he knew about it, but I was wrong about a lot of things those days. He gave me the picture and a pack of spearmint gum that Brandon always smelled like, and he led me to the spare bedroom. He gave me space to endure my heat alone, and the closest thing to a loved one that he could get. And you know what?"

Cambry leaned back, licking the tears from his lips. Jeremiah's eyes were red-rimmed and glassy, his lips shaking as his body trembled. Cambry whined, shaking his head.

"I survived, Wolfie. Even when everyone said that a heat alone would be the worst experience of an omega's life, I got through it. I could imagine him there with me and look at his face every time I got lonely. I slept with that pack of gum against my nose, leaking slick everywhere. My husband, Dylan, paced outside the door, but he never tried to get to me or force himself on me. If I hadn't already belonged to Brandon, I would have loved Dylan at that moment."

Cambry dropped to his knees as he shifted, dirt and pine needles clinging to his damp skin as his fur melted away. Tears streaked down his face as soon as they were able to form, just as uncontrollable as the slick between his thighs.

"What do you think, Wolfie? Can Jake and I help you to your room? We won't touch you — not like that. I have a feeling that no one will touch you without a few people tearing them apart." He winked as if there weren't pink impressions of teeth fresh on his neck.

Cambry nodded, letting his eyes fall shut. He couldn't help but wonder if the same thing would work for him. He didn't have someone who loved him, after all, and not a single keepsake photograph to his name.

Chapter Fourteen

Bryce

Bryce paced the clearing as he waited for the couples to return, his thoughts more tangled than they had been an hour before. A stray pinecone crunched beneath his sole, a spider scuttling across the grass to flee his stomping sandals.

He mustered a smile as Braxton and Edward returned, but they hardly noticed. They could barely look away from each other, both reeking of arousal and sweat from the chase. Bryce should have been congratulating himself, or at the bare minimum reaching for his back to give himself a pat. He tried not to do the latter too often because he usually pulled a muscle.

The fisher alpha and his mate appeared next, giving him a quick wave before they disappeared toward their cabin. They had been one of the easiest couples he'd ever dealt with, and barely memorable. They had probably chosen the place because of the name — just like Wilfred Parsons had.

Feral Woods was supposed to be about finding your beast and making peace with them with your mate at your side. Sex usually solved itself once a person stopped holding back or tried to live a life that someone else had decided for them. It wasn't about forcing someone.

He growled, toeing off his sandals so he could feel the grass beneath his feet. He dealt with bigoted assholes all the time, so why did this one bother him more than any other? Maybe because Cambry had snuck under his skin the moment he'd stepped into the house, his scent seeping into everything as if it belonged.

Jake had been right. He should have never let an omega into their house. It didn't even feel like theirs anymore.

Glancing at the door, he glared at the frame that was just a tad cock-eyed. The house looked the same as it always had, but for some reason, he couldn't imagine it without Cambry inside.

He couldn't picture what it had been like to have an empty bed in the room beyond the bathroom, with Jake curled at his side and snuffling in his sleep. He couldn't imagine waking up without wondering what two men were thinking instead of just one. It had only been a few days, but he knew those days had changed him forever.

A staggering growl echoed through the forest, his hair prickling as the sound struck him. It was Jake — louder and with more desperation than Bryce had heard in a long time.

Did something trigger him? It hadn't been all that long since Jake had fought other alphas in illegal cage matches, and rage like his never truly disappeared. Bryce had helped him harness it and pour it into beautiful things, but everyone had their limits.

He darted into the forest, a stray stick stabbing the soft arch of his foot after only a few steps. He staggered as his eyes watered from the sharp sting, gripping the bark of a nearby tree as he hopped.

How many times had Jake told him that he needed to wear proper footwear in the bush? Rattlesnakes aside, there were so many things that could hurt him.

Glancing down at his foot, he paled as he spotted a twig sticking out like the biggest sliver in the world. He grabbed the base, glancing through the trees in the direction that he had heard Jake's bellow. He didn't have time.

He tugged as hard as he could, pulling the branch free in a spurt of blood and relief so deep that it was nearly orgasmic. It only lasted a moment before the ache sunk in, pounding to the beat of his heart in stinging throbs. His vision wavered as he spotted his blood dripping down to the forest floor, soaking into the leaves and needles.

Oh. He blinked the red from his vision, almost falling as his grip on the tree went weak. There was a singular reason that he hadn't gone through medical school, much to the disappointment of his parents. Without the help of his slumbering beast, a single drop of blood could sometimes send him to his knees.

Pounding footsteps reached his ears a moment later — too soft to be Jake's or Cambry's. Dark hair came into view and Brandon's terrified gaze locked onto him.

"Help!" Brandon ran toward him, grabbing Bryce's shirt and tugging him off balance. "Jeremiah — he heard them and he went and, oh God, he's going to get himself killed!"

Bryce stumbled toward the spot that Brandon was pointing to—the same spot the noise had come from. His mouth went dry, his heart pounding. "It's okay, Brandon. I know Jake seems scary, but he won't hurt anyone." He crossed his fingers, hoping against hope that he was right.

"Not Jake, you idiot...Cambry. That fucking wolf!" Brandon growled, a tiny sound that barely made Bryce shudder. "He's dangerous. He's going to get my husband killed!"

"Hey!" Bryce said sharply, more to stall his own panic than Brandon's. "Yelling and name-calling aren't going to help anyone. Take me to them."

Brandon scowled at him, cursing under his breath with something that sounded a lot like 'knot-head'. Bryce let it slide, seeing as he was terrified himself and doing everything not to show it. Panic did terrible things to people, especially when loved ones were involved.

Wincing, he followed after Brandon, trying to go as fast as he could with pine needles jabbing into his sore foot with every step. Brandon didn't seem affected by his own naked feet, but in Bryce's experience, omegas usually weren't.

They didn't get far before Bryce's breath caught in his throat, a powerfully sweet scent sinking straight into his chest and making his groin throb to life. Brandon paused, his own nostrils flaring before a glistening, clear fluid appeared between his cheeks, adding to the scent.

"Jeremiah?" asked Bryce, hoping that he was wrong.

Brandon shook his head. "My husband has monthly heats, and we hardly even know it's happening until we find ourselves screwing like bunnies for a couple of nights."

Which left one option. *Crap.*

Bryce touched the nearest tree, grounding himself as sugar seeped into every part of him, his bear blinking awake and grumbling in his chest at the pure irresistibility of it. He didn't usually find himself attracted to omegas or their scent, but something was different about Cambry. Something had been different since the very beginning.

Wilfred's words churned through his mind, his gut clenching with nausea. He couldn't give Wilfred exactly what he wanted and manipulate Cambry like that without him even knowing his father's wishes.

A thorn bush twitched, its branches creaking before they snapped to the side, bent beyond repair. Jake pushed through the gap, clutching a pale Cambry to his side. Jeremiah followed slowly, Cambry's hand in his worried grasp.

Cambry looked as if he'd been run through by a jumbo jet. He was barely hanging on, with his arm thrown over Jake's shoulders and his naked body pale against his flushed and feverish cheeks. His hair was soaked, sweat beading on his skin, even as he trembled.

Jake looked up, his face etched with the same tension that Bryce was feeling in every bone. His chest heaved, his lips parted and he snuck his tongue out every few moments to lick his lips. He was naked and obviously aroused but somehow hanging onto his sanity.

"We need to get him to his room," said Jeremiah, maybe sensing that the alphas could barely speak.

Squeezing Cambry's hand once, he let go, stepping toward a waiting Brandon and throwing his arms around him. "Take care of him or I'll string you up by your knots."

Bryce didn't doubt it for a moment. Jeremiah was tiny and utterly adorably, but he had a strange fierceness about him, like he'd seen too much of the world but had still managed to come out on top.

Moving to Cambry's other side, Bryce ducked under his arm, easing some of the load from Jake's shoulder. Cambry was built like a tank, and he was nearly dead-weight, his eyes barely open as he fluttered his lashes. Cambry let out a soft groan, the sound barely a whisper of sound.

"Jake?" Bryce asked, checking in as he nearly lost his footing. The pain in his foot had magically disappeared, the throbbing fully in his pinned cock. At least he wasn't on display like Jake, who was hard and leaking, his cock jutting out from his body like a red flag.

"Just get him to his room. We'll figure the rest out when we get there," said Jake, tugging Cambry along toward the house.

The few minutes it took to get there was like the agony of begging for Jake's knot and knowing he wasn't going to get it because Jake got more fun out of teasing him than fucking him. He couldn't imagine how Cambry was feeling, strung between two alphas with his rational thoughts lost to the murk of his beast.

Bryce had been exposed to numerous cases during his classes, with stories of omegas who had gone mad during their first heat. It was as if something snapped in their mind or perhaps their fever had gotten too high and had melted their brain. The fever was needed to induce ovulation, but nature was cruel sometimes.

It happened to alphas when their hormones surged, and they entered a rut. They didn't eat, they didn't drink and they only thought with one head — the one with the least amount of hair. Bryce could feel his rut surging beneath his skin, his body temperature climbing to match Cambry's.

No matter how far society had come, there were still beasts at their core. Sliding his hand along Cambry, he touched Jake's shoulder, his skin alarmingly cool to the touch. Jake gave him a sharp look, his forehead creasing as they ascended the stairs three-wide. His pupils were blown wide, his teeth too big for his mouth as he let out a snarl.

Jake dipped and lifted Cambry bridal-style, carrying him to his bed before pulling the covers over his frame. The book was still there, marked with Bryce's spot, but it tumbled to the floor, spilling open and bending the pages. Jake didn't seem to notice, tucking Cambry into the sheets before placing a soothing palm against his forehead.

"I need to blow off some steam, pup," said Jake, smoothing his thumb over Cambry's sweaty cheek. He fluttered his lashes under the touch and groaned, turning his head to the side. "Call for us if you need us. We'll be right next door."

His calm façade dropped the moment he turned away from Cambry's bed, his gaze pinning Bryce where he stood. Snarling, Jake rushed at him, grabbing him by the shoulder and forcing him through the adjoining bathroom to their bed. Bryce let out a whine as Jake dug his claws into his shoulder, the ache piercing through his haze.

"I hope you're ready for me, sleepy bear, because you are about to get fucked six ways from Tuesday." Jake pushed him to the bed, following seconds later and bringing their lips together. His lips had grown hot as his own fever started — the unbidden response of Cambry's heat.

Bryce tilted his head to the side, deepening his kiss and sucking Jake's tongue into his mouth. Any other time Jake came at him so violently, he knew he was in for a fight for dominance before Jake ultimately took his knot. The grizzly was fierce, but he was afraid to fight dirty.

Bryce lay back, drawing him closer, even as Jake clawed at their pants, pushing them from their hips until their cocks burned together, the molten heat engulfing him completely. He wasn't sure if the slickness was from Jake or himself, but it poured between their cocks, smoothing the way as Jake thrust harshly.

Jake was everywhere all at once, stripping the last sane thought from Bryce's mind. He sucked at Bryce's nipples, licking and biting his chest while squeezing his ass in his large hands. Pushing between Bryce's thighs, he nudged his cock against Bryce's entrance, lurching forward as the head caught.

"Fuck!" Bryce arched away from the touch as Jake managed to sink in a few inches, twisting to the side to get away from the sudden pressure. He may have been lost in the throes of the rut, but he still needed prep to take something like Jake's cock. Jake snarled, biting at Bryce's neck in an attempt to subdue him.

With a deep growl, Bryce batted the side of Jake's head, boxing one ear and hooking his leg over Jake's hip to reverse their positions. Jake fought him, bucking and writhing as he was pinned with his back on the mattress, nearly tumbling them off the edge as he struggled.

Bryce reached for the artificial slick, but Jake was faster, grabbing his arm and twisting it behind Bryce's back before scrambling to get behind him again. He rutted his cock between Bryce's ass cheeks as he searched for his hole with animalistic accuracy. With a deep groan, he found Bryce's entrance with the head of his cock and jammed forward a second time.

At least it doesn't hurt as much the second time. Bryce let out a laugh at Jake's whimper as he twisted to the side again, pushing Jake's cock from his body. Shooting an elbow back, he struck Jake's ribs before tipping until they were keeling over backward.

They landed on the edge of the bed, but Bryce had pushed too hard, sending them to the floor in a heap of limbs and claws. He lunged for the drawer as Jake shook his head, momentarily stunned. Grabbing the slick and popping the cap open, he shoved it against his entrance and squeezed. The neck of the bottle popped through his loosened hole and slick flooded him, dripping down his thighs as he was filled.

He pulled it free, shoving three fingers into himself before wincing at the sting of his own claws. Trying to push his bear back, he shook his head as it refused, snarling and grunting as Jake lifted himself to his hands and knees. In a rush, Bryce popped a fourth finger inside, the quick stretch all he was going to get.

He would hurt tomorrow, enough that he would probably have to cancel his last one-on-one sessions with each couple, unless he could convince them to keep talking as he stood uncomfortably.

"I thought you liked it rough," said Jake as he crawled closer, his voice a deep growl. "You love it when I split you open on my knot."

Bryce was a touch surprised that Jake wasn't beyond words at this point. Then again, he had better control than most men Bryce knew. There was a reason that omegas were asked to isolate themselves from all but their intended during their first heat.

Most alphas claimed that they couldn't control themselves, even if that had been disproven in court time and time again. The first heat was always the most powerful, designed by nature to attract the biggest and baddest mates so they could fight it out.

Yeah, nature was a dick—and not the fun kind.

Hissing, Bryce turned away, reaching for the bed so at least his knees would be comfortable when Jake knotted him. Jake wrapped his arms around him from behind, pulling him until his cock nestled back where it belonged between Bryce's cheeks.

Jake growled low as he nudged forward, finding Bryce's hole with unerring accuracy. The man took tracking way too seriously.

He sank inside, pushing a broken groan from Bryce's lips as he was split wide faster than his body could adjust. The first time Jake had taken him in a feat of rage, Bryce had torn, splitting on Jake's knot as he'd nudged it inside.

But that had been years before, when neither of them had known what they were doing, and when they both had been alphas at the edge of their frustrations, just trying to get through life. Bryce had been split open with excruciating slowness so many times since then that he didn't have a hope of counting how many. His body knew just how to stretch, and he had never torn since that first time.

It didn't mean that it didn't smart a bit, though.

Letting out a deep growl, Jake humped all the way inside, until his hips were flush against Bryce's ass and the swelling of his knot had started to stretch him even wider. Bryce whimpered, thrashing in Jake's hold as his own cock throbbed, unable to release without any pressure on it.

Jake's knot was huge enough that Bryce usually questioned his sanity when it reached its max. Could he really take it?

Heat seared through him as Jake started to shoot, his knot locking and his seed pushing fast and deep until Bryce started to bloat. It was too much and not enough, but it was only just beginning. He didn't know how many times Jake was going to knot him, but it was definitely going to be more than once.

"Fucking take it, bitch," Jake growled, biting down on Bryce's neck until he whimpered. As much as he hated being called *bitch*, he also really loved it— especially when Jake was already deep and locked with no chance of pulling out any time soon.

A low growl had Jake tensing above him. Bryce whipped his head around, peering over his shoulder. Cambry was standing in the bathroom doorway, his cock hard and weeping and slick soaking his thighs as he stared at them. His skin had flushed with heat, the paleness dropping away since Bryce had laid eyes on him last.

"Did you hurt him?" asked Cambry, walking up to Jake before crouching beside him. He dropped his gaze to Bryce, reaching beneath him and stroking Bryce's cock once before he withdrew.

His eyes were unfocused and glazed, fresh sweat on his forehead.

Jake shook his head with a grumble. "Sometimes we need it hard and fast, just like we need it slow other times." He bit down on Bryce's opposite shoulder, sinking his teeth in for a second time before straining as his cock flexed again.

Cambry hummed, his hand disappearing as he touched Jake. Jake let out a gasp against Bryce's ear as he disengaged his teeth, thudding his hips against Bryce's ass and dragging him along with his knot.

Bryce let out a huff as he was tossed around like a rag doll, his ass aching with every pull. The throb wasn't nearly as bad as his cock, though, which must have been purple.

"Does that hurt?" asked Cambry, rubbing his fingers through his own slick before his hand disappeared again, and Jake let out a long groan.

What is even happening? Bryce gasped as Jake's knot somehow swelled farther, pushing him beyond his breaking point until his head was swimming.

"Can I?" asked Cambry, gathering his slick and smoothing it down his cock until he glistened in the bedroom light. He tilted his head, his blown eyes filled with so much lust that Bryce had to shudder. Jake nodded against his shoulder, and Cambry moved in behind him.

Bryce's mottled mind finally caught up when Jake started to rock against him in slow lulls that were nothing like his usual thrusts. Cambry groaned deep in his chest, matching Jake's own sound as his knot swelled that much farther.

"Oh God." Bryce grabbed at the edge of a nearby blanket, bringing half the bed down on them as he scrambled for purchase. Cambry was fucking Jake. He was *fucking* him with Jake was still buried knot-deep in Bryce's ass with no sign of deflating in sight. The stimulation of Jake's prostate must have been mind-blowing, because Bryce could feel his stomach bloating beyond anything that it had ever done, his ass aching as he tugged against Jake's knot in the beginnings of panic.

"More slick," said Jake, huffing once at the squelching noise before the rocking began again. Cambry groaned low in his throat, the movement grinding to a halt as he whimpered.

Bryce's knot was going to explode. He didn't care if it were impossible. It was going to happen. With the weight of two men on top of him, moving his hands would have meant a broken nose and maybe a concussion when his face came crashing down.

Jake sighed and Cambry appeared a moment later, his cock softening and dripping with slick and cum. The sight was mesmerizing, even more so at the scent of Jake mingled with Cambry's sweetness. Cambry smoothed a hand down his own chest before he reached for Bryce, tugging his cock with aching slowness.

"Can I?" Cambry asked, addressing Bryce this time. Bryce nodded through ragged breaths, shouting as Jake dragged him upward, using his cock alone. *It's not a handle, buddy.*

Cambry smiled, low and sweet, his strange eyes glowing as he shuffled toward Bryce. Bryce had been expecting a hand or a mouth, but at the last moment, Cambry turned, butting his ass against Bryce's cock until the head slipped between Cambry's soaked cheeks.

"Whaaa—?" Bryce bit his tongue as Cambry grabbed his cock and pushed the head against his hole, flexing his back until it popped inside. Yelping, Cambry tried to pull away, but Jake reached around his hip, tugging Cambry back onto Bryce's cock.

"Hurts," said Cambry, the joy in his voice cutting through the tears on his cheeks as he turned his head, locking his gaze with Bryce, then Jake.

"Do you like it?" asked Jake as he drew Cambry steadily back until Bryce was buried all the way inside the tightest hole he could have ever imagined. He could picture the ache that Cambry was feeling as he was split apart, because it was the same in his own ass as Jake humped against him.

"I—I like it," said Cambry, throwing his head back to rest on Bryce's shoulder before he turned, biting Bryce's ear and leaving open-mouth kisses there. Jake grumbled his approval, leaning in to capture Cambry's mouth in a brief kiss that probably tested their mutual flexibility.

"It's going to hurt more," said Jake, holding Cambry's hips steady as he thrust, using his knot to fuck Bryce's cock slowly in and out. Bryce grunted with each stroke, the tingling in his gut telling him that he wouldn't last long.

"Knot me, Bryce. Show me what it's supposed to feel like."

How can I say no? As Jake pushed Bryce ahead and his cock sank to the hilt, his knots throbbed to life, starting to lock Cambry to him. If Cambry somehow escaped the first knot, the second would hold him tight, refusing to let go until Bryce had spent every drop of his seed.

"That's it, bitch," Jake rumbled in his ear. "Show the omega how it's done."

Chapter Fifteen

Cambry

Was Bryce even real? There was no way that an alpha's cock was supposed to be that big. It had to have been nearly ten inches long, and the knots were about to split him apart, the second one pushing against something inside him that threatened to turn him to mush.

His mind had cleared after they'd entered the house, the scent of two familiar alphas calming his beast until it pulled back, letting Cambry take control as Jake laid him out on the bed. Terror had coursed through him when Jake had lunged at Bryce with such brutal intent, taking Bryce through the bathroom to their own room.

He'd crept from the bed, not even sure if the alphas knew he was alive—or if they even cared at that moment. What greeted him was like something out of his deepest imagination, mixed with the cage fight from his memory. The only difference was that it was *real*.

He could taste their power in the air as they grappled, Bryce giving way more than once, even as Jake tried to shove his cock inside without slick or preparation. Cambry had almost leaped to Bryce's aide at that point, remembering everything that Bryce had told him.

But Bryce seemed to keep the upper hand, even as Jake sprouted a touch of fur along his arms. He'd stood frozen as Bryce had reached for the bed, and Jake caught him, hilting his cock and knotting him in one single thrust. The noises Bryce had made were pure bliss with a gnarled edge of pain as Jake cursed at him, humping his cock even deeper.

Cambry hadn't been able to stop as his wolf took over.

And there he was, with a cock so far up his ass that he swore he could feel it in his stomach, and two knots swelling within him as Bryce flooded him with cum. It wasn't exactly *nice,* but Cambry couldn't find a single part to complain about, even as his stomach started to cramp from the sheer volume.

It was also new, exciting and exactly everything he'd been missing out on for his entire life. His books had been wrong about one thing, though. There were no fireworks or sparks beneath his skin. He felt so close to himself that it was nearly blissful, with no need to hide from the men behind him. Embarrassment wasn't even a concept.

But no fireworks.

He let out a sigh, wincing as Bryce's cock pulsed again, his tummy going taut with pressure. *That* was something that he would probably be okay living without, but he'd wanted to try it at least once, especially since his wolf had urged him on, and Bryce had seemed so willing.

If he were completely honest, he had enjoyed taking Jake more, the alpha so tight around his cock that he'd thought he might be inadvertently castrated. How did Bryce stand it with his extra inches and girth? They seemed completely unnecessary in Cambry's opinion.

"You okay?" asked Bryce, huffing against Cambry's neck and sliding his hands so they were braced on either side of Cambry's head. Cambry nestled between them, turning his nose to Bryce's wrist before he shrugged once.

"I didn't hurt you, did I?" asked Bryce, a touch of panic in his voice.

"No." Cambry stared at the wrist before him, tilting so he could run his nose along the tanned column. "Just wasn't what I was expecting." There was something enticing on Bryce's wrist that begged him to close his lips on it.

Following his instincts, he did just that, sucking the skin into his mouth. It was delicious. He hummed, nibbling on the spot. *More.*

"Cambry, that's —"

Bryce's voice cut off as Cambry bit down hard enough to break the skin, his teeth suddenly sharper than they really needed to be. Something that wasn't blood filled his mouth, the earthy tang to it reminding him so much of Jake that he was momentarily confused as to whose wrist it was.

Something snapped inside him as he swallowed, locking behind his navel before bursting along his spine and wrapping around his heart. It tugged tighter until he was sure that his heart would burst. His jaw locked up as Bryce let out a startled yell, a feral growl piercing the air a moment later.

"Fuck!" Jake yelled from behind him, pulling back violently and tugging Cambry along on Bryce's knot. Somehow, he must have pulled himself free of Bryce, because he was in front of Cambry, snatching Bryce's wrist from his weak grasp.

Cambry looked up, horror and uncertainty flooding through every pore. His body clenched in fear as he struggled, trying to free himself from Bryce, to no avail. Although he'd stopped coming, Bryce's knots hadn't started to shrink yet.

Jake's face twisted into a brutal snarl, his eyes wide with disbelief. Bringing up his clawed hand, Jake backhanded Cambry across the face. Cambry's head snapped to the side, Bryce's knot so close to being tugged free that he was about to break.

"Fuck you!" Jake yelled again, closing the space between them. Cambry thrashed with everything he had, screaming as the first knot popped free from his ass. Whatever genealogical link had created knots, he wanted to travel back in time and murder them.

The second knot was still locked deep inside, stretching him even wider than the first. Bryce had doubled over, his full weight attempting to pin Cambry to the floor.

Maybe he had overestimated himself. He had lost against two alphas before, but somehow his beast had been filled with the utmost confidence that he would be safe. He didn't feel safe, though—not when he was pinned at the hips and attached to one alpha while the second looked like he was about to gut him, the sting of his slap still sharp on his cheek.

He dodged the second slap by sheer will alone, grabbing onto Jake's arm with both hands and pulling it to him. That same spot pulsed under his lips as he brought it close, the taste thick as he bit down and pierced straight through Jake's resistance.

His mating gland, Cambry realized with a delay. He let go, flinging himself away from Jake, but it was already too late. His mouth was filled with him, the bonding fluid already trickling down his throat and mingling with Bryce's.

The bond snapped into place in the same way Bryce's had, squeezing his chest so tight that his vision swam. His wolf howled in triumph at the same time he screamed, tearing himself free from Bryce in a move that definitely tore something.

Seed dripped from his hole, sliding down his thighs and mingling with the slick from earlier. Terror seeped into him, pulling his chest even tighter as he backed against the wall. He kept his gaze locked on the two alphas — his *mates.*

Of course, he'd been taught about mating in high school, and he'd paid attention and everything. But bonding had been the last thing on his mind when he hadn't been able to get within ten feet of an alpha without someone getting hurt.

Whether it was a coincidence or it was mother nature throwing omegas a single bone in life, bonding could only ever be initiated by an omega. Alphas could nibble and bite every scent gland in an omega's body and suck them dry, but a bond would never form. It was the same reason that Jeremiah and Brandon were bonded, and yet Jake and Bryce weren't. It simply wasn't possible for them.

Jake pulled Bryce to his chest, reaching between his legs then tilting his hand to the light, checking on his partner, even as he trembled. His large body looked like a stiff wind would blow it over. Bryce appeared barely conscious, something leaking from his wrist and dripping over Jake's chest and matting his chest hair.

Jake's wrist didn't look much better, pouring over Bryce's back and dripping to his crease.

"I'm so sorry." Cambry shook his head, trying to scramble away, without anywhere to go. Jake leveled a weak glare at him, stripping the excuse from his mouth.

There was no excuse. He had just bound two men to him—two wonderful men who didn't deserve his shit show of a life. There was no going back, and even if they chopped their arms off to remove the scars, they flowed through Cambry and they were tied until the end of their lives.

He could *feel* them. Bryce's flickering consciousness was like a fluttering lightbulb that hadn't decided whether it was going to go out or burn the house down. Jake was pure rage and horror.

Cambry looked to Jake, his eyes pleading. "I didn't mean to." It was the least he could say. "Don't be angry at Bryce. It wasn't his fault." Every ounce of that fury should have been directed at Cambry. Cambry was the one who had stepped between them, and Cambry was the one who was going to tear them apart.

"I'm not angry," said Jake, leaning against the bed as he closed his eyes. "I'm so fucking pissed off that I'll never be able to describe it with just one word. Get your ass over here, omega, and see to your mates." His voice was shaky, and it looked like his grip on Bryce was failing fast.

Cambry shuffled forward slowly, then faster when Jake didn't strike out. His cheek was still stinging from the blow, a bruise probably sinking in already.

Raising his hand slowly, he set his palm on Bryce's shoulder, letting out a gasp as every nerve sang with life. He reached for the floor to steady himself but struck Jake's leg instead. The feeling doubled at the contact, until he could almost taste and hear everything they were experiencing. It jammed into his own brain as if it belonged to him.

"I can hear him," said Jake, letting out a soft sob as he turned to Bryce. Bryce blinked, sliding his hand over Jake's chin and itching his scruff with the edge of his thumbnail.

"I can feel you," said Bryce, his eyes wide as he looked at Jake as if he'd never seen him before. "Are you always so angry?" He turned his gaze on Cambry. "Are you always so scared?"

They both nodded, and Cambry swallowed at the strange taste in his mouth. The ringing in his ears faded at the same time his chest eased, something settling as he touched the two men.

"I never really knew," said Jake, touching Bryce's chin and tilting him up before bringing their lips together in a brief kiss. "I mean, I knew you loved me, but I never really *knew*. Not like this." He touched his chest at the same place Cambry's heart was ready to burst with how full it brimmed.

"Of course I do, buddy," said Bryce, shuddering as lightning passed through him at the touch. Cambry knew it because he felt it in his own body, zinging down his spine to swirl around the base of his cock.

Stumbling back, Cambry pulled his hands back to his sides, nearly crying with relief as the sensations dulled to a warm glow. They were still there, brimming at the edges of his mind, but they were muted, his own thoughts easy enough to decipher. The space between them didn't hurt this time, and Bryce and Jake didn't seem to feel the difference.

A smidge of relief snuck through Cambry's panic. Perhaps he hadn't screwed up entirely. Jake and Bryce were happy, and they had the bond that they never would have been able to achieve on their own. Cambry was just the third wheel — the third mate who didn't matter all that much in the grand scheme of things.

It didn't matter that they were the only men that he'd ever trusted. Trust was overrated. He'd gotten through worse with no support system, and honestly, the sex had been one step above terrible.

Bryce snapped his head up, tilting to the side as he stared at Cambry, the exhaustion melting away from his gaze. He pushed away from Jake, turning to stand before Cambry with a look of utter wonder.

"You thought the sex was terrible?" asked Bryce. Jake spluttered behind him before a laugh let loose.

Cambry flushed, inching back before Bryce grabbed his arm, his nerves zinging back to life. He let out a gasp as Bryce tugged him, pushing him down into Jake's lap and curling up behind him so Cambry was between the two of them, ensnared inside and out. Groaning at the overload, he collapsed against Jake's chest.

"Yeah," Cambry managed, closing his eyes as things started to lull again, giving him back his independence with a few deep breaths. "I thought it would feel really, really good. It was okay, I guess, but I don't get all the hype."

Bryce kissed Jake on the forehead before their gazes locked. The look was a thousand words shared between them. "Do you remember what I told Braxton when he accused Edward of disinterest?"

Cambry thought back to their first introductions — a day that felt like more than a lifetime ago. He'd been terrified of hurting anyone, and so naïve about what the next few days had in store for him. "Something about foreplay."

Bryce nodded, tilting Cambry's chin and bringing their lips together. The touch was so unexpected that Cambry gasped, Bryce's tongue touching his as his mouth opened. It was a pressure of lips and damp tongues, but it was so much more.

The intimacy floored him. He was giving Bryce a part of himself, and Bryce was taking it, judgment-free. He groaned as Bryce deepened the kiss, his skin flushing as the heat started to build again. It was hot, wet and he never wanted it to end.

Whining as Bryce pulled back, Cambry flushed at Jake's chuckle, his lips aching and tingling. He could still taste him and feel him in his mouth, his hot breath like fire against his skin.

"That was better than the sex," said Cambry, blurting it out before he could stop himself.

"At least I've still got it," said Bryce, grinning at Jake. "But you can't expect to stick your cock in someone's ass, then jump on a knot when you're finished there and be blown away, especially when it's your first time. You need someone to romance you, treat you right and touch and kiss every part of your body. Sex and mating aren't about fucking, even if sometimes our beasts fight us on that."

"But I saw you," said Cambry. "You were pinning each other, and Jake hurt you. You looked like you really enjoyed it."

Bryce sighed, sharing another look with Jake. "Come on." He grabbed their hands, tugging them to the bed before pulling back the remaining covers, patting the mattress and settling down. Jake eased in right after him, placing himself on the farthest edge with Bryce in the middle.

Staring, Cambry took a step back. "I've never slept with someone before. What if...?" There were a thousand possibilities. He was pretty sure he wouldn't spontaneously attack them while he was awake, but what if he had a nightmare and woke up confused?

"You don't have to sleep here, but I need you to listen," said Bryce, sitting against the headboard. Jake slid his head into his lap and Bryce threaded his fingers into his hair as if it were second nature. "That feels so much better than it used to." He let his head fall back, a smile on his lips.

Cambry perched on the edge of the bed, sliding closer when Bryce patted the space next to him again. Pulling the blanket over his legs, he pressed his back to the headboard, leaving a foot between himself and the other men.

"I figure you should know the men who you are bonded to," said Bryce without opening his eyes.

"Do we have to?" asked Jake. "He could just figure it out on his own."

"There's no time for that," said Bryce. He didn't leave Cambry time to wonder what that meant before he let out a small laugh. "I met Jake when I was completing my thesis for my degree in psychology. Most of my classmates were focusing on more traditional studies, like the risks of mating bonds, strangely enough, and physiological causes of heats or psychological attributes of beast-forms—super fun stuff with lots of technical terms, but so boring that I wanted to cry. Everyone wanted to study omegas, but nobody seemed to care about the mentality of alphas."

"You really gonna tell him this?" asked Jake.

"So I thought, where are alphas at their most feral?" Bryce continued as if he hadn't heard Jake, and Jake let out a long sigh. "It's harder than you think to find an alpha in rut. It usually only occurs if their sexual needs aren't being met or if there is an omega nearby in their first heat. Even then, most alphas just get horny."

Cambry swallowed, dipping between his legs to the slick that had started to dry. The strange cramping had stopped, and somehow most of Bryce's cum had managed to stay inside him, although he didn't feel nearly as bloated as he had.

"Your heat is over," said Bryce, as if sensing his worries through their new connection. The idea was mind-boggling. "The moment we bonded, your heat ended. The next one will be different, too, but we'll talk about that later."

"Anyway, I looked high and low for pumped-up alphas who were fighting, fucking and rutting, and there Jake was," said Bryce as Jake grumbled. "He was in a cage match. This was ten years ago, when they were still on the line of legal. Back then, there weren't rules like there are today in the few legal matches around the world. It was fight or die, and the victor got his pick of who to fuck. It was bloody, brutal and nobody cared if you shifted or not." He let out a wistful sigh.

"I watched Jake win his first three matches, turning away his prize after every round. He fought like a wild animal, but he never shifted, even when his opponents played dirty. He dropped every one of them to the ground and went for the next one like he wasn't even fazed. I could see his frustration, even from the sidelines, and I knew I had to interview him. I needed to know what was going on in his mind."

"What did you do?" asked Cambry breathlessly. He could remember the cage match that he'd snuck into and how the air had been charged with heat and fire. He could only imagine Jake fighting in one, his strength pinning another man to the mat while blood seeped down his naked chest from a shallow cut from his last opponent.

Only, it wasn't his imagination. He could see it in the minds of his mates and could almost taste the sweat in the air as Jake pinned another challenger and knocked him unconscious.

"What did you do?" asked Cambry again, licking his lips as his mouth ran dry.

"I challenged him," said Bryce. "He laughed at me when I waved him down from the side, but the crowd loves a good amateur fight, so they let me fight him. The only problem was that I didn't have any money. So I offered up the only thing that I had." He shrugged.

"Which was?" asked Cambry, tilting his head. *A pen and paper for the interview? The shirt off your back?*

"His ass," said Jake, shifting on the bed. Cambry's jaw dropped open as Bryce nodded in agreement.

"It was the first time I saw Jake look excited about a fight. I'd known for years that I was attracted to both alphas and omegas—although only males—but Jake had no idea. He hadn't realized why he could fuck and fight his way through an entire night and still feel empty. But his eyes had shone when I offered myself to him, and I knew I'd made the right decision."

Bryce looked down, tugging Jake's hair until he leaned up for a kiss.

"What happened?" asked Cambry, his nails biting into his palms as he caught flashes of the fight in his mind. It was intense, with no small amount of pain, but more adrenaline and freedom than he could ever imagine.

"I won," said Bryce, grinning.

"You cheated, bitch." Jake grumbled, turning to Cambry. "He tried to mount me during the fight and I got a bit...distracted."

"Fair is fair," said Bryce, ignoring Jake as he rolled his eyes. "I pinned Jake to that mat face-first, ripped his shorts off and fucked him right there in front of a hundred people. I've never heard cheers that loud."

"Uh-huh." Jake crossed his arms.

"I didn't knot him, even though I wanted to. I didn't want to hurt him too much, after all. An alpha's ass is like a virgin every time." He grinned like a Cheshire cat. "When I pulled out, I asked him back to my place, and the rest is history."

Chapter Sixteen

Jake

Jake let out a grunt, rubbing the back of his arm over his face to try to erase a night's worth of sleep and drool. His chest was like a swimming pool, with one head on each pec and two mingling breaths keeping him warm.

He wouldn't need to chop nearly as much wood for the winter if he had two men in his bed. Or maybe he would anyway, just to watch Bryce's jaw drop every time he split a log into three with one strike. He'd never told Bryce how he managed it, mostly because he loved his mate's eyes on him.

My mate. Grinning, he looked at the two mops of dark hair that had greeted him every morning for the past four days. Cambry's hair was a touch darker and longer, his hand paler where it touched Jake's hip. He was getting more tan with each day they spent together, but Jake wasn't sure if he'd ever catch up to Bryce.

If Bryce had the option to live outdoors and wander around naked at every turn, he probably would. As it were, he'd kept his clothes on until the moment the last of his therapy group had pulled out of the driveway. Seconds after they'd disappeared, Bryce had stripped down to his boxers before he'd cleaned up the cabins for the next group.

Cambry had watched them go, tears flowing down his cheeks when he had hugged Jeremiah to him, promising to text.

Jake had almost expected Cambry to disappear into the woods when the three of them were finally left alone, but he had surprised him yet again.

Cambry shifted as Jake's bear grumbled in his chest, the sound bubbling up from his throat. He hadn't really expected Cambry to stay in the same bed as them, either, especially with the constant fear he'd felt through their bond that seemed to overrule his own anger.

He'd dreamed of his mates every night since Cambry had bonded them. Sometimes, he would be trapped in Bryce's memories of classes and camping when he'd grown up, and other times he was locked in Cambry's distorted thoughts, his fear flooding every part of him until he was on the edge of a panic attack when he woke.

He'd thought he was losing his mind the first time it had happened. He'd dreamed of being restrained, struggling and shifting as he'd broken his own arm to escape. But when he'd woken, he'd seen the scar on Cambry's arm, the pale pink mark in the exact spot that the bone had jutted through his skin in his dream.

It was true. Every moment of it.

What do they see when they dream of me? His life hadn't been one of excitement, unless one counted a cage match as excitement. Jake hadn't really felt that way about them. Fighting had been a means to an end, burning off his excess energy at a time when his life had been numb. He didn't regret them for a moment—not when they'd found him his true love.

Bryce snuffled in his sleep as if he sensed Jake's thoughts. Maybe he did. There were so many new things between them…things that Jake had never thought would be possible. Before, there had been no way for them to bond. Now they had the strongest bond that could happen, their thoughts and emotions mingled along with their memories.

And Cambry.

Jake swallowed uncomfortably, easing from between his two mates and stepping away from the bedroom. He splashed water on his face, glancing at the mirror as he closed the bathroom door and flicked the light on.

Droplets fell from his face and down his neck, the thickest one making it all the way to his navel before it dried out. He was wearing the same skin with the same lines and scars, but he was a different person.

It wasn't just the bond. Cambry had started to change them before he'd bitten them, soaking the house in his scent and flooding Jake with desires that he never thought he'd have.

When Bryce had volunteered him, he had thought of it as more of an annoyance than anything else. He'd never found himself attracted to an omega before, just like he'd never been attracted to a woman. Why have a slick hole when he could wrestle for a tighter one?

But it wasn't just that. Most alphas he'd met in his lifetime had left him with a poor taste in his mouth. Bryce was different in every way. He wasn't afraid to speak his mind, and he didn't care what others thought of him. He was himself and only himself. There was no boasting, no carrying on and no pretending.

He had his weaknesses, just like he and Cambry did, but Jake couldn't help but love him more for it.

He tugged on a pair of pants from the bathroom floor, heading down to the kitchen through Cambry's room so he didn't wake the two sleeping men. Cambry's room had the same untouched feel that it had had before he'd first arrived, his scent almost faded from the fresh linens, and his books untouched where Bryce had stacked them in a small bookcase that Jake had built the day before.

Flicking the coffee pot on, he grabbed two mugs from the cupboard, returning for a third as he shook his head. As much as Cambry had become a part of their daily lives, it had been Bryce and him for so long that sometimes he forgot.

Cream for himself and Bryce, and milk for Cambry, because he didn't like how light the cream turned his coffee. Jake suspected that he would drink it black if they had a better brand than one that had been on sale.

"Couldn't sleep?"

Jake looked up at Cambry's sleepy voice, unable to hold back his smile. His light eyes were like something out of a magazine, his dark lashes making them stand out even more. The soul of his wolf shone through, even when it slumbered.

"Slept in," said Jake, grinning at Cambry's wince. His omega wasn't used to getting up before the sun or greeting the birds as they took to their perches and started to sing. Bryce was probably in agreement with him.

"I'd like to help you again today if I could," said Cambry, dropping his gaze to his coffee cup as Jake slid it to him. "Thank you, Jake. You don't have to do that."

Jake grunted. A cup of coffee was nothing. It wasn't like he was the one chasing the cow for the milk.

"I'll be off in the far cabin today," said Jake, taking a long sip of his drink before setting it on the table. Perhaps he was a masochist, but he truly did hate the taste of coffee. Going through a day without it was beyond imagining, though.

"Oh." Cambry flushed, the bridge of his nose going bright pink. "Is that the one with all the snakes?"

Jake wasn't sure why Cambry blushed as often as he did, but he hoped it never changed. There was something endearing about how he went pink every time Jake spoke.

"Don't listen to Bryce," said Jake, taking another swallow. "The brush pile with the snakes is a good hundred yards away from the cabin. Just don't wear sandals like him, and you should be fine. If you hear a buzzing sound like a really big bee, just call out and I'll rescue you."

Cambry snorted, smiling into his coffee. Jake had slowly been chipping at his shell over the last few days, and he'd managed to find a passionate young man who was almost as sarcastic as himself. It was keeping him out of his shell that was the real trick.

Finishing their coffees, Jake waved Cambry to the door, pulling on a pair of steel-toed work boots. The one and only time he had done any construction work in sandals, he had broken two of his toes.

"Can I borrow a pair?" asked Cambry, looking to his sneakers that had seen better days. There was a hole in one of the toes that made Jake want to snarl every time he saw it.

"Sure," said Jake, turning to the closet and pulling the door wide. "I think Bryce's might fit you better than my backup pair. What are you, a ten?"

"Eleven."

So, his sneakers were too small for him, too, which explained the hole in the toe. If Jake ever managed to meet Cambry's father, he had a few words and maybe a new asshole to tear into him.

"Here." Plucking the boots from the closet, he double-checked the size. They were twelves, but they would have to do. His own feet barely fit into fourteen double-wides, so Cambry would probably be left swimming in them, even if the laces were pulled tight.

Jake dropped to his knees, reaching for Cambry's foot. He hesitated at Cambry's gasp when their skin made contact, the touch searing up his arm and into his core. His bear grumbled, urging him to deepen the contact.

"You don't have to do that," said Cambry softly.

The thing that pissed Jake off more than the ratty shoes and clothes and the hidden books, which he had definitely read when Bryce had told him about them, was how terrified Cambry was to be doted on. It wasn't even the touching so much anymore, but the simple things, like coffee in the morning or brushing his hair out for him before bed.

Jake had done it for Bryce so many times, and Bryce had returned the favor, so it was as natural as breathing between them. There was no question that he was going to help Cambry, even if their bonding had been a bit unorthodox. The guy deserved it.

"I don't have to, but I will, little pup." Sliding his hand to Cambry's calf, he dipped his finger along the top of his sock before moving to his ankle and propping it up against his thigh. Cambry reached for the wall as Jake slid the first boot over his foot, pulling the laces tight and double knotting them.

There was no resistance when he reached for Cambry's other foot, but his breathing had changed from steady and deep, to shallow and rapid. Placing a kiss against Cambry's knee, Jake leaned back before standing.

They made their way to the last cabin, tramping down the freshly bent grass under their shoes. He hadn't heard of any problems from the latest couple who had stayed in the cabin, but he'd wanted to check on the plumbing situation again before Bryce decided to overbook them.

At least they only ran the sessions every other week in the summer and once monthly in the winter. Jake couldn't imagine having people around at all times, watching and analyzing his every move as he tried to stay out of the way.

Bryce was fine with his sexuality and didn't seem concerned that their relationship might become public at some point. Jake wasn't quite sure if he was ready for that, though. It was probably a moot point. Between Bryce and Cambry, no one had to know who he'd fucked first.

Something tugged at his chest and Jake paused, rubbing at the spot. It wasn't exactly heartburn, but something else deeper that almost brought tears to his eyes. He turned to Cambry, the feeling getting worse at the sight of him on his knees.

"What is this?" Cambry asked, touching the tiny little makeshift cross that Jake had thrown together with a couple of twigs and some string he'd had in the bottom of his pocket. The earth was still fresh in the rectangle that was barely a foot long and half-a-foot wide. The little daisies Jake had plucked from the ground and had placed across the grave were wilted and curled like the tiny corpse beneath the turned dirt.

"One of Bryce's chipmunk friends got jammed in a pipe and died. I buried him with all the peanuts I found in that damn pipe. If he believed in an afterlife, he won't go hungry." Jake scuffed his boot along the path, erasing the footprints that he'd just left.

"Oh. Does he have a lot of chipmunk friends? I only ask because I swear something ran across my foot the other day, and I was hoping it wasn't a rat." He touched his fingers to the base of the grave before he started to rise.

"Not many rats around here. Too many snakes." Jake grinned as Cambry looked up and down the path. "But Bryce has made friends with pretty much every creature that's around. There was a fox momma that was rooting through the trash every night last year, so Bryce started leaving out a plate of scrambled eggs for her. That brought in the raccoons, but they took off for good once they got a good look at his shifted form one morning. And there is a loon in the pond that will steal a fish right off your line."

Cambry winced.

"Haven't seen her around this year, though." Jake tapped his chin. He'd hardly made it out to the pond at all since spring. "Well, anyway, let's get to work before it gets too hot today." Jake turned, but the same tugging pulled him back. Cambry hadn't moved, his gaze locked on the tiny grave.

"Do you make graves for all of them when they pass?"

"Well, yeah, of course." Jake shrugged. "They are important in their own lives, and they made an impression on ours. They deserve some remembrance, even if it only lasts a few days." He glanced to the flowers that would have probably disappeared already if it hadn't rained the day before.

Cambry nodded, something passing over his features before he started walking again.

The inside of the cabin was thankfully cool, even with one window that had been left open by the last couple. Luckily, the trees were especially thick on that side and only a few drops of rain had made it through, drying in a pattern of water spots on the rustic flooring. Jake scratched them with his fingernail before he trudged deeper within.

While Bryce had been screaming his head off as the toilet flooded the last time Jake had been in the cabin, he'd noticed that the window hadn't been sitting right. He hadn't stuck around to fix it.

Propping the door open, he looked around the bathroom floor first. There were a few spots of darker wood right around the base of the toilet, but Bryce had done a surprisingly good job with his clean-up. He would have to mention it the next time Bryce pulled the blankets halfway up the bed and called it 'made'.

"What are we fixing?" asked Cambry as he nudged his way through the door. The space was small enough with just Jake inside, but Cambry's presence didn't add the expected claustrophobia.

"That," said Jake, pointing at the window that was open just a hair. He grabbed his level from his toolbelt, testing the top and bottom of the frame. "Looks like the cabin shifted a bit during the last thaw. Any more and the window would have cracked." He tapped the glass, noting the clouded corner.

"What can I do to help?" asked Cambry.

Jake grinned. He had longed for those very words from Bryce for the last ten years when it came to anything physical, not that he would trust Bryce with a hammer. They would both end up with concussions.

Cambry braced the window for him while he pried the trim off, setting each piece on the edge of the bathtub so he could reuse them. More than once, he brushed against Cambry as he worked, heat floating through him at each gentle touch. Cambry must have felt it, too, from the flush over his nose that deepened when Jake leaned close to pry a particularly nasty nail from the wall.

"What kind of sadist installed this window?" asked Cambry, sweat pouring down his forehead as the small space grew warmer. His breath tickled against Jake's neck, and he leaned into it, telling himself that it was for the breeze alone.

"That would be me." Jake grinned as Cambry blanched, almost dropping the window as it finally came fully loose from its shims.

"I'm s—"

"You better not be about to apologize," said Jake, letting out a snarl of frustration. "You're actually a funny guy when you aren't so worried. I won't hit ya, and I'm not going to tease you, either. So come on, tell me a joke, and make it brutal."

"I can't...like not at the moment, I mean," said Cambry, ducking his head. His knuckles were nearly white where he clutched the edge of the window.

Jake let out a sigh, scrubbing through his damp hair. His cock was throbbing harder from every innocent touch, and he wasn't sure how much more he could take. Tossing his pry bar, he stepped closer to Cambry until Cambry had no choice but to look up.

Jake dipped to run his nose along Cambry's neck, committing him to memory with a single lungful. Cambry had always been overpowering and sinful, and that hadn't changed since their accidental bond. Since they'd started sleeping together, Jake took his fill every time he could.

"Do I smell? Sorry." Cambry took a step back, wobbling to hold the window steady with his arms extended.

Jake braced the glass with one hand, looping an arm around Cambry's hips and pulling him tight. *God, he smells good.* Jake rumbled, licking a stripe up Cambry's neck and gathering the sweat on his tongue. *Good enough to eat.*

Jake shook his head, taking a step back and turning to the window. He cleared his throat, his legs wobbling uncomfortably. "Sorry. Sometimes I forget."

Grabbing a fresh stack of shims, Jake fitted the window until it was level. Slapping the trim back in was way easier than removing it, and within half an hour, Jake had the window opening and closing to perfection.

"I'll have to do the glass soon," he said as he polished the corner. "Probably in the spring or next fall. Maybe you could help?"

Cambry blinked at him from his new perch on the tub, his mouth dropping open.

"I would have been out here all day if it were just me, and Bryce is just about as useless as an actual bear with these types of things." Jake rubbed his sternum at the strange feeling that spread there. "He's a good cook, though, so I keep him around."

"He's passable at best," said Cambry, grinning as he pushed his way to his feet. Hopefully, he wasn't reeling over Jake's slip-up as much as Jake was.

But picturing Cambry there with him in a year felt like the way things ought to be.

"Are you claiming to be an undercover chef?"

"Hell no," said Cambry, squinting as he looked at the clouded glass. "My father's cook on the other hand? He could cook a steak perfectly while blindfolded with one hand tied behind his back. I do miss his risotto."

Jake laughed, licking his lips as he leaned away. His clothes were clinging to his body in every crevice, and even his feet had started to sweat through his workmen's socks.

"Any chance I could get you in the pond again?" asked Jake, taking a deep breath of fresh air as they stepped outside the cabin. Cambry nodded, trailing behind as they made their way along the looping path that led in the general direction of the water.

Jake paused as a call cackled through the trees, a troop of blue jays hopping from branch to branch above their heads. A few needles shook loose, one landing at the top of Cambry's head, the sap sticking to his fine hair.

Cambry watched the birds play and jostle, the one at the lead of the flock with a peanut in their beak. The rest followed like a bunch of ravenous hyenas.

"Bryce must've found my stash of peanuts again," said Jake wistfully as he watched his afternoon snack disappear as a jay swooped in and plucked the peanut right from the beak of the other bird.

"They're pretty. I think I've maybe seen a dozen in my life back home, but here, they seem to be everywhere." He tracked as the last bird took flight, letting out an angry caw before it trailed after its siblings.

"Here." Jake plucked the stray needle from Cambry's hair, tossing it to the ground. The sticky sap clung to his fingertips, a tiny bit of it still stuck in Cambry's hair. "I have a special soap back home that gets sap out a lot better than the regular stuff. I used to stick to everything until Bryce found it for me."

He touched Cambry's hair with his clean hand, separating the few strands that glimmered with stickiness. "Or I could just rip the fuckers out." Cambry smacked his shoulder, and Jake stepped back with a chuckle.

The breeze picked up as soon as they reached the pond, filtering out a few shades of humidity that kept his sweat from drying out. *I don't get out here often enough.*

Everything about the place was rustic, from the soggy west bank with reeds higher than his head to the little beaver dam along the south that kept the pond from being a lonely little puddle. He could smell the wildlife and knew that he would see different tracks on every single shore.

"She came back this year," said Jake, pointing to the loon that was near the middle of the pond. "Her mate must've dumped her, though. She likes to bring back a new guy every year, but sometimes they don't stick around long." Cupping his hands over his mouth, he let out a howl. It sounded nothing like a loon, but it worked every time.

The loon turned in the water, her powerful strokes bringing her closer to Jake as he let out another howl. She answered with a warbling call, the sound sinking straight into him.

"Umm." Cambry stepped out from behind Jake, moving to the edge of the water where the loon was headed. The bird let out a startled call, turning in the water before beating its powerful wings and taking off.

"Oh." Jake scratched his head as he watched the loon disappear out of sight. "She's usually really friendly."

"I maybe tried to eat her when I was a wolf." Cambry flushed bright as Jake laughed, the sound letting loose from his chest.

"Is there anything you don't try to eat when you're a wolf?" asked Jake, shaking his head as he looked out over the water. His chest stung just beneath his sternum as Cambry fell silent.

Jake's humor fell away when he saw the sorrow etched into Cambry's every feature. *Fuck.* He hadn't even thought what those words would mean to his shy wolf. *That's why Bryce should do the fucking talking.*

"I'm sorry. I didn't mean it like that. I was really just wondering what you could catch us for dinner." He relaxed at the tiny peek of a smile on Cambry's lips. "I don't know about you, but I'm going swimming. Don't look if you don't want to see a full moon."

Peeling his boots and clothes from his body and laying them out on the rock, Jake slowly stepped into the water. After the brief rocky shore, the bottom squished beneath his feet with each step, oozing between his toes as he moved deeper. A stray leech undulated by, probably pissed off that they had chased away the tasty loon.

"You coming?" asked Jake, calling over his shoulder when he was waist-deep. Cambry had stripped his shirt off, revealing enough pale skin to temporarily overload his brain.

"Too many leeches. I got one between my toes last time," said Cambry, leaning against the rock as he let out a sigh.

"That's nothing," said Jake, letting out a breath as he eased the rest of the way into the water before kicking away the weeds that tangled around his ankles. "I had to get Bryce to sprinkle salt on my asshole once." He chuckled at the memory.

"What?" Cambry perched on his elbows, lifting his lips into a grin.

"I didn't even know it was there until I got out and felt something wriggling. My first thought was that Bryce was trying to get frisky, but then I realized that he was a few feet away. When I bent over, sure enough, I was getting rimmed by a leech."

Cambry cackled, leaning back against the rock as he kicked off his shoes. "And that didn't stop you from going in again? I would be scarred for life."

"Nah." Jake leaned back, taking a few strokes into deeper water that was just above his head. "I was hoping I would get one on my dick next. Bryce felt so sorry for me that after the thing fell off, he cleaned me up and ate me out for an hour." He hummed fondly at the memory.

Jake had never talked to anyone about his relationship with Bryce but saying it out loud was the most freeing experience of his life. The only moments that competed were when he was one with his bear, sparring with Bryce and hoping to be pinned.

Cambry shook his head, shutting his eyes against the sun as his breathing evened out.

Slowly moving back to shore, Jake eased from the water, checking every crevice and cranny for little suckers. He found one on the soft sole of his foot, but he scraped it off on the rock, wincing at the twinge. The spot seeped blood, leaving little impressions as he made his way to Cambry and lowered himself to the rock.

The water quickly wicked away from his skin, the sun glowing against him. It was the perfect summer's day, with only the sound of their breathing and a few animals.

Cambry looked like he was dreaming, with his dark lashes on his cheeks and his eyes moving back and forth behind his closed lids. His chest rose and fell softly, his breath as quiet as the gentle breeze through the rustle of trees. He didn't have a single scar except for the one on his arm where his bone had broken.

Jake forced his gaze away, touching the damp sole of his foot. His fingers slid through the gritty muck left behind by the pond. It wasn't a beach, but it was the best way to cool off on a hot day.

"What did you mean when you said that sometimes you forget?" asked Cambry, his eyes staying shut as he spoke. "Back in the cabin, you said that sometimes you forget."

Jake turned away, running his hand over his own leg so he didn't reach out. He wished he never would have said anything at all. He let out a sigh, closing his eyes against the sun. "You didn't mean to bond with us, even if you gave us something wonderful. I forget sometimes that you're not really mine."

Chapter Seventeen

Bryce

"Okay, so how far back have you actually been?" asked Bryce as he eyed a sleepy Cambry, who was cuter than an actual wolf pup. His hair was fluffed, and his eyes were half-lidded and everything.

"Just to the pond," said Cambry, letting out another yawn that cracked his jaw before he rubbed the back of his hand over his eyes.

"You've been here almost two weeks, and I haven't even given you a proper tour," said Bryce, sighing dramatically. "The pond is just the tip of the iceberg. Did you know that we have an actual waterfall near the back of the property? I mean, it's probably just a trickle right now, but in the spring, it's glorious."

"That's nice," said Cambry flatly, blinking against the sun as Bryce led him outside.

The morning was a touch crisper than the previous few, and the humidity had finally taken a tumble to the mid-fifties instead of the mid-nineties.

The forecast had said that it would push thirty Celsius by noon, so Bryce had dragged Cambry out of bed at six o'clock when the first blue jay had started trilling outside of the bedroom window as it begged for peanuts.

Hopefully Jake hadn't found where he'd hid the stash. He'd been up at four-thirty as if that were a reasonable time for a human being.

"We can go back to bed if you want to instead," said Bryce, his enthusiasm starting to wane. He'd tried to get Cambry on his own over the last week, but every time he'd managed, his thoughts had instantly filled with other things.

"No, really, it sounds neat," said Cambry with a touch more enthusiasm. He squinted at the sun, putting a hand above his eyes to shield himself from the worst of it. "But do we have to go so early? It's not even seven."

"I was hoping to introduce you to the deer," said Bryce, grinning. "There are a few does that hang around back there. I take them apples sometimes." He lifted the bag that he'd hidden at the bottom of the fridge when he'd gotten back from a grocery run the day before.

Bryce paused at the tree line, pressing a finger to his lips before closing his eyes and taking a deep breath. He would never get used to the smell of the outside — always different and only very rarely awful. It changed from day to day as things grew, died, pollinated and budded. Cambry was mixed in there too, his sweet scent almost a touch floral when he was surrounded by trees.

"Can you hear that?" asked Bryce, keeping his eyes closed as he reached for the bark on the nearest tree. It was rough and smooth under his palm at the same time, snagging his nail as he dug too deep. He drew his claws back, not realizing that he had started to shift.

"I hear…"

Bryce peeked one eye open to watch as Cambry tilted his head, closing his eyes to concentrate. It was so wolf-like that Bryce barely held back a chuckle.

"A couple of crickets, because it's still kind of nighttime, and I think that's a robin? I'm not great with bird songs. I can hear your heart, too." Cambry's eyes shot open as he stared at Bryce. "It's louder than mine."

"Wow. A-plus, buddy." Bryce let out a chuckle, self-consciously listening for his own chest sounds. *I'm not having a heart attack, am I?* He shook out his left arm, just in case. *Feels fine.* "It *is* a robin, by the way. What I was really going for was *nothing*—no cars, no lawnmowers or chainsaws or dogs barking, just nature."

Cambry grunted, leaning against the tree and closing his eyes as he tilted his head against the rough bark. "I can hear a car. It's really far away but it's definitely going over the speed limit. Sounds like the transmission is on its way out, too."

Bryce's mouth flopped open and Cambry chuckled, shaking his head as it turned into a full-blown laugh.

"Seriously?" Bryce leaned up on his toes, straining for the sound with every part of him. There was definitely a frog somewhere, but no car that he could hear.

"No." Cambry snorted. "I was just joking with you. You were having a very 'one with nature' moment, and I thought you might need a reality check. Jake said he gives you one per day, so I thought I would give it a shot."

Bryce spluttered, crossing his arms as he looked Cambry up and down. Something about him had changed since their bond, even if it had come on so gradually that Bryce couldn't nail down exactly what it was. He wasn't so afraid anymore, and he only really blushed around Jake…except the one time Bryce hadn't thought before heading down for breakfast in the nude. Jake had thrown a blanket at him, growling once and pointing him right back up the stairs.

"I like it." Nodding once, he turned into the forest, Cambry still chuckling as he followed. The path grew damp as they moved deeper, some spots still muddy from the rainfall three nights before. A frog perched at the edge of one puddle, hopping away as he slapped by it with his bare feet.

"Wrong direction, buddy," he called to the frog, frowning when it headed back toward the cabins. He turned to Cambry, who was looking at him curiously. "Rattlesnake alley is about ten meters that way." He pointed off into the thickening bush.

"Do you think they'll be out now?" Cambry perked up, his eyes going bright. "I was worried the first time you mentioned them, but I think I want to see them now."

Bryce wilted, shuffling his feet across the forest floor. He'd gone barefoot in the hopes that he could convince Cambry to shift with him, but he wasn't getting any closer to the poisonous demons without three layers of protection – *or claws.*

"I can show them to you on one condition," said Bryce, dropping the bag of apples to the ground. He would have to come back for them later…if he was still alive. Lifting the edge of his shirt, he tugged it over his head. "You ride me."

It was Cambry's turn to splutter, his face nearly crimson when Bryce finally tugged his shirt free from his ears where his piercings always managed to snag.

"Um, okay? It's a little chilly, but I'll work with it," said Cambry, tugging his own borrowed shirt free and tossing it next to Bryce's. He scrambled for his belt that was holding his jeans up that were a size too big.

"What?" Bryce froze, his pants halfway down his legs and Cambry's not far behind. "What are you doing?" His heart picked up at the sight of all that pale skin. Cambry had darkened a touch, but he was still so pale and pure. It was a miracle that he hadn't burnt to a crisp.

"Getting ready to ride you," said Cambry slowly, playing with his boxers with his gaze locked on the forest floor. "I didn't bring anything, though."

"What are you — I mean, you can if you want. I'm all about au natural, but it might be a bit chafing." Bryce scrubbed at his back. Jake had mentioned that his fur was always coarse except around his ears. Not like Cambry, who was like a fluffy doll.

"I t-think we're talking about two different things." The words rushed out of Cambry's lips, and he dove for his pants, tugging them back up his legs before Bryce could blink.

What? Oh. Oooooh. Bryce rubbed at the spot just below his ribs where his stomach liked to flare up when he ate too many tacos. It had been acting up over the last few days and he'd forgotten antacids on his last trip out.

"We can do that, too," Bryce said in a rush, tugging his underwear off, despite the fact that his cock had started to plump up. "I just didn't want you on the ground with the snakes, so I thought I could shift and you could ride me while we check out the nest. My bear has a better sense of smell than me." He pointed to his nose. "But sex later. That's cool."

Bryce nodded, even as his heart threatened to beat out of his chest. Despite sleeping together, they hadn't gone beyond simple good night kisses since their first time. He had started to get antsy, even though Jake hadn't shown his usual horniness cues — grumpiness, insomnia, shifting for no reason and, Bryce's personal favorite, initiating a wrestling match while pretending to fight over something unimportant, like where his peanut stash had disappeared to.

"I wasn't sure if you were ready for something like that, but if you want to, we can. I can talk to Jake about it when we get back," said Bryce, scratching the back of his head again. Sex was something he could talk about for literally days, and showing Cambry the ropes properly was at the top of the to-do list. *Pun intended.*

Cambry's eyes flew wide as he stumbled back. "Please don't tell Jake."

Cambry's shoulders went instantly tight, and his lips thinned. Bryce's stomach flared as his heartburn chose that moment to make itself known.

"Okay," Bryce said slowly. He'd honestly thought that Jake was closer to Cambry than he was, but he wasn't about to push.

"Jake is yours, and you're his," said Cambry, reaching for his shirt and tugging it on. A few needles clung to the front, sticking through the fabric and probably pricking Cambry's skin. "I don't want to come between you guys."

"Coming between us could be really fun," said Bryce, his smirk spreading wide. "Sorry, I couldn't resist. You got me once today, so I had to get you back.

Seriously, though, don't worry about it. If you want something to stay between us, then it will. I am technically your therapist." *I am breaking so many rules when I say it like that. Bye-bye, license.*

Cambry nodded once, looking away with the bridge of his nose tinted bright.

Just when I thought we were making progress.

Crouching, Bryce gave in to his bear, shuddering as fur sprouted over his body and his limbs rearranged themselves. It wasn't exactly painful for him, but more like stretching a slightly sore muscle after a workout. He sneezed as his nose transfigured itself into a snout, scents pouring in and making up for his less-than-stellar vision.

"I forgot how big you are," said Cambry, every sign of tension falling away as he approached Bryce and ran a hand through his scruff, digging in deep to the corded muscle below. Bryce let out a grumble, leaning into the touch. "I'm not sure if you can carry me, though. I'm not a small guy."

Bryce huffed. *Well, excuse me, Mr. Manly. Get on.* He nudged at Cambry's leg, leaning against him until Cambry had to put his weight on Bryce to keep his balance. *Okay, so maybe he's a touch heavy. Too late.*

With a narrowed-eyed look of hesitance, Cambry swung his leg over, jostling onto Bryce's back as if he were mounting a horse. Clenching his hands in Bryce's fur, he wobbled a moment before finally getting his balance. His feet were only a few inches off the ground, but it would have to do.

Holy shit you're heavy. Bryce was a little glad that Cambry couldn't actually hear him. Cambry was heavy for an *omega* but perfect at the same time. He didn't want to give him a complex.

"So are we going to look at some snakes or am I just going to sit here getting itchy thighs for the rest of the day?" Cambry scratched behind Bryce's ear, chuckling as he let out a soft growl.

Okay. I can do this and not fall over. Bryce took his first step off the beaten path, heading directly to where his nose was pointing him. Snakes had a dank, earthy smell that was unique to reptiles and happened to give him heart palpitations. After he started walking, it got a touch easier, Cambry's weight shifting smoothly between his four legs as he moved.

Too close. Bryce slammed on the breaks, locking his front legs so he didn't take another step. Something slithered in the grassy undergrowth about a foot away from his paw. He relaxed at the yellow stripe down its black back.

Reaching out, he pointed the best he could with his broad paw, tapping the ground softly when the snake paused. It flicked its forked tongue out to taste the air, blinking its dark eyes as it considered them for a moment. It was awfully intimidating for only being about twelve inches long.

"Wha—oh! Oh, wow." Cambry leaned forward and Bryce had to put his foot down to keep his balance. "It's beautiful. How can you be afraid of such a tiny thing?"

Bryce rolled his head back and forth. Garter snakes, he was completely okay with. It was their toxic cousins that terrified him. They were twenty minutes away from the nearest hospital with antivenom, and he wasn't sure if he'd last that long if a rattler actually bit him. He might die of shame before he even got out of the driveway.

He could almost hear Jake grumbling about it. *"Maybe the snake wouldn't have bitten you if you hadn't paraded past its nest naked every day. It's just taking out the competition."* Or *"Stop feeding the rodents, because that's what feeds our snake population."* Jake just didn't want to share his peanuts.

The snake slithered away as Bryce took another tentative step, his eyes locked on the ground to try to pick up any movement. A gentle buzzing reached his ears, getting louder as he hit a soft patch of undergrowth. Huffing wildly, he flung backward, Cambry clutching at his shoulders as he pitched to the side.

"Warn a guy."

He scrambled on Bryce's back as Bryce took a step sideways, the buzzing intensifying. He couldn't see them in the underbrush with their patterned backs tricking his eyes successfully, but he could smell and hear them clearly. *This was stupid.*

"I see them," Cambry whispered, gripping Bryce tight. "There are a lot of them. Maybe we should go back? Slowly."

Bryce blinked, searching again and not knowing where the hell he was even supposed to step. *This was a really bad idea.*

"Hey. Hey, Bryce, it's okay." Cambry stroked the smoother fur on the top of Bryce's head, dipping his hand over his muzzle. "I can feel you're afraid, but it's okay."

You can feel me?

"Yeah, it's okay. I can kind of hear you, too." Cambry shook his head, before rubbing one hand down his own face. "I couldn't before, but as soon as you shifted it started, almost like a whisper. But don't worry about all those nasty thoughts you were thinking of me. Just take a step back with your left front paw."

Bryce snorted, lifting a paw.

"No! The other left. I don't think you can see how close they are right now."

Bryce lifted his other paw, blinking through his panic as he realized that he couldn't tell left from right at the moment. Sometimes he lost things when he was a bear, and if it got any worse, he wouldn't be able to understand what Cambry was saying. Being one with his animal was not his issue.

"Okay, now the other one. Good." Cambry patted Bryce's neck, twitching his fingers through the thick fur. "Okay, you can turn around now. You're clear of them."

Bryce looked back, peering through the place he'd just been standing. Suddenly, he saw them. There had to be a dozen of them, all curled together in a pile that looked like a rock and not a slithering promise of death. His paw had only been six inches away at the absolute maximum. If he would have taken another step, he wouldn't have had to wonder if their fangs could pierce through his thick coat.

Cambry let out a deep breath, flopping down on Bryce's shoulder as he started to chuckle. "That was pretty cool."

We almost died. Bryce rolled his eyes as he headed away from the reptilian smell.

"Don't overreact so much. You kept me safe," said Cambry, rocking with each movement. Each step was slow and soft, Bryce using every muscle to try to keep himself steady. Trees passed them by until he couldn't smell the snakes at all, his apples lying forgotten behind them.

"I'm going to have a nap, okay?" He shoved his face into Bryce's scruff, breathing deep so Bryce's skin went cool.

Screw the waterfall. Bryce turned, stepping carefully when Cambry relaxed his grip. He wasn't sure if Cambry would actually fall asleep or not, but he didn't want to take the chance that he tumbled off onto the forest floor — not to mention that Bryce's adrenaline was giving way to something much more intense.

"I feel it, too," said Cambry softly, scratching at Bryce's ear before he went lax again. "I'd like to think that I've found a real friendship with you and Jake, but I don't want to kid myself, either. I know I'm only here because my father paid you more than I'm worth."

Bryce grunted, shaking his head. With a sneeze, he shifted, drawing his fur back under his skin as his bones and muscles reformed themselves. Cambry fell on top of him with an *oomph*, pushing the air from Bryce's lungs.

"Oh." Cambry flushed, rolling off Bryce and holding his hands up in surrender. "I'm not even looking. Sorry… I should have gotten off."

Getting off would be excellent. Bryce pushed himself to his feet, brushing the pine needles from his chest, and taking particular care to pluck the ones that had managed to plaster themselves to his groin. Sometimes foreskin was more of a curse than a blessing.

"Nope, that's not why I shifted. Come on." Instead of leading the way again, Bryce reached for Cambry's hand, threading their fingers together. His palm was sweaty and hot, but Bryce squeezed tighter, the zing at their touch soothing some of his lingering panic.

"I didn't grab your clothes," said Cambry, craning his neck to look for them. *Good luck.* Bryce had deliberately avoided them. Jake could only make him wear them when he was around.

"Clothes, smothes." Bryce waved him off, wincing as his cock bobbed along. Usually, he wasn't hard when he was walking, but hey, that's what kept life interesting.

He tugged Cambry along the perimeter of the pond, keeping well back from the squishy shores and flinching every time a pine needle stabbed into his foot. His cut was still healing, and the little buggers seemed to know just where to poke when he was walking.

Cambry's flush had subsided by the time they reached the little fall, which was more of a trickle, if Bryce were being fair. Even a trickle was generous. The slab of rock that probably existed since the last ice age, jutted up through the trees at the base of a hill, water trickling down from above at a sparse drip. In the spring, everything fell from the hill at once, creating a pool in the rock below that was crystal-clear and so frigid that it had almost castrated Bryce when he'd taken a dip.

With the summer heat bearing down on them, the pool had shrunk to a sludgy couple of feet deep, the rimmed rock edges sheer and smooth. The water fell into the middle, each drop sending circles from its core like tiny little waves. It was a wonder to think how long it had been dripping to carve out a bowl that Bryce could drop into without being able to touch the sides. The distant bottom was out of reach, and the bit of water that was in it was a shimmer within a shadow.

"Wow." Cambry moved to the edge, extracting his hand so he could crouch down at the edge and look into the cylindrical hole. "Where does the water all go?" His voice echoed off the walls of the concave surface, startling an animal that had been hidden in the brush nearby. *So much for showing him the deer.*

"I don't know," said Bryce, sitting on the edge and dangling his legs over the side. The water was more than six feet down, and if he ever fell in, not even the vultures would be able to find his body. He swung his toes through the cooler air regardless, before scraping his heel over the smooth edge.

"When it rains, it fills a bit, but it doesn't really drain." He pointed up to the jutting outcropping and the eroded notch where the water dripped from. "In the spring, it fills to the top and it slowly starts to go down as the season gets longer."

"I'm surprised nothing's fallen in," said Cambry, shuffling closer before sitting next to him.

"I pulled a deer out of it last year. I was too late to save it, but it hadn't been down there long. Most animals steer clear of this spot, though. They have good instincts." He kicked the ledge, letting the sting in his heel take his grief away. "Who knows? Maybe you'll toss me in in a few minutes."

Cambry gave him a strange look, tilting his head to the side as he scrunched his nose.

"Your father is coming tomorrow," said Bryce. There it was—everything that had been haunting him since he'd spoken to Wilfred Parsons. So much had changed since that conversation, and he could barely believe it had even happened.

But it had. Despite his shattered phone, his call records were easily accessible. Every time he looked, that private number glared back at him.

"Oh. I guess my time is up?" asked Cambry, his voice strangely soft. He shuffled closer to the precipice, then dangled his feet over the edge.

"He called me a week ago," said Bryce, scratching at the back of his head. *How do I even say this?* "He wanted me to break you."

He'd never been ashamed of being a sex therapist before, but he'd never had reason to be. He'd never had someone turn his life upside down and risk his license. Was it such a bad thing that he was at a loss? Was it terrible that he would do it all again?

"What did you say?" Cambry asked gently, his expression closing off as Bryce's gut let out a pang. Rubbing the spot, Bryce shook his head.

"I don't even remember. I broke my phone, though. Jake was not impressed." That was a conversation he had no desire to revisit. Jake was supposed to be the one with the anger problem who was allowed to break stuff and swear if he needed to.

"What did he say when you told him about us?"

What would I say? I don't really care what he would have to say about it. "He doesn't know. No one knows." Bryce bit his lip to keep the sudden surge of emotion at bay. As much as he wanted to announce their bond to anyone who would ever listen, it had been an accident. He wasn't going to hold Cambry to something that he hadn't meant to do. "He'll be here tomorrow, though. Probably early, if I had my guess." Bryce plucked a dead leaf from the forest floor, tossing it into the pit.

"Thank you, Bryce."

Bryce looked up, his chest going tight as he saw the tears streaming down Cambry's cheeks. He ached to reach out and pull him in for a hug, and if it were anyone else, he would have.

"You and Jake have done so much for me." Cambry shook his head, wiping his cheeks with the back of his hand. "I owe you everything." Pushing himself to his feet, he turned away, heading back along the same path that had brought them to the fall.

Bryce stayed where he was, glaring down at the deep pit. Their bond may have been an accident, but why did he feel like a hole had just been blown through his chest?

Chapter Eighteen

Cambry

He avoided the house as long as he could, until the sounds of lunch dishes were quieter than his growling stomach. He'd never managed to skip breakfast without getting seriously hangry, but he'd hoped that he could fall asleep in the bed at the cabin he'd been helping Jake fix up.

Jake's and Bryce's scents were everywhere, driving him and his wolf mad. His wolf was grumbling at him to get up and go to them, but his mind was stuck on what it would be like never to smell them again. Scent had always been his weakest sense, but he seemed to be specifically tuned to them, as if he'd suddenly been switched on with no hope of ever turning off again.

Stumbling through the door, Cambry crouched to remove his work boots that Jake had insisted he keep after he'd worn them the first time. He couldn't remember the last time someone had given him shoes for more than just necessity, and he found himself wishing that they were a touch more comfortable so he would have the excuse to wear them all the time.

"Bryce? Is that you?" Jake called from the direction of the kitchen, his deep voice carrying through the house with ease.

Cambry trembled as he let the words wash over him, committing them to memory so he would never forget the way Jake sounded. He tended to roll his r's a bit, giving his voice the edge of a growl, even when he was speaking normally. It was as adorable as it was sexy.

"It's just me," Cambry called out, reaching for the wall and pausing with his hand on the wooden slat.

"Hey, puppy, did you see Bryce out there anywhere?" Jake peeked around the corner, the smile on his lips twisting Cambry's belly. "I haven't seen him since breakfast."

"I'm here."

Cambry stiffened as Bryce pushed his way through the door, the wooden screen falling shut with a splat as Bryce bent to rub a towel over his feet. His feet were filthy, with mud between his toes and sandy earth clinging to the hairs on his legs. He'd dressed since Cambry had last seen him. Brushing himself off quickly, Bryce sent him a nod before he continued into the kitchen.

Swallowing, Cambry stepped in after him, taking a deep breath to calm his beating heart. If Bryce and Jake could act normal, then so could he. He rubbed his chest at a pang of what felt like heartburn, cursing himself for not eating sooner. The cupboards were stocked, and he would have been able to sneak something.

"Where did you two disappear to this morning?" Jake asked as he stirred something in a pan that smelled of garlic and onions. Cambry's mouth watered, and he couldn't stop from moving close and gazing into the pan. There was bacon, too, and hunks of what looked like chicken breast in a creamy sauce.

"I wanted Cambry to ride me in the woods," said Bryce, pulling out a chair.

Cambry's mouth dropped open, a betrayed protest on his lips that was quashed as Jake chuckled and turned to him with a smile. He hooked an arm around Cambry's shoulders, hugging him close as he stirred the pan with steady sweeps.

"And how did that go?" Jake ruffled Cambry's hair with his nose, breathing deep as Cambry shivered and went lax. His beard scratched against Cambry's cheek, so much softer than it looked.

He should have been used to the small touches, especially the ones from Jake, as the grizzly didn't seem to be able to keep his hands to himself. But with each one, his heart picked up, his skin bursting with warmth.

"Less sexy than you'd think," said Cambry, his voice low as he struggled to breathe normally. The bacon splatted in the pan, and he hissed as the grease landed on his arm.

Jake chuckled, lowering the heat before pulling Cambry back from the danger zone of continued spatters as the sauce bubbled. "That pretty much sums Bryce up — less sexy than you'd think."

"Hey!" Bryce called, his voice filled with indignation. "I am a sexy beast — and you both know it."

"Says the man who has to explain every little detail while his partner is just waiting for him to get on with the *fucking* part." Jake gave Bryce a pointed look before smirking at Cambry. "You know he does that when it's just the two of us sometimes? I start moaning from something that he's doing, and he starts explaining the purpose of the prostate."

"Prostates are important!" Bryce slapped the table, sending a fork flying.

"And so is dirty talk," said Jake, leaning down to Cambry's ear. "Sometimes I think I should buy him a gag for Christmas."

Cambry flushed, leaning into the whispering heat of Jake's breath. He could picture Bryce with a black gag in his mouth, pinned beneath Jake as he kissed down his neck, plucking at his nipples, even as Bryce begged for more through the rubber. Cambry closed his eyes, the picture going into sharp focus behind his closed lids.

Bryce would have his legs spread wide, his hole already dripping from where Jake had claimed him a few minutes before. Jake was holding his knot, still coming and marking every inch of Bryce's skin. The air would be thick with their arousal, Bryce's cock still hard with nothing to hold his knots. One touch would be enough to get him off, but he wouldn't be able to move under Jake.

"Holy fuck," said Jake, letting out a gasp as he stumbled back and clutched at his head as if he were in pain. Bryce whined from the table, his head in his hands as he let out a pained noise. "What?"

"It's the bond," said Bryce lowly, peeking through his fingers as he spread his hands. "I can't believe how strong it is."

Cambry took a step back, bumping into the stove with his ass as he backed himself into a corner. "I'm sorry." They looked like they were in pain, both of them, the healed bite mark on their wrists flaring red. Cambry couldn't look away, his scars calling to him.

"Don't be," said Jake, giving his face one last scrub before he touched Cambry's hip, easing him away from the stove and turning the heat off. "You have an imagination, that's for sure. I'm excited to see what you can come up with if you have real inspiration."

What? They couldn't possibly have —

"I'm not sure I like the gag idea, though," said Bryce, tapping his temple as he grinned. "But Jake claiming me with his cum? That's just about the most feral and wonderful thing that anyone has ever suggested. I should think about adding that into one of my therapy sessions."

Jake spluttered, his spatula clattering to the floor and a piece of bacon leaping from it to *thunk* against the cupboard. It stuck to the solid surface before slowly easing down the stained wood.

"Your partner's semen has physical and psychological benefits that have been well documented," said Bryce, nodding as he perked up. "Ingesting one ounce per day can reduce your risk of a heart attack by twenty-four percent, and it stabilizes your blood sugar as well as providing a rich source of protein."

"You have got to be fucking kidding me," Jake growled, grabbing pasta from a second pot and draining it in the sink. Steam billowed from the pale noodles, a fresh wave of humidity clouding the kitchen. "This is what I have to deal with, kid," said Jake, turning to Cambry as he buttered the pasta and started to dish it out. "I'm trying to get kinky, and he's educating me. You get him a ball gag for Christmas, and I'll get you the *Kama Sutra*. Between the two of us, we're bound to find something that shuts him up."

Christmas? Cambry swallowed, looking to Bryce as his panic rose. Bryce had a similar look on his face, his eyes wide and his mouth opening and closing. *Jake doesn't know.*

His eyes burned as tears suddenly threatened, his chest aching as reality came crashing back. For a moment, things had almost felt normal for him — well, at least his new normal, which included waking up with two alphas who were his best friends and still strangers at the same time.

"Did the steam get you?" Jake's concerned voice reached him.

Cambry nodded, wiping the tears from his cheeks before he forced a smile on his face. He wasn't going to ruin their last day together. "Yeah, sorry, I guess I was standing too close."

"I'll be more careful next time. Gotta take care of my little guy." Jake gave him a grin before turning a fake frown on Bryce. "Not like this bitch. He'd ask me to lean closer so he can explain the difference between evaporation and sublimation, like I fucking care."

"I could tell you the difference between *ejaculation* and evaporation," said Bryce, grinning as Jake placed a bowl in front of him. Cambry snorted a laugh, shaking his head as he took his own seat.

Cambry looked between the two alphas as they ate, a companionable silence settling over the table. Jake caught his eye, furrowing his forehead in question. How could Cambry explain that he didn't want to look away? He wanted to make sure he never forgot the way they looked, not even ten years down the road when he was…wherever he ended up.

"He's quiet," said Cambry, glancing at Bryce, who had both cheeks stuffed with pasta in a good impression of a chipmunk. "Maybe he doesn't stop talking because he's hungry? That's what happens when you give half of the food to the animals."

Jake tapped his beard, scratching at his chin as he appeared to think very hard. "I think you have a point, puppy. He just needs to keep his mouth occupied."

Bryce mumbled around his mouthful of food, a noodle peeking out between his lips and threatening to escape. Cambry hardly saw it. He was caught on Jake's words, the image painting itself as he shut his eyes.

Bryce was sitting at the table, about to start talking again, when Jake shoved his shorts down to expose his hard cock. Bryce stuttered, his mouth dropping open as Jake threaded a hand through his hair and tugged him close, until Bryce closed his lips over the head of Jake's cock and sucked him deep in the warm, tight cavern of his mouth.

"Fuck, puppy." Jake's fork clattered to the table, a piece of chicken falling from Bryce's mouth as he gaped and touched the center of his forehead. "I think I've had enough to eat."

Jake's chair clattered to the ground as he shoved himself to his feet, the table jumping a few inches as he banged his knee. He prowled the few feet over to Cambry's chair, his hips swaying with each predatory step. Cambry swallowed his mouthful of food, his own fork slipping back into his bowl.

"Jake?" Cambry asked, his throat tight with longing. Jake's lips were wet, a bit of sauce lingering at the corner, which he quickly gathered with his tongue. His shoulders were wide enough to make Cambry feel small, which was the strangest sensation he'd ever had. He'd always been the biggest, baddest and most terrifying.

Jake sank to his knees next to Cambry's chair, cupping his hand before bringing it to his lips and placing a kiss at the center of his palm. The spot tingled, even as Jake leaned away and licked his lips.

"Can I touch you, Cambry? Can I take you to bed and make you ours?" Jake's voice was thick and dark, his throat bobbing as he swallowed.

Cambry's cock throbbed to life in an instant, every terrible part of his day and life draining away until joy surged through him. His wolf howled in delight, all previous rejections forgotten, even as Bryce let out a startled noise.

Jake looked to Bryce, his eyes narrowed. "You've been wanting him since the first time he slid his ass onto your knot. You're just too scared to ask."

"Yes," said Cambry, reaching for Jake before he could pull away. He clutched Jake's hand, cradling him and rubbing his cheek over Jake's wrist where his claim bite still looked fresh. "But can it be sexier than expected?"

Jake snarled through a laugh, grabbing Cambry and hefting him up. "When I'm done with you, you won't even remember your own name."

Please make me forget. Cambry let out a gasp as his groin settled against Jake's, his own hard cock meeting an alpha's that made him look insignificant in comparison. He was already aching, his balls going tight as his groin tingled. How long would he last when he was already on the edge?

Jake brought their lips together, and Cambry wondered if his heart would explode by the time he took his next breath. Jake's lips were firm, the scratch of his beard like fine-grit sandpaper on Cambry's chin and tickling at the edges of his lips.

Groaning, he sucked Jake's tongue into his mouth, Jake's taste filling him with the smokiness of bacon and chicken right behind. Their tongues touched in a burst of slick heat that had Cambry whimpering and wanting to beg for more.

He dragged his tongue over the inside Jake's mouth, mapping out every part as Jake pulled him closer, lifting him up and setting him on the sturdy table so they were at the same height. Cambry looped his arms over Jake's neck, kissing him until his lips ached from the unbearable pressure. It wasn't enough.

He tore his mouth away at a touch to his chin, Bryce leaning against his back. Stretching, Bryce brought their lips together. The angle was all wrong, Cambry's neck aching from turning so far, but he wouldn't have changed it for the world. He was on fire, his cock aching. But it was nothing to the burning in his chest.

Dragging in a breath, he let it out again as Jake kissed down his neck, sucking and biting into the sensitive glands that Cambry had never cared to pay attention to before. They throbbed in time with his heart, the pleasure spiking as Jake's beard dragged over his oversensitive skin as he sought out a fresh spot to suck and kiss.

"Ahh," Cambry called into Bryce's mouth, the cry muffled with teeth and tongue as his cock reached its limit and he came between them. Both alphas grumbled in approval as Cambry slicked the inside of his borrowed pants with cum, jerking his hips as he lost control.

"Did you know that an omega can have up to twelve subsequent orgasms?" said Bryce, nibbling at Cambry's lower lip as he continued to quake. "Alphas can only have one — or two, if we are really, really lucky."

Jake grumbled something that sounded a lot like *'can't wait for the ball gag'* before he bit down on Cambry's neck harder than before, his sharp canine teeth piercing the top layer of skin with a zing of pain. Cambry writhed, not sure if he was even standing anymore or if his alphas were simply holding him up between them.

The warm liquid of Cambry's cum cooled as he whimpered, quickly becoming almost unbearably sticky against his sensitive cock. He couldn't imagine having more than two orgasms in a row, which was his record in the past. But he'd never felt even remotely similar to how it was being in their arms. The kissing alone was better than every part of his first experience with them combined.

Jake popped off his neck, tugging Cambry's T-shirt free with a seam-tearing pull. Cambry whimpered at the display of strength, his wolf urging him to bare his neck. He complied, turning his head to offer Bryce the untouched side and whimpering as Bryce sucked his earlobe before moving lower.

"You want to do this here?" asked Bryce as he pulled his mouth free, tracing small kisses down Cambry's neck before he bit into his shoulder. He wasn't as rough as Jake, his teeth only grazing Cambry's sensitive flesh, but somehow, it was just as intense.

His head was foggy with their combined scents, their arousal pushing him back to hardness in his uncomfortable mess. He longed to kick his pants free and cursed himself for not opting for track pants earlier in the day.

"The living room has the most space." Jake looked over his shoulder to the room where the single television lay, its dark screen glaring yellow from the sun cutting through the windows. "Or the yard would be best."

"Oh, outside. That sounds good," said Bryce before sucking a fresh line of bruises on Cambry's shoulder. "I want to fuck you in the grass and see you tear it up as I lock you on my knot."

Cambry trembled as Jake laughed, licking the other side of Cambry's neck until he was close enough to trap Bryce's tongue with his own, kissing Bryce against Cambry's skin.

"Who goes first, puppy?" asked Jake, his chest rumbling. "We're both going to take a piece of you. I've never fucked an omega before, and I want you to be my first."

A gasp pushed through Cambry's lips as he opened his eyes, Jake's honey-colored ones swimming into view. Jake was one of the two most handsome alphas that he'd ever met. It didn't make sense that he'd never slept with an omega.

"There's only been Bryce," said Jake, cupping Cambry's chin. "I never even gave an omega a second look before you found us. You're different in all the right ways."

"I'm a freak." Cambry shook under the weight of the words that found their way from his mouth. Bryce froze with his teeth against Cambry's skin, and Jake let out a feral growl.

"Don't. Ever." He didn't explain anything further, just crushed their lips together in a kiss that was more teeth than tongue. Cambry was sure he was bleeding by the time Jake pulled back. "You're exactly who you're supposed to be."

He couldn't remember how they got out of the house and onto the grass, but suddenly he was outside, the crickets hopping away from him as he dropped onto the ground, Jake beneath him and Bryce kissing a line down his spine as his clothes disappeared. The hint of dominance from the position sent a thrill up Cambry's spine as he ground down onto Jake's cock, his hips loose and free.

"Can I kiss you again?" asked Cambry, his own voice deep and breathless as Bryce spread his cheeks wide and kissed in between. A second of shame passed over him and his wolf growled, his body going tense as Bryce touched his hole.

"You okay?" asked Bryce, pulling back, even though it must have been nearly painful for him. Jake looked up in concern, his chest heaving with exertion.

"I don't know." Cambry touched his chest, the presence of his wolf just as strong as the bond to his mates. It thrummed beneath his skin like sweet ambrosia, pushing his instincts to the forefront of his mind.

He closed his eyes, listening to the call with all his might. Practically, he had no idea what he was doing, but Bryce and Jake had already shown him so much. Beneath his arousal was utter terror — the same terror that had lingered since the first time he'd been exposed to an alpha and had tried to tear them to pieces.

"Bryce, I need you to kiss Jake." Cambry eased off Jake's lap, scampering back a few steps to give them room. His arousal had quelled, his mind clearing enough that his rational thoughts were starting to poke holes in his fantasies.

Bryce let out a hesitant grin before he climbed onto his lover's lap, bringing their lips together in a kiss that would light most panties on fire. It was wet and loud as they explored each other's mouths as if it were new and unfamiliar territory. Heat rushed into Cambry's groin, bringing him back to the edge in moments as he watched the two alphas together.

Their skin was slick with sweat, beads of it gathering and dripping until it landed in the grass below. Jake dug his heels into the ground as he thrust against Bryce, bringing their naked cocks together. Cambry couldn't remember the moment that they had undressed, but he saw the trail of clothes that led from the front door.

He moved closer, reaching to touch Bryce's flexing back and digging his nails in to test how thick and strong he was. Bryce hissed beneath the touch, bucking harder against Jake as Cambry let his wolf take the reins, his claws dragging a white line over Bryce's flesh. It wasn't a cry of pain on Bryce's lips, but pure pleasure, Jake groaning beneath him as he responded to his lover's enthusiasm.

As Bryce spread his legs wider, something else caught Cambry's eye. He'd seen Bryce stretched around Jake's cock and even his knot, but with nothing inside him, his furl looked so small and unassuming. How had he taken something so big?

Reaching out, he slipped his fingers over Bryce's dry entrance, the wrinkled skin soft and warm to the touch. Bryce gasped, presenting himself to Cambry. Would any alpha do the same thing? Cambry doubted it. He doubted the average alpha would ever let anyone do something like that to them.

Bryce seemed even tighter than Jake had somehow, his furl resisting as Cambry slowly pressed at his center. He needed something slick or he would never get inside.

He dipped his fingers into his own mouth, lathering them with spit the best he could before he brought one finger back to Bryce's entrance, easing inside with a steady push. Bryce writhed at the intrusion, Jake tightening his grip on Bryce's ass and pulling him wider for Cambry.

"Curl your finger," said Bryce, pushing himself back onto Cambry's thick finger until he was all the way to the last knuckle, heat and silky walls clutching Cambry from every angle. He traced the walls, exploring the impossible warmth with so much more care than he had with Jake. He felt almost bad for his behavior with the grizzly, even if he hadn't complained.

There was something firm beneath his fingertip and the moment he touched it, Bryce let out a long moan, a stream of pre-cum dribbling from his cock and onto Jake's belly. Jake growled, reaching for Bryce's mouth and crashing their lips together.

"What does it feel like?" Cambry asked as he pushed the spot again, his cheeks heating as he watched Bryce unravel. "I need to know." He clenched his hole as his gut suddenly cramped, a few drops of slick seeping from him. The scent of it hit the air — sweetness and coconut.

"Come here." Jake beckoned him with his huge hands, his nails looking sharper than Cambry remembered. At least he wasn't the only one having trouble holding his animal back.

Cambry crept closer, pressing into Bryce's side so he could look into Jake's face, his lips still glistening from his kiss.

"Tell me what you're afraid of, puppy," said Bryce, leaning back. Cambry caught sight of his cock, fully engorged with the smallest hint of his knots starting to form. He was massive, the sight causing a few more drops of slick to leak from his hole, staining his thighs as it dripped down.

"I'll hurt you. Every time you touch me, I remember." Cambry looked to his arm at the permanent scar that would always remind him of his last close call with a strange alpha.

"The room," said Jake with a nod. "I've seen it in my dreams. I've felt my arm break in the same way yours did."

Bryce frowned, a look of realization crossing his features.

"We would never force you," said Bryce, slowly easing off Jake and pushing his erection down as if that would quell it. Jake lifted himself from the grass, brushing a few strands from his front.

"*I* know you won't, but he doesn't." Cambry tapped his chest where his wolf was still grumbling half-heartedly as it fought against him.

"Then listen to him," said Bryce, cupping Cambry's face in his hands. "Listen to him and give in. He knows what's best for you on every instinctive level, and if that means that we can't knot you, then that's fine. If it means we stop this right now, then that's what we'll do. Close your eyes, buddy, and tell us what you see."

Cambry leaned into the touch, dragging in a deep breath of his mate's scents. His wolf perked up, taking the freedom and rushing to the forefront of Cambry's mind.

Only, he didn't shift. He didn't even get any hairier. Instead, he grabbed Bryce's hand, pinning it in place as he sank his teeth into their bond mark. Bryce's groan was a distant symphony to the blood rushing through his ears and the gentle release in his chest and groin.

His tastebuds surged to life as everything pinpointed to Bryce...his first.

Mine. Always.

Cambry shuddered with the strength of his wolf's claim, pushing his worries to the side as he let himself *be.* He reached for Jake, pulling his arm close as he released Bryce, biting into Jake's yielding flesh with Bryce fresh on his tongue. Their tastes mingled, their essences becoming one as the bond surged.

He needed them now...both of them. But this time he wasn't spurned with the rush of heat, and his mind was clear — startlingly so. Pulling back, he grabbed his closest mate, slamming their lips together in a kiss that took his breath away. It was Bryce, his lips yielding yet fierce as their bond glowed and pleasure shivered over Cambry's skin.

It was over before he could bear it, and he pulled Jake to him, claiming him in the same way — begging them to be his without words or thought. He dragged his mouth free, gasping in a breath when his thoughts blurred around the edges, his cock throbbing as he came from the force of their kiss. Bryce bent down, wrapping his lips around him and drinking down every drop as he emptied himself over and over, his orgasm stretching beyond anything he'd ever felt.

Jake stroked down his sides as Cambry started to come down, his belly aching as slick flooded between his cheeks. Jake pried his cheeks wide, licking a stripe up the crevasse within before prodding his tongue deep and piercing into Cambry's center.

He came again as Bryce swallowed his cock, which hadn't softened in the least. Jake fucked him from behind with his tongue, sucking at his rim and cupping his balls as they lifted and went tight. Bryce moaned as he drank down Cambry's release, the sound matching Jake's bliss as he tasted his slick.

He could feel them and nearly hear their thoughts as if they were his own. There was no disgust, no judgment, only adoration and bliss that matched his own, ten-fold. He may have been an omega, but he was *their* omega, slipping into their alpha partnership as if he'd always belonged.

Jake pierced him with one finger, then two, spreading Cambry wide as Bryce moved to his chest, biting at Cambry's nipples that he hadn't even realized would ever be so sensitive. His hole ached for more, even as Jake prodded deep, twisting his fingers until he touched something.

Cambry had touched an electric fence once when he had been younger. Jake's fingers on his prostate had the same effect as his hand on the live wire. His back arched and his muscles locked tight as a grunt pushed its way through his lips, his eyes rolling back in his head. The only difference was instead of tingling pain, the shock was pure pleasure, wrapping around his cock until he was exploding all over Bryce's chest and belly.

His balls ached from the repeated orgasms, his belly going tight as slick dripped from him, only for Jake to catch it on his tongue. He couldn't breathe, and he could barely think with so many hands and mouths on every part of him.

When his books had mentioned fireworks, he hadn't quite expected the explosive quality of his orgasms to exceed his imaginations. He hadn't expected to beg.

"More, please." Cambry tilted his hips to drive Jake deeper, roughly grabbing Bryce by the hair to bring him in for a brutal kiss. He growled into Bryce's mouth as a hint of blood flowed over his tongue when his teeth caught Bryce's lip. Bryce moaned, giving in and letting Cambry take control.

Jake bit into the back of Cambry's neck at the same time he lined up the blunt head of his cock. He felt bigger than Bryce had the first time, so much so that there was no way he would ever fit inside.

Grabbing him by the hip, Jake steadied Cambry as he slowly rocked forward, pressing against his entrance until he finally gave way.

There was a moment of heat and an ache so intense that Cambry cried out, sinking his claws into Bryce's sides and dragging red lines into his flesh. Bryce growled, biting Cambry's shoulder as he rutted into his belly.

Every inch split him apart until he was sure he would break. Jake had to have been some kind of beast, his cock an entity unto itself. "I can't."

Shaking his head, Cambry tried to tug free, even as the pain faded and something much more dangerous filled the gap. He wasn't built for so much. He didn't deserve it.

Jake growled low in his throat, fucking into Cambry until his groin settled against Cambry's ass. "This is the part when Bryce tells you what knots are for, omega."

Cambry whimpered, his body going lax, even as terror filled him. It wasn't anything like when he'd driven himself onto Bryce's knot, his cock still wet from Jake's hole. That had been a drop in the ocean in comparison.

That was when Cambry felt it—Jake's knot engorging and starting to lock them together. Growling, he tried tugging free before it grew too large, his head pounding. He remembered the terrible ache from when he had pulled free last time, and how long it had taken for it to stop hurting every time he moved.

Bryce snarled, biting into Cambry's neck before grasping his hips just above Jake's hands and shoving Cambry back into Jake's cock. Licking his lips, he cupped Cambry's chin in his hand. "You're going to hurt yourself, buddy. You were lucky last time because I had started to soften. Jake was mostly soft, too, when he pulled out of me, but it still hurt, didn't it? I know it's scary, but we've got you, and you aren't going anywhere."

The words were like a magical potion that plucked Cambry's resistance right from his bones. He sagged against Bryce, who caught his weight and kissed up and down his neck as the stretch inside went from tolerable to beyond. How much was it going to hurt? Especially since Jake was bigger.

"We've got you, Cambry," said Jake, kissing between Cambry's shoulders before licking a stripe between. "It feels good, right? You're so tight around me, holding me just right."

Cambry shuddered as the first hint of warmth flooded him. It seemed almost impossible that he could feel it, flowing deeper and deeper as something released inside him. With every shot, Jake swelled bigger inside, until Cambry knew there would be no way to separate them. He could imagine twisting and turning to try to free himself, but why would he try?

He wasn't sure when he came again, only that Bryce was licking him clean, his cock so sensitive that he whimpered from the softest touch. Jake sucked at his shoulder, the ache adding to everything else until he was floating. He could hardly feel his limbs anymore, his lips numb as he smiled and looked up to the sky.

The sun had peeked out from between the clouds, bathing them in scorching summer sun that made Cambry's body prickle with sweat, his lips dry as he longed for a drink. And still Jake stretched him wider, his body yielding impossibly as his belly grew heavy.

Bryce panted against them, his lips moving in time with his hands as he touched and tasted every part of them, including ducking between Cambry's legs to lick at the slick where they were connected. Jake growled in his throat as his knot was no doubt stimulated from the outside, the bulge probably visible as Cambry tugged ever so gently, just to make sure they were still locked together.

Grabbing for Bryce, Cambry pushed him back until he fell to the ground on his back, his legs splayed wide and his cock throbbing and nearly purple. It was dripping a near-steady line of thick pre-cum, the fluid nearly clear as it glistened in the sunlight. It had to have been painful, and Cambry didn't envy him for waiting for so long, unable to come without anything on his knots.

Tugging Jake forward by their connection and hissing at the welcome ache, Cambry crawled close enough to drop his mouth over Bryce's cock. His mouth watered at the first taste—just like Bryce smelled, only thicker and so much deeper. It leaked over his tongue as he swiped at the head, swallowing down every drop as his mind started to blur.

"Breathe, buddy."

Bryce's voice sank into him, and Cambry dragged in a deep breath through his nose, shuddering at the pure scent of his mates. Tucking his teeth away, he sucked down Bryce's cock, only getting a few inches before he couldn't go any farther. How some omegas managed to take it all was beyond him. And the idea of Bryce knotting his mouth was terrifying. *How would I breathe?*

Something released inside his belly, and suddenly something was leaking from him, trickling down his thighs as Jake leaned heavily onto his back. Cambry whimpered as Jake tugged free, his knot slipping through his entrance with a low *pop*. He hadn't even noticed it getting smaller with how full he still was.

"He still open?" asked Bryce and it took a moment for Cambry to realize that Bryce wasn't speaking to him.

"Yeah. He wants more." Jake grumbled once, scraping his teeth over Cambry's spine before retreating.

He nearly panicked when Bryce pulled away, trying to tug him closer by his cock again. Bryce soothed him quietly as he moved behind him and lined himself up. He tugged Cambry up by his shoulders as he started to sink inside, his cock like an instant plug to keep Jake's seed from leaking.

"Remember how hardly anything dripped out last time?" asked Bryce as he seated himself before giving a few gentle thrusts, the beginnings of his knots rubbing against Cambry's walls with delicious intent.

Cambry nodded, reaching for Jake and pulling him in for a kiss. He remembered wondering where it had all gone. He had been so full, but only a few drops had leaked from him.

"An omega's biology is actually really smart," said Bryce, his thrusts becoming longer and deeper as he steadied Cambry's hips, popping in and out of him as his knots remained small. "When an omega is receptive, their womb stays open for however many times they want to be mounted, but as soon as they're satisfied, both physically and mentally, their womb closes off and holds everything inside."

Cambry flushed, his whole body burning between them and beneath the sun as his shoulders started to ache with the beginnings of sunburn. They *knew* he wanted more. How terribly embarrassing.

"The nice thing about Jake is that I can keep fucking him fuller and fuller and his body never closes off to me. I can go all day if I want to and take him as many times as I want until I've got nothing left to shoot." Bryce chuckled, nipping at Cambry's ear before he cupped Jake's chin, bringing their lips together in a quick kiss.

"And the nice thing about Bryce," Jake growled, tilting Cambry's face to him as he grinned, "is that I can knot Bryce over and over and he'll act like a bitch in heat every time. He loves it when I fuck him full and pull him around on my knot while he can't get away."

"Oh God. Oh fuck." Cambry's eyes rolled back as he came again with a full-bodied shudder, nearly screaming as Jake cupped his cock and eased him through it. He had been sure that he would never be able to come again, but Jake and Bryce had managed to sum up every one of his fantasies.

"Yes," Bryce hissed, locking himself inside as he started to shoot, filling Cambry even fuller than before, if that were even possible.

Tears streamed down Cambry's cheeks as he clawed at Jake, pulling him as close as possible before seeking out their mating mark and biting down. Jake swore, tearing his wrist free before slamming their lips together in a kiss that was more consuming than any fuck.

"Was it better that time?" Bryce whispered against Cambry's ear as he finally started to pull out, only a few drops of slick escaping.

Cambry nodded, his teeth chattering as he trembled between them, so overwhelmed that he was certain he'd never be the same.

The real question was how he was ever going to live without them.

Chapter Nineteen

Cambry

Glancing back at the bed for what felt like the hundredth time, Cambry wiped his cheeks with the edge of his shirt sleeve. The entire sleeve was nearly soaked, his eyes and chest aching as he swallowed sob after sob.

He'd barely been able to get into the bed with Jake and Bryce the night before without starting to cry, knowing it would be the last time he was in their arms. Even a call to Jeremiah earlier in the day hadn't helped. He didn't know about their relationship, so there was only so much Cambry could say, but speaking to Jeremiah over the phone was nothing like talking to him in person.

"Come stay with Brandon and me, and we'll make sure your father can't touch you." Jeremiah's offer had less appeal than it had a week before. Because if Cambry's father couldn't find him, then Bryce and Jake wouldn't be able to, either.

Not that they would look.

They appeared so peaceful together, snuggled on a bed that had probably never intended to support the weight of two muscled men, let alone three. It was as if the mattress company even knew that Cambry was never bound to stay.

Without the other couples around, Cambry had been able to pretend that he was in a loving relationship with two mates who cared for him as much as he regarded them. They were so different in their own right and absolutely made for each other. He'd almost imagined that he fit into their complicated puzzle, matching up to their corners and edges until they made one whole portrait.

But he was that little piece from a different puzzle that had managed to make it into the wrong box. There was never any chance that he would be welcome to stay longer than what his father paid for. He wasn't at a resort or a vacation getaway, even if it felt like that most days.

Sure, he'd come a long way from where he'd been, but his wolf was unpredictable at best. He would end up in an institution before the week was over.

Even if Bryce hadn't wanted to break him, he had, and Jake along with him.

Cambry touched his chest where he felt the connection the strongest to his two mates. He could feel them slumbering, even when he closed his eyes, and he could hear the tiny whisper of their beasts as if they were his own. His wolf was silent in comparison, content in a way Cambry had never experienced.

The wooden walls of the house were the same ones that he'd been looking at for so long now, but they'd become as suffocating as his trapped sobs.

Standing from the chair slowly so it didn't squeak, he grabbed his bag that he'd packed when Jake and Bryce had been out of the house before dinner the night before. It was an empty shell, his books still proudly displayed in the room he'd slept in for almost a week. He'd pulled his own clothes back on around midnight when he'd first crawled out of the bed to watch his mates.

Jake grunted, planting his face into the pillow before throwing his leg over Bryce's hips. Bryce let out a little grumble in response, lifting his hands above his head as he tried to get comfortable again. They were beautiful in their vulnerability, their strength and size meaning nothing with their defenses down.

Plucking the note from his pocket, Cambry crept to the bed, setting it on the side stand for Jake.

"Pup?"

Cambry froze at the sleepy grumble, slowly turning to Jake with his hand hanging empty above the note. Jake had one eye half-open, his face still mostly buried in the pillow as he blinked.

"I just have to use the washroom. I'll be back in a minute," said Cambry, the lie like acid burning along his tongue. Hopefully, it was the first and last time he'd ever have to lie to Jake.

Jake's eyelid slowly drooped, his eyes rolling back as he let out a soft snore. With any luck, he wouldn't even remember come morning.

Lifting his nearly empty bag over his shoulder, Cambry turned from them, fresh tears rolling down his cheeks as he closed the door softly behind him. The house passed in a haze until he was standing outside, looking down at his phone in the low light. He hit the power button, starting toward the property entrance to where the cab was hopefully already waiting.

The cab's tires popped against the gravel, dipping into the tip of the lane just as Cambry reached it. Sliding into the back seat, Cambry shut the door as softly as he could, the sound of the first blue jays starting to sing morphing into AM radio.

He gave his address, leaning against the seat and ignoring the cabbie's lingering looks. He was aware that he looked terrible, his eyes puffy and probably glassy as well, his cold palms doing little to help with fresh tears rolling down every time he looked over his shoulder.

His wolf grumbled, either from the distance from his mates or because it couldn't understand why he was leaving their sides.

The cabbie seemed to sense it, too, shifting in the driver's seat and accelerating a tad as he looked over his shoulder. "You okay?"

"Just drive," said Cambry, his own abruptness nearly shocking him. Cold sweat poured down his neck, gathering in his T-shirt until it stuck to his skin uncomfortably. He'd spent the last two weeks without air conditioning, but just a few minutes in a temperature-controlled car and he was sweating.

"Jeez, buddy, I was just asking." The cabbie held up one hand in defense as he shrugged, keeping his eyes locked on the road as the meter clicker higher.

"*Don't* call me that," Cambry growled, his wolf surging up so quickly that it took his breath away. He panted, trying to stay calm as his nails lengthened, growing into sharp claws that he had no chance of controlling. *Calm down!* He closed his eyes, counting in the way Jake did when Bryce managed to push him too far.

His house was nearly a mansion compared to the cabins and lodge he'd just come from, but it had never looked more distasteful. The exterior was a soft gray brick that could be found on the cover of a design magazine, with lights every few feet just to illuminate its greatness. Inside, the rooms were white and stark and reeked of chemical cleaners and scent diffusers that centered around his old room.

He'd always thought that it was his own nose that was dulled, but as he typed his password in and opened the front door, he realized that the entire place was saturated in a blanket of nothing—no trees, forest, just a hint of his mates that still clung to his clothes like greedy fingers. He'd have to find a way to keep them from the cleaners.

He rounded the many corners into the kitchen, passing three housekeepers who he didn't recognize and one who gave him a fearful glance before they scurried away. He looked at the carpet, the familiar rejection settling deep.

Setting his bag on the table, he pulled back the nearest stool, shaking his head when the butler offered him a choice of hot beverages that would make any barista swoon. His stomach was in his throat, even though his tears had finally dried, leaving his cheeks sticky and tight.

"Well, at least you have the decency to save me the time," said Wilfred Parsons as he strolled into the kitchen, the paper already tucked under his arm.

Cambry looked up, his gut so tight that he was sure he would vomit what little was left in his stomach from dinner the night before. His father had gone from gray to silver in his absence, the last few dark hairs disappearing from his usually slicked-back style. His mustache was impeccably trimmed, hiding the scar from the surgery he'd had as a child. He only shaved it when he needed to garner sympathy from somebody — usually somebody political.

"You could have at least let someone know so we didn't send a driver out already. We'll have to call him back here now so he can get you on your way." Wilfred tapped the paper on the island between them, very obviously keeping his distance.

"On my way?" Cambry asked when he finally managed to drudge up the courage. His heart picked up as he touched the phone in his pocket, Jeremiah's offer echoing through him once again.

"Don't speak to me like that." Wilfred scowled, even as he took a step back. "You should be thanking me for all the trouble I've put up with over the years. But I won't have to anymore."

His stomach dropped like a stone as his mouth went dry. Which institution was his father sending him to? He clutched his bag tight, trembling with the effort of keeping his wolf at bay.

The chair clattered to the ground as Cambry stood, his father's flinch just pushing his wolf further to the surface.

"Did those useless fools do anything that I asked them to?" Wilfred's scowl deepened as he looked Cambry up and down. "Well, if he didn't have the gall to break you, I'm sure your new mate will. He was the one to recommend the place, after all."

Mate? The word was enough to knock the wind from Cambry's lungs, his chest aching as everything drained away. Trembling, he looked to his father, the grin on Wilfred's face sending him spiraling.

"Yes," said his father, his grin stretching wider. "He's expecting you this afternoon, but I don't think he'd be averse to getting you a touch early." He turned serious as he brought his finger up to point one gnarly digit Cambry's way. "This arrangement cost me ten percent of my business. The sooner you get out of here, the sooner I can forget the utter waste."

Wilfred turned away, grabbing his paper and coffee before storming out of the kitchen. The butler gave Cambry a glaring look before following after Wilfred like a lost puppy.

Cambry went to ease back into his chair, falling on his ass on the new tile instead. His hole ached from the hit, where he could still almost feel his mate's knots inside him when he closed his eyes.

But they weren't his mates—not really. His father had seen to that. *Fuck, I can't breathe.* He grabbed his chest, letting his head thud to the floor as his vision went dark.

Chapter Twenty

Bryce

He's pissed. Bryce rolled out of bed, rubbing at his chest as heartburn set in yet again. *I have to make an extra trip to get some antacids. This is getting ridiculous.*

His heartburn hadn't let up, even when he'd cut the spicy in half on the tacos he'd whipped up for dinner the night before. Maybe it was the salsa, but that didn't explain the same feeling that he'd had before he'd eaten half a jar.

"He's gone." Jake whirled into the bedroom, his chest heaving after he must've sprinted through the house completely naked. Bryce wasn't one to complain, but Jake rarely went without clothing unless he was planning to shift. Their bedroom floor was already scratched up enough without an angry grizzly tearing through it. "Why are you smiling? If this is a joke, it's not funny." Jake paced the edge of the room, grabbing a pillow and tossing it to the ground as he went by the bed. It fell with a burst of fluff as his claws tore through the pillowcase.

"I know he's gone. I didn't expect it until later, but he must've slipped out while we were asleep." Bryce scooted up the bed, leaning against the headboard as his stomach rolled. He grimaced as he rubbed it, cursing the tacos again. He must've undercooked them by accident.

"What the fuck are you talking about?" Jake's eyes flashed as he snarled, showing off his teeth as he rounded on Bryce.

"His father picked him up this morning."

Jake stared at him, his eyes wide and incredulous.

"You knew, but you let him go anyway? You know what kind of man his father is. How long have you known?" Jake clenched his fists tights, his claws probably biting into him.

Bryce pulled his feet under himself as his gut clenched, his world tilting as he clutched the sheets. "A week. I had a week to break him, and I wouldn't do it. His father took him back home."

"We've been bonded for a week!" Dark hair sprouted over Jake's arms as he drew closer. "You didn't say anything! How could you let him go?"

Each question struck Bryce in the gut until he knew he would never make it to the bathroom in time. He stumbled from the bed, pushing past Jake as he cupped his mouth, his sides heaving as he started to gag. He was only a few feet from the toilet when he lost the meager remains of his stomach.

"His therapy was over. He did what he came here to do," said Bryce once he finally stopped gagging. There wasn't much on the floor, but his hands were disgusting. Lifting himself from the tile, he staggered to the sink, his stomach still not sure which direction it wanted to go.

"His *therapy*?" Jake asked softly, his voice cracking as he followed Bryce's every step.

"He didn't come here for therapy. He came here because his father was looking for any excuse to get rid of him, and he found us instead."

Bryce leaned over the bathroom counter, refusing to look into the mirror for fear of what he might see. He couldn't imagine that Jake felt as broken as he did. It wasn't possible to ache so much for a person that he'd only known for a short time.

"We helped him with his fears and calmed the rage of his beast. We did everything we could for him." Bryce turned on the sink, rinsing his hands and watching the last of his sickness flow away. If anything, his stomach felt worse.

"And the bond?" Jake asked.

Bryce looked up, finally meeting Jake's gaze in the mirror. Jake was rubbing at his chest, his face scrunched with the same ache that Bryce felt. He blinked as realization finally dawned on him.

Every time he'd felt the ache, Cambry had been in some sort of distress. The only time it had calmed was when Cambry had been asleep in their arms, wrapped close on a bed that was much too small for three men.

Well, crap. Antacids weren't going to help at all.

"You know as well as I do that it was an accident," said Bryce, keeping his voice low so the situation didn't get out of hand. He didn't want to know what would happen if Jake let his anger overwhelm him. "I won't bind him to something that he didn't mean."

"But what if he *did* mean it?" asked Jake, grabbing a cloth and wetting it in cold water before wiping it across Bryce's chin. Closing his eyes, Bryce leaned into the touch, letting out a breath as some of his nausea eased.

"You're my mate, Jake, and I love you with everything I have. Cambry gave us a connection that we never would have been able to have any other way, but it was an accident. He left us, and he's not coming back."

The bathroom light was too bright, the mirror showing off his pale visage.

"But we didn't even ask him to stay," Jake murmured, pulling Bryce close as he dropped the cloth. He was trembling, his claws digging into Bryce's skin with each shiver. "If I would have known...things would have been different. I never would have said what I did." Jake shook his head, burying his face deep in Bryce's neck. "I pushed him away when we were at the pond, and I told him that he wasn't ours. I shouldn't have said it, but I was too stupid to understand what I was feeling." Jake leaned back, cupping Bryce's chin. "I never thought I would ever love another man the way I love you, but I think I was wrong. He belongs here with us, between us and alongside us."

"He can't." Bryce let out a breath as Jake put words to the same thing that was rising in him. He wasn't certain of the exact moment it had happened—maybe when Cambry had stepped out of the cab on that first day and Bryce had looked into his pale blue eyes that had enough sorrow for two lifetimes. Or maybe it had been when he first saw Cambry shift, his body flowing into something so perfect that it took his breath away. "I'm his therapist." *That excuse is getting old.*

"Not according to you, you aren't," said Jake, hugging Bryce tighter. "Think of something better, and

I might believe that you don't want him to come home."

Home. That was the only place he wanted Cambry. To open his eyes early in the morning and see his omega curled up in the chair with a book in hand, reading in the low light of the sunrise with Jake in his arms keeping him warm. Now *that* was a dream come true. It was too bad that Cambry probably rarely saw a sunrise with how little he liked mornings.

"I want him here," said Bryce softly. There was no use denying it anymore.

"Why did we send him away?" asked Jake, his words choked with a sob.

"I think we were afraid," said Bryce, wiping the tears from Jake's cheeks before they could fall. "New bonds can cause treacherous emotions and can induce a heat in almost twenty percent of cases. Cambry was lucky that he was already in heat, and it ended with the bonding."

"There's my walking Wikipedia," said Jake, tapping Bryce on the nose as he smiled softly. "Any mention in there of how to get him back?"

Bryce's heart sank at the thought. Wilfred Parsons was a dangerous and powerful man — only dangerous because of his wealth and his pitiful lack of empathy. There was no way that they would ever be able to fight him financially without putting *Feral Woods* on the line. Would he risk his lifelong dream for Cambry? It didn't take long for him to think of the answer.

"We would have to sell this place to get a good enough lawyer to bring him back to us. Mating bonds are more legally binding than actual marriages, but I wouldn't put it past Wilfred Parsons to be able to wiggle his way out of it somehow — unless he just wants to get rid of his son." The words were like acid on his tongue. Cambry was a man to be held and treasured.

"Okay," said Jake, seemingly completely at ease about giving up his home for his new mate. Warmth bloomed in Bryce's chest as his nausea finally started to fade. "Give him a chance, or we'll bring his empire down on his head."

Bryce grabbed his new phone, still fresh from the box with a glow that hadn't had time to fade from his fingerprints. His heart pounded as he connected the call before it plummeted as he spoke with the secretary. He could barely speak by the time he hung up, and Jake's forehead was pinched with concern.

"He already sent him away," said Bryce, hardly able to believe it. "He promised him to another alpha while he was still sleeping in our bed."

Jake's mouth dropped open before his features twisted and he let out a roar that boomed against Bryce's eardrums. "Then I'll challenge him to the death."

Oh dear. Bryce let his head fall into his hands as Jake drew back, fur sprouting from his body as he shifted. "You won't fit into the car like that!" Bryce grumbled as Jake loped out of the bathroom, slamming into the door frame and nearly tearing it from its fastenings.

They would get there in time. They *had* to. Cambry had never let an alpha lay a hand on him before, and Bryce had to trust that he would be able to defend himself. *He shouldn't have to. We should be there. Better yet, he should be here with us.*

Grabbing some clothes, Bryce winced as he caught the sound of breaking glass followed by the car alarm blaring over and over. Panic surged through him. Both of his mates were losing themselves.

He ran for the door, hitting the stairs at a run and hoping he had the strength to save them both.

Chapter Twenty-One

Cambry

Cambry pressed his face to the glass as the familiar landscape slowly disappeared.

The neighbor's concrete fountain was one of his favorites with its naked winged angels surrounded by bears and thorns. But it had passed by a while ago, and he wasn't sure if he was going to see it again or not. It was the bear that he had always liked about it because it was one of the only alpha forms that he had ever imagined taming his beast.

Others had tried and failed—anything from an overconfident lion to a sweet bobcat that had backed away as soon as Cambry had growled at him. He tried not to wonder what his new husband was at the same time he yearned for *his* bears.

A facility was one thing, but a husband? People stood outside of facilities and protested the cruelties within, calling for omegas to be released. He doubted anyone would stand outside his home, no matter how poorly he was treated.

And he had no doubt that his future husband was cruel. No one would accept a bribe for a marriage, not unless they valued the marriage so little that it really meant nothing to them — not unless they had only one use for him.

He didn't have a choice. His mates didn't want him, but he had to get away before he reached their destination. The bulky guard beside the driver, along with a second across the seat from him, wouldn't make it an easy task.

Sliding his phone from his pocket, he checked to make sure the nearest guard was looking away before he unlocked it and went to his contacts. Jeremiah's name was at the top of the list. He pressed the call button, bringing the phone to his ear as he ducked against the glass, trying to conceal it as best he could. Between the music and the tires, he just caught the sound of the ring.

"Hey, Wolfie! Long time no speak. Catch any good tail lately?" Jeremiah's voice was the first hint of brightness in his day, his voice so loud that Cambry winced, sending a quick look to the guard who was enthralled with his own phone.

"I need your help." He cupped his hand over his mouth and the speaker.

"I can't hear you, just a second." There was the sound of shuffling and a few elated shouts before a door slammed and the line finally went quiet. "Brandon's family is here for his birthday, and they are totally nuts." Jeremiah chuckled.

"I need your help," Cambry said a touch louder. He held his breath as the guard shifted and cleared his throat.

"What do you need? I can pick you up in half an hour at *Feral Woods*. Did Bryce do something? Did Jake?" Jeremiah's voice pushed further into panic with each word. He had known that Cambry was staying, but not for how long.

Cambry let his eyes fall shut. The two men who he had fought in the beginning, then imagined would never hurt him, had wounded him the deepest. He would never be theirs and they would never be his, no matter how much he longed for them.

"My father paid another alpha to take me off his hands. I'm on the way to his house now. I can't, Jeremiah." A sob caught in his throat. "Either my beast will kill him or it won't, but either way…"

His mates fell farther away as the driver accelerated. He could scarcely breathe.

"Tell me where you're going. I'll bring everyone I know out there if I have to. You're going to be okay."

Cambry forced his eyes to open. The scenery had changed from trees and fields to huge houses and endless driveways. The car slowed and he picked up the sound of the flicking turn signal.

"I don't know. It has a black gate at the front. I can't see the house from here," said Cambry, his voice rising as the driver started to turn into the driveway.

"Is there a house number? How long were you driving?" Jeremiah's voice seemed to double in panic.

"I don't know, like an hour or two. It just has a fire number." The guard perked up as Cambry listed off the address. He lunged toward Cambry, calling out in alarm. Cambry ducked to the side, growling and snapping his growing teeth at the guard.

"Give me your phone, little bitch. You're not going to need it where you're going." The guard lunged at him again, moving across the seat and pulling the phone from Cambry's hand. His finger must have touched the speakerphone button because suddenly Jeremiah's voice was filling the car."

"Does it have an eagle at the gate?"

Cambry scrambled back to the window, looking for any sign of the bird. It was nestled beneath a bush, one wing partially concealed with bright flowers.

"Yes!" Cambry shouted as he twisted to the other side of the car. His father had hired professionals to take him and he knew he had no chance against them.

"I know where you are. You are going to be—"

The phone call cut off as the guard caught him by the back of the neck.

"Trust me, kid. I know who lives in that house. If there was one place in the world that I would never send my child, it would be there." The guard frowned, clamping down on Cambry's throat as he struggled. "But my job was to deliver you, not to ask questions."

"Ease up on him, Jack. Can't you see that the kid is terrified?" said the second guard from the front seat as he turned to face them. He looked nearly identical to the first, and just as jacked, his arms nearly bursting from his suit jacket.

"Do you want to get bitten? The kid's practically feral." Jack pinched something behind Cambry's ear and his entire body went tight. His wolf growled, fur prickling against his skin.

"Fuck. Knock him out."

* * * *

Cambry woke in a cool room with silky sheets against him and a throbbing headache. It took him a moment to realize that he had shifted, his fur holding some heat against his body. The surface under his cheek was soft and moved as he tried to lift his head.

Oh. He squinted against the light, his head pounding as he looked around. There was only one lamp, thank goodness, but it bathed the large room in warm light. The tattered shadows around the edges called to him. He needed to run and hide, and the large bed he was on wasn't going to help him in the least.

The walls were decorated with paintings that had to be original, their thick frames an antiqued bronze. The wooden trim gave the room an almost dated feel, the richness coming from the massive fireplace that was cold and dark.

Whimpering, he stood, trying to find his balance on the thick pillow top as he slowly made his way to the edge and jumped down, his nails clicking on the hard floor. He turned his head slowly, gazing around as he tried to get his bearings. Moments before, he had been in a car, but from the way his stomach was rumbling and how the sun was cutting through the curtains, it looked as if hours had passed.

He circled the bed, sniffing the subtle scent of sandalwood that seemed to permeate the room. There were blue slippers at the side of the bed, along with a stand that was topped with unfamiliar glasses. A blue robe was tossed over a hook on the nearby door.

He nosed his way through the crack in the door, wincing as the lights turned on automatically. It was a polished marble bathroom that looked so familiar that he must've seen it in a magazine. The sinks were black and set into the silky white of the smooth countertops, the tiled floor chilled beneath his feet. A clawfoot tub stood next to the shower that was big enough for three men.

If anything, he had expected to wake up bound, his nightmares finally given life. He hadn't expected... luxury.

He circled out of the bathroom, heading for the second door he had spotted. The handle was a circular knob that he had no chance of turning with his paws, but his wolf showed no sign of retreating. He was in an unfamiliar territory that smelled of an alpha who wasn't one of his mates. His wolf simply didn't understand.

Pawing at the door, Cambry let out a whine, startling as the knob turned and the door was slowly pushed open. He growled, backing toward the bed as a tall alpha that put Jake's size to shame, entered the room. The frown on his lips didn't help calm Cambry's terror as he slowly closed the door behind him, flicking the second bedside light on and flooding the room with more excruciating light.

Snarling, Cambry backed toward the bathroom, tucking his tail as he found himself in the corner instead. The man was huge, which meant that his beast had to be something utterly massive. His stomach churned as he ached for his mates. He could almost hear them if he closed his eyes, like a whisper on the edge of his thoughts.

"My name is Dylan. I'm sorry for the way you were brought here. If I'd had any idea about the situation, I would have come to get you myself," he said, holding his hands out in a peace offering. "I think there are a few things that I wasn't told." He smiled, the grim twist to his lips putting Cambry further on edge.

"Can you shift so we can speak? I have a robe you can wear until I can send for some clothes for you."

Cambry shook his head, remembering the warning from the guards. His beast had claws and teeth, but he was no match for Dylan in his human form.

"Okay… That's okay." Dylan took a step back, sitting on a settee that was next to the bed in its own little area. He leaned back, steepling his fingers before he let out a sigh.

"Your father offered me one million dollars if I signed a marriage contract," said Dylan, crossing his legs. "That's a hard offer to refuse from anyone, especially a man like Wilfred Parsons. I may have been looking for a husband, but I didn't want some kind of backward slave, so I turned him down."

Cambry let out a breath, tilting his head. His father had always kept their financials from him, probably believing that Cambry didn't have the head for it, but he knew that a million dollars was nothing to what his father was worth — probably because Cambry himself was worth so little.

"So I took him to the board and threatened him instead. He gave me ten percent and you, so I would keep quiet about a few dealings he's involved with. With ten percent, I have enough pressure over other shareholders that soon I'll have the majority, and I get a husband, too." Dylan licked his lips, his eyes going bright. "Something I've been hoping for for a long, *long* time."

The air grew heavier between them, sandalwood soaking into every surface.

"I should tell you that I've signed the marriage contract, but I had no idea that you were coming here against your will until you arrived." Dylan lifted himself from his seat before walking to the window. He held his arms behind his back, his posture rigid and straight. "I have no desire to go through that again. I think I deserve to know why you're here, though."

Strolling to the bathrobe that hung on a hook, Dylan grabbed it before tossing it toward Cambry's paws. It was fluffy, floating to the ground like a giant tissue caught in the wind. The straps brushed against Cambry's paws, and his wolf growled.

"I'll let you shift. Just knock when you're ready." He moved to the door, letting out a sigh before he opened it, stepped into the hall and shut it behind him.

What other choice do I have? Cambry closed his eyes, reaching for the sound of his mates' whispered voices one last time before he let his wolf fall away. They were his mates, but not really. Like Jake had said, they didn't really belong to each other.

He could only wonder about Jake's reaction when he'd woken up without him. Hopefully, he hadn't been too upset with Bryce and had stormed off to fix something instead of getting angry. Or maybe he hadn't been angry at all, and more relieved that his pretend partner was finally gone.

Cambry shivered as the air conditioning overwhelmed him, pulling the robe over his shoulders and tying it tight. It was shorter than he would have liked, ending just above his knees and showing off his thick calves along with enough leg hair to make any omega blush.

There was a bruise just above his kneecap that was dark and nearly purple. He blinked as he looked at it closer. Not a bruise at all, but a love bite.

After knocking at the wall, he waited for the door to open, shuffling back as Dylan let himself in right away. He was just as tall and intimidating with Cambry's head only reaching his collar bone. He swallowed as he thought about the guard's warning, his wolf growling as it tried to free itself again.

Dylan sucked in a breath, his eyes going wide as he looked at Cambry. His cheeks flushed pink, his pupils dilating, even as Cambry took a step back, the smell of sandalwood growing thick. Dylan raised one hand, scrunching his nose as his breath cut off.

"You're quite potent, aren't you? I'm sorry, that was rude. You just aren't what I expected at all," said Dylan, seating himself on the same chair. "I'd offer you a seat, but I doubt you'd accept it. The door isn't locked if that makes you feel any better. I just thought you would feel more comfortable with it closed, in case any of the staff walks by."

Staff. Dylan is worse than my father.

"Cambry. May I call you that?" Dylan asked, leaning forward ever so slightly in his chair at Cambry's nod. "May I ask where you got such a unique name?"

Chewing his lip, Cambry shook his head. His mother naming him after her favorite band had been the last motherly thing she had done for him. His father had already turned away from him at that point. A few hours old and he'd already been a disappointment.

"Okay then. Can you tell me why you're here?"

Cambry looked around the room, doing everything he could to not look at Dylan. He tugged the tie on the housecoat tighter, wishing it was long enough to reach the floor. "I didn't have a choice."

"I see that now, but one would think that three weeks' notice would give you some time to get used to the idea."

"Three weeks?" Cambry looked up, searching Dylan's face for a lie. The flush was still there, and the dilated pupils, but his gaze was steady. Three weeks meant that his father had already made the arrangement before he'd gone to *Feral Woods*. It had probably been a last-ditch effort to try to tame him for his new husband, so he didn't tarnish any reputations.

"He didn't tell you," said Dylan, frowning. "When he asked for a recommendation, I didn't realize it was for *you*."

"He told me when I got back this morning," said Cambry, looking to the shuttered window as if it would tell him the time. He wondered if he'd missed lunch as well.

"In the spirit of being forthcoming, I'll tell you that you aren't my first husband. I had thought that you might be different, but—" Dylan paused as a soft knock sounded at the door three times. He furrowed his brow, apologizing once before he rushed to the door, opening it a few inches and using his body to shield Cambry from view.

Cambry trembled, shifting farther into the corner just in case the door did open. It was bad enough being nearly naked in front of one person. It was strange. His nudity had almost become second nature at *Feral Woods*, as if Bryce had finally lifted the stigma.

Bryce. He swallowed, squeezing his eyes shut as his chest tightened. He took a few deep breaths before opening his eyes again, not wanting to take his eyes off his new husband for too long.

"I told you I was not to be disturbed," said Dylan, looking over his shoulder at Cambry before he turned back to whoever was on the other side of the door.

"But, sir, they insisted. I've already told them four times that you would call them back." It must've been one of the *staff*. At least they sounded like they had a touch more of a backbone than his father's servants.

"Who is it?" Dylan's voice was sharp, an edge of anger seeping into his tone.

Cambry couldn't catch what the other person said, but Dylan took a step back as if he'd been slapped. When he looked back to Cambry, his eyes were wide, his lips in a firm line.

"Do you know Mr. Keller by chance?" asked Dylan, his surprise smoothing away to polite indifference. Cambry blinked at the change, tilting his head as he ran the name over in his mind.

"I don't—"

"His friends know him as Jeremiah, but I know him as my first husband." Dylan smiled, the curve to his lips flickering away after only a few moments. "Apparently he's been trying to reach me since you arrived."

"He's my friend," said Cambry, letting out a breath as he sagged against the wall. He remembered what Jeremiah had told him as they'd lain by the pond.

"Well, he's here to see you. I guess when he couldn't reach me on my phone, he did what he does best. May I let him in?"

Cambry nodded and suddenly he was sobbing, his shoulders shaking as his body quaked from the force of it. He couldn't remember the last time he had cried so hard, not from fear or grief, but from relief. He'd lost his mates, but at least his friend had found him.

"Hey, Wolfie, hey. You can cry as much as you need to. I've got you now, buddy." Jeremiah kneeled before him as soon as he arrived, pulling Cambry into his arms and ducking his fingers into Cambry's robe. His hands were warm, his touch so soothing that it was as if he were lifting a physical ache from Cambry's skin.

Cambry hissed as Jeremiah skimmed over his ribs, touching a bruise that must have been left by either Jake or Bryce. His sobs turned to uncontrollable laughs as he tucked his head into Jeremiah's neck, taking a lungful of his light scent as he hugged him tight. His beast calmed, slumbering with much-needed rest.

"I thought Dylan said he didn't touch you," said Jeremiah softly so that only Cambry could hear. He touched the same spot again and Cambry flinched as Jeremiah peeled back his robe, drawing back as his pale skin was exposed.

A few love bites was an understatement. He looked like he'd gone to the fair and instead of the tilt-a-whirl, he'd taken a ride through the love tunnel with a bunch of horny guys. A few spots had bruises that were definitely from someone's hand, and the bite mark on his belly was a dead giveaway.

He knew there were more around his neck and shoulders, but he tugged the robe tighter, forcing it closed as Jeremiah gaped. Dylan was still in the room, seated at the couch with an angle where he could probably see everything. His frown deepened until Cambry was sure one of them was about to get slapped.

"Who did that to you?" asked Dylan, his voice tight with rage.

"It's none of your business," Jeremiah quipped back before Cambry could speak. "He's a single omega and he can fuck who he wants."

Cambry flushed. The word '*fuck*' on Jeremiah's tongue was so out of place that he was mortified. His cute bunny was apparently part raccoon and was even more fierce than the little scavengers.

"It's my business when he's *my* husband." Dylan stood but paused when Cambry let out a low growl and wrapped an arm around Jeremiah protectively.

Jeremiah pushed back with a hand to the center of Cambry's chest, rounding on Dylan. "I don't even want to know how you got sucked into it this time, D. I know you've always had a big heart." Jeremiah grasped Cambry's hand, pulling him from the floor before leading him to the bed. "Come on, Wolfie. Let me take a look at you, and you can tell me *what* or *who* happened."

Cambry followed, his stomach in his throat as he looked at Dylan. If Jeremiah trusted him, then maybe he was worth a second chance and a touch of honesty.

Sitting on the bed, Cambry shivered as Jeremiah slowly eased the housecoat from one shoulder, exposing the worst of the love bites. They were still sore and flared with heat as Jeremiah slowly probed them.

"Is this okay? I don't want to upset you," said Jeremiah, his voice soft and low.

It was strange. Cambry should have been terrified, or at the very least, ashamed of the bites, but Jeremiah's touch was having the opposite effect. It was almost as if they were in the snuggle-pile again, with each touch soothing his body and soul.

"It's nice," said Cambry, clearing his throat when his voice cracked. It was nice to be naked again and not worry about modesty.

"It's because we're both omegas," said Jeremiah. "I looked it up after Bryce told me about it. It's the same reason that most therapists are omegas, Bryce aside. It calms our beast when we touch, skin on skin."

"Oh." Cambry swallowed, closing his eyes and leaning back as Jeremiah pulled the robe wider.

"We should report this to the police, Cambry. Whoever did this to you, it looks like it was rough." His hands were warm, bringing the heat back to Cambry's skin. It wasn't the same as the touches that he really wanted, though.

"I wanted it. I asked for it, then begged for more when they wouldn't give it to me." Cambry kept his eyes closed, unwilling to look at Dylan whose gaze was burning into him.

"Who?" Dylan asked, his voice strangely calm. Cambry peeked one eye open, looking at his future husband. His face was carefully blank, with only a hint of fire in his eyes. At least his desire was gone.

The sound of a small slam cut Cambry's answer off, the wall of the room nearly trembling as a roar lit the air. Grabbing his chest, Cambry pushed Jeremiah back, jumping from the bed and making for the door.

He knew that roar. It vibrated within him, filling the empty gaps that had widened as soon as he'd run from his mates.

Jeremiah fell to the ground at the side of the bed, letting out a fearful squeak as the roar came a second time, so much louder and closer than the first. There was yelling in the halls and the sounds of running footsteps along with a few screams. Cambry's heart pounded as he reached the door, tugging against Dylan's grip as he caught his arm.

"Stay back." Dylan dragged him from the door, tossing Cambry back as if he weighed nothing before he threw the door wide. His skin rippled, his clothes tearing into tiny shreds as he shifted and *oh*.

Cambry had never seen anything like it. He didn't even look real, with fur so dark that it was nearly purple and green slitted eyes that narrowed as a third roar blasted through the air. Dylan let out a hiss, darting out of sight and presumably toward the approaching danger.

Danger for *Dylan*. Cambry pushed himself to his feet. Dylan had no idea who he was going up against, and even though Cambry barely knew him, he didn't seem like a bad person. That aside, Jeremiah looked positively terrified, hidden half under the bed and his eyes wide with fear.

"Whatever you do, don't come out. Hide, Jeremiah." Cambry dragged the robe from his shoulders, shifting at a dead run.

Chapter Twenty-Two

Bryce

If anyone had told him that he would find himself caged in his trusty rusty with an enraged alpha grizzly on a Sunday afternoon, he would have called them insane. Extra points to the one that predicted that the grizzly would hang his head out of the window and slash at the dashboard every time he caught Cambry's scent.

They'd driven to Wilfred Parson's estate first, and the man had nearly pissed himself as Bryce calmly interrogated him and Jake paced behind him, tearing up a few pieces of furniture and gouging one wall when Wilfred refused to answer. After that, Wilfred had been reduced to a puddle of tears, and unfortunately piss as well, hiding in a corner as he begged for his life.

He'd pointed them toward the home of Cambry's apparent husband, yelling for mercy as Jake snapped his teeth just short of Wilfred's face. Bryce had almost lost it a few times, his sleepy bear an enraged beast that clawed to get out.

But someone had to drive the damn car — not that there was much left to it now. Jake had seen to that.

When they'd pulled through the iron gates of a legitimate mansion, Bryce had swallowed, slamming the car into park as Jake pushed his door open with brute force, tossing the tattered door to the ground with a roar that shook Bryce to his bones.

But then he'd caught it — the sweet scent of Cambry that was better than freshly toasted marshmallows and peaches on a sunny afternoon. His mouth watered at the same time his chest went tight, every inch of his body begging him to shift and smash down the door of the mansion before dragging Cambry home where he belonged.

Jake smashed through the front door before Bryce could struggle back into his sandal that had slipped from his foot when he'd stumbled from the car. The car lurched as it stalled, but he couldn't bring himself to care. It could have blown up in front of him and he wouldn't have blinked. The love of his life had just crashed into another alpha's territory, his mate waiting on the other side and hopefully unharmed.

Darting for the door, he stepped through the broken frame, his heart pounding as a few people ran past him screaming. Enraged, Jake was closer to a wild animal than a person, and with his mate at risk, Bryce had no idea how far he would go. Jake had been trained to fight, and he'd come on out top every time until Bryce had stepped into the ring.

A piercing yowl cut the air as Bryce stumbled up the stairs, the deep claw marks in the wood showing him the way. His breath stuttered as he finally caught up with Jake on the landing. A few feet away was the largest panther he'd ever seen. The *only* one he'd actually seen in person, as they were the rarest beast-form and one of the most dangerous.

A blur of white and gray caught his eye, and he thought his heart might burst. *Cambry.* His pale blue eyes were narrowed with focus as he went straight for Jake, his tail over his back and his hackles raised.

"*Stop.*"

Bryce's eyes went wide as he heard Cambry's voice in his head. He stumbled back at the sheer force of the command as Cambry stopped between them and the panther.

Jake snarled, taking a step forward as his eyes rolled back, and he flashed his teeth. Fur rippling and drool dripping from his open maw, he was an intimidating sight, even for Bryce. But Cambry didn't back down, he barked high and loud, the command rippling through a second time.

This time Bryce fell to one knee, clutching Jake's side so he didn't fall flat on his face. Whatever Cambry was doing to them, he had never been taught about it in any of his lectures. Alphas were the ones with the upper hand in every piece of literature, the omega prey fleeing and escaping, not standing and taking command.

Jake whimpered, tossing his head before he seemed to shake off the order. With one last roar, he leaped for the panther, his claws outstretched.

Cambry intercepted, his teeth latching over Jake's wrist to the mating scar that resonated as a white crescent, even in his beast-form.

The change was instantaneous. Jake went utterly limp, shifting into his human form faster than Bryce had ever seen. Sweat dripped down his body as he fell on the carpet, his large body taking up most of the hall. Cambry wasn't far behind, every love bite and bruise they'd left, laid bare to the onlookers.

Perhaps we went a bit overboard. Even when Bryce had been denying the bond, his beast had obviously taken over enough that he'd left his mark nearly everywhere. If he wasn't mistaken, Cambry was still wearing their scents, too, inside and out.

Bryce hobbled to them, lifting Jake's head into his lap as he grinned at Cambry, the elation at seeing him overwhelming every bit of fear and trepidation.

"Are we done being dramatic?" Bryce chuckled as Jake blinked slowly, his eyes still glazed over with half-bliss and half-confusion. Cambry pulled Jake's wrist from his mouth, sucking it clean with a smack before leaning back on his heels, a matching grin on his face.

A low hiss broke through their bubble, the single noise bringing back the *where* of the situation. They weren't at a cute reunion where they could pause for a few kisses before jumping into the back seat of the car. They were in another alpha's territory.

Cambry turned on the panther before Bryce could move, letting out a growl that sent a shiver down his spine. Even Jake blinked as he tried to stand, his limbs obviously still wobbly.

"They're mine," Cambry hissed, placing one claw-tipped hand down and shielding them from the panther's view. It would have been adorable if it hadn't been so damn sexy at the same time. Their mate protecting two big bad alphas? Now *that* was what *Feral Woods* was about.

The panther took a step back, then another, his skin rippling as his fur fell away to an intimidating man. He held his hands up on either side in surrender, even as he stood, towering over them.

"Bryce? Jake? What are you —? Oh."

Bryce shook his head, scratching the back of his scalp as Jeremiah appeared at the end of the hallway, a blue robe clutched to his chest. The bunny looked terrified, each step slow and careful.

"*Mine.*" Cambry growled again, slapping the ground with his hand and tearing into the hardwood.

"I'm not going to touch them, Wolfie. I just thought you might want your robe. I only brought one, sorry." He looked to Jake, his gaze anything but apologetic. "So these are your mates, right?"

Cambry smiled, his blue eyes so bright that it was heartbreaking.

"Yeah."

Bryce chuckled, pressing his forehead to Cambry's shoulder.

If anyone had told him that this was how his day would have gone, he probably would have hugged them.

Epilogue

Bryce

"Come on, Jake. You promised," said Cambry, kicking Jake under the table and sending his coffee flying when he startled. "Sorry."

Jake glowered, wiping his shirt with a napkin before he leaned back in his chair. Setting his mug on the kitchen table, he narrowed his eyes at Cambry. "No."

Bryce snorted, shoving his own mug into the sink and rinsing it. A car door slammed in the distance, calling him from the relative peace of the breakfast table. Another week and another set of couples.

"Well, I'm off to greet this week's batch, guys. If you manage to settle the argument, let me know. My bets are on Cambry, though, Jake. Eighty-two percent of omegas can convince their alphas to do something if sex is on the table."

Jake blinked, looking to Cambry. "You never said sex was on the table."

"Sex is always on the table, and maybe *actually* on the table this time. I want to test out your craftmanship," said Cambry with a grin before he stood, circling around the table like a vulture—a sexy vulture.

Sure, he'd thickened around the middle a bit, but that had only added to his appeal.

Jake slid a hand over Cambry's belly, echoing Bryce's thoughts. "On the table? Are you sure?"

Cambry crossed his arms, pulling away from the touch. "You've got to be kidding me. It's just like the counter and the back of the new pickup. How about this, Jake? You help me show these new couples how it's done, and you can pick the time *and* the place. It will be like old times."

Bryce grinned behind his hand. There wasn't a day he didn't want to spend with his two mates, even if they were just holding hands by the pond. They were all around him and in his thoughts, their thoughts almost as loud as his own after their year together.

"Hold hands?" Jake asked, turning to him. "Who the fuck wants to hold hands if sex is on the table?"

Cambry snickered, shrugging. "He has a point, Bryce."

Bryce chuckled, kissing them both and sliding a hand over Cambry's belly one last time before he turned for the door. "Come on, boys. Clothes off and claws out... We've got work to do."

Want to see more from this author? Here's a taster for you to enjoy!

It's a Kink Thing: Dupli-Kinked
M.C. Roth

Coming February 2023

Excerpt

Copley

The ring burned a hole through the pocket of his jeans, drawing his attention with every step. It was supposed to be a symbol of his love, which had simmered for three years and burned bright for another two. Instead, it was the sole representation of his humiliation.

He'd been so excited when he'd strolled into the jewelry store while wearing his best dress shirt and a pair of slacks that had fit him just right. He dressed well for his work, but he'd never really worn something truly expensive before.

He'd kept his jaw sewn tight as he looked at the price tags on every ring, going from glass case to glass case until he'd finally found the dismal selection targeted for men. A simple gold band had barely been within his budget, but he'd needed something. He hadn't been able to go another moment without telling Spencer how he felt about him.

They'd hardly spoken during the whispered moments at night when they had lain together in the most intimate embrace. But what was he supposed to say to someone who had started as his roommate but had stolen his heart instead?

It had all begun so innocently as a way to blow off steam. The tension had seemed to build as soon as they'd settled in as roommates, even though they'd been strangers at the time. Outside the apartment, they'd become friends who were perhaps more affectionate than most, but as soon as the apartment door had closed behind them, their walls had come down.

Spencer had been *his*. He would slip into Copley's bed and lie with him until the sun peeked through his bedroom curtains when he had to roll out and go to work with his ass aching and his lips still bruised from their kisses.

"Copley, come back to bed."

How many times had he fallen for that? How many sick days had passed with them in bed as they kissed and made love until they simply couldn't anymore?

That was why the ring had been so important, and why he'd purchased the simple gold band from the clerk, who had given him a slightly disappointed look, as if he should have spent thousands instead of hundreds.

He was in love, but he still had to eat.

His heart had been ready to pound out of his chest by the time he'd arrived home, pulling the ring from the tiny box and clutching it in his hand. He had bitten his tongue, pushing himself through the door before he could chicken out.

And everything had come crashing down.

He'd grabbed his packed bag from his side of the bed, wiping the tears from his cheeks before he'd fled the apartment with Spencer staring after him looking so confused and concerned that it had nearly broken his heart a second time.

The bag was heavy on his shoulder, thumping against his back as he took practiced steps toward the main street. He'd packed light for the second part of his would-be surprise—a camping trip just for the two of them.

The bag contained a single change of clothes with one tent and an extra-large sleeping bag that would have zipped around them just right. It was the perfect way to celebrate a new engagement.

Only he'd been wrong from the very beginning. While Copley had been falling in love for five wonderful years, Spencer hadn't felt a thing. Their stress relief had been just that and nothing more to him—which was why Spencer had introduced him to his girlfriend while Copley had clutched the ring in his hand like some clueless idiot.

Wiping his cheeks with the back of his hand, Copley looked out onto the street and the zooming traffic that was slowly starting to thin. For a gloomy fall Saturday, the road was surprisingly busy, with people rushing here and there as they prepared for winter.

It would have been near freezing in the tent on their impromptu trip, and they would have had to snuggle so close to share their bodily warmth, fogging the air as they breathed each other in.

Copley sobbed, cupping his hand over his mouth as he stumbled to the nearest bench. He sagged onto the slatted wood frame, dropping his pack as he pressed his face into his hands. A wail seeped past his lips as his chest pulled so tight that he wondered how he could still breathe.

"You okay?"

Sniffing, Copley turned to the man next to him, who looked rather startled at his new bench mate. His hair was gray, a few age spots peeking from under his waterproof cap that matched the poncho around his shoulders.

"Yeah." Copley sniffed, wiping his hands over his face to try to squish the sobs at the source. It didn't quite work, but the stranger's eyes on him stalled his tears where they were. He'd already humiliated himself enough for one day.

"I get like that on rainy days, too, sometimes." The stranger tipped his cap as he gazed up at the cloudy sky. "Not sure if it's the best weather for camping, though, son." He eyed Copley's bag and the sleeping bag nearly bursting from its packaging. "It's going to be a mighty cold one tonight, and you don't look like you're dressed for it. I can feel a storm brewing in my bones."

Copley's lips twitched in the briefest of smiles as he let out a breath. "You sound just like my mother. '*Don't forget your sweater, Copley.*'" He shook his head, pulling his arms around himself as a gust of wind stripped him of warmth. The guy was right, though. In his haste, he hadn't grabbed a jacket, and with the nightfall only a short time away, it was already starting to get chilly.

"Sounds like a wise woman, like my Nancy. I would forget my pants if my wife didn't remind me every morning." He smiled, rubbing his hand over his knobby knee and grimacing. "I'm surprised she even lets me take the bus anymore. Some days it's just nice to meet new people, but she's more of a homebody. Always was."

Smiling through the last of his tears, Copley leaned against the bench and shuddered as another wind gust swept over him. The blue and yellow bus sign blared above his head, but there were no vehicles in sight. The routes went every fifteen minutes in the city, and he could hop from one to the next with his eyes closed. He'd never even thought of having his own car before.

"Where are you headed, son? Up toward Forrest Lake? Or maybe down by the flats? We used to party there in my day. Don't tell my Nancy, but there were quite a few ladies that liked to tag along, if you know what I mean. I played football back then. Nothing like a bit of pigskin to get the fire started."

Copley blinked, chuckling awkwardly as he looked around for an escape. Listening to an old man talk about his young and straight escapades was slightly awkward, if he were honest. He didn't want to be rude, but that generation tended to be a tad…ungentlemanly to him when they found out he was attracted to men.

"I wouldn't know, actually. And as for where I'm headed…? I haven't figured that out yet." *I couldn't catch a football if it was covered in glue.*

He looked to the bus sign. Route fifteen looped around the north side of town before it hit low-income housing and some spots that he didn't dare step into while he was dressed the way he was. As much as he tried to be open-minded and non-judgmental, he clutched his keys tighter when he passed by graffiti or a few gang members on a corner.

"Well, this bus will take you to some of the best spots," said the old man, tugging his cap back over his brow as the sun peeked out one final time before clouds consumed it again. It was starting to get low in the sky, bronze blushing to pinks and reds as a few lamplights buzzed to life.

"My Nancy was raised on South Street, just next to the old inn. Not much to it now, but in its glory, it was a beautiful place. Do you know it?" He looked to Copley, his bushy eyebrows scrunching as he slowly blinked.

"I do. I was raised up that way, actually," said Copley, tugging his shirt tighter around his belly as a raindrop landed on his knee. The rain was cold, sinking straight to his skin as a second drop landed on the bench next to him.

He had been raised near Highbury Street, which was only two blocks from South, and he knew exactly why he shouldn't travel there. He remembered the noises in the night and the shouts that had kept him awake. His mother and pop had done their best to raise him and his brother and keep them safe in that neighborhood, but sometimes he wondered how he'd ever made it out.

When he'd been old enough, he'd left the neighborhood behind, and his parents had followed shortly after, only they had moved so far south that he rarely saw them in person anymore.

"My brother is still down that way, actually. He's in the old apartment building near the corner of Highbury...the one with the yellow brick and the steeples," said Copley. The brick had been all but crumbling the last time Copley had seen it, the shingles on the peaked roof barely hanging on.

"That's the old McGuire place. He used to own the old bus line in town before it went out of business. Committed suicide not long after that, and his wife went into a nunnery."

"Oh dear," said Copley, trying to keep his face blank. *Do nunneries still exist?* He used to watch *The Sound of Music* with his mother all the time, and he still knew the songs by heart. The man nodded, his mouth set into a grim line.

"We lost a lot of good men to things like that back then. Not so much now with people my age, but then, half of them aren't alive anymore, anyway. There are only two people left from my high school graduating class." He let out a long sigh, finally stilling his hand where he rubbed at his knee. "But I should be going before Nancy sends the search party out for me. I hope you find your way, son."

The old man stood with a groan, his shoulders stooped as he grabbed the cane that was sitting next to the bench. "And be careful in that part of town. There are a lot of sons of bitches out there." He walked off, slowly shuffling his feet against the sidewalk.

Copley looked to his pocket where he could still feel the ring like a blazing halo of misfortune. He wasn't close to feeling any better, but at least he had a touch of perspective.

"Well, I guess I know where I'm headed."

He grabbed his bag as the bus pulled up to the stop and parked with a burst of air brakes before the doors swung wide. Stepping inside, he clutched the strap of his pack as he paid and slipped into a seat near the front. He hadn't seen his brother in years, so he was woefully overdue. Hopefully, he had a couch that still had its cushions where Copley could sleep.

He let out a sigh as his eyes began to burn again, his tears budding afresh as he looked back to the bench and his neighborhood. *It's going to be a long night.*

About the Author

M.C. Roth lives in Canada and loves every season, even the dreaded Canadian winter. She graduated with honours from the Associate Diploma Program in Veterinary Technology at the University of Guelph before choosing a different career path.

Between caring for her young son, spending time with her husband, and feeding treats to her menagerie of animals, she still spends every spare second devoted to her passion for writing.

She loves growing peppers that are hot enough to make grown men cry, but she doesn't like spicy food herself. Her favourite thing, other than writing of course, is to find a quiet place in the wilderness and listen to the birds while dreaming about the gorgeous men in her head.

M.C. Roth loves to hear from readers. You can find her contact information, website details and author profile page at https://www.pride-publishing.com

PUBLISHING

Sign up for our newsletter and find out about all our romance book releases, eBook sales and promotions, sneak peeks and FREE romance books!

www.ingramcontent.com/pod-product-compliance
Lightning Source LLC
Chambersburg PA
CBHW031451260626
47154CB00016B/835